THE MACARTHUR FAMILY
SERIES COLLECTION

KATIE REUS

Cover art: Jaycee of Sweet 'N Spicy Designs

Editor: Julia Ganis

Author website: https://www.katiereus.com

Publisher's Note: This is a work of fiction. Names, characters, places, and incidents are either the products of the author's imagination or used fictitiously, and any resemblance to actual persons, living or dead, or business establishments, organizations or locales is completely coincidental.

The MacArthur Family Series Collection /Katie Reus. -- 1st ed.

KR Press, LLC

ISBN-13: 978-1-63556-281-1

CONTENTS

FALLING FOR IRISH

CHAPTER ONE

Kathryn Irish's heels clicked across the lobby floor of the Davis Building as she headed for the bank of elevators. She felt weird being in her ex-boyfriend's building but the chances of running into Daniel MacArthur here were very small.

Daniel's company had hired Tony Domínguez, head of the East Coast division for Security Solutions and Analytics, Inc., to do a diagnostics check of their new security system and protocols. And Tony had hired her, since she was one of his preferred contractors. She wasn't exclusive to him—wasn't exclusive to anyone, and she liked it that way. It was just dumb luck that this was one of Daniel's buildings.

Under normal circumstances she wouldn't have taken a job at her ex's place, but the money was too good to pass up. He didn't work out of this building even if he did own it.

So here she was, posing as an engaged woman to talk to Helen Marr, owner of White Sands Event Planning. She just needed to get to the eighth floor so she could work her magical hacking skills. She'd done an analysis of the new security and the building itself, and had deemed this the easiest way to infiltrate and pinpoint any security holes.

As she waited in line at the bank of six elevators, she swore she could feel eyes on her. A little tingle started at the back of her neck and she automatically reached up to rub it. She looked at the others waiting for the elevators, wondering what was wrong with her.

Then she glanced over her shoulder and froze for all of a second before turning back around. *Oh, God!*

"Kathryn." That deep voice was nearly too much for her to handle.

She inwardly winced as the big, imposing man slid up next to her. His familiar masculine scent teased her nose. It was a woodsy, citrusy scent that made her think of Daniel and sex. She went weak in the knees, just like that. She couldn't believe he was here, but she pasted on a smile and turned to look up at sexy Daniel MacArthur. Since he was six foot four, she always had to look up, even though she was wearing heels today. For a moment all she could see were his pale blue eyes, staring down at her with an intensity she felt to her core. "Daniel," she rasped out, then cleared her throat. "I, ah, didn't think you came into this office very often." And never on Fridays. She knew that from simple recon. On Fridays he always, *always* worked out of the building on Prescott Street—well, apparently not. And planning the job today had hinged on him being gone.

He watched her with an unnerving intensity. "I had some stuff to take care of today. What are you even doing here..." His words trailed off as he glanced down at what she was holding.

Yikes, her stack of bridal magazines. And oh yeah, she was also sporting a huge engagement ring on her left ring finger. It was real too, though it wasn't hers.

He blinked once when he saw the ring, his expression darkening. Damn, the man was good-looking. It was no wonder he'd been voted one of the top twenty-five sexiest bachelors in the city the last five years in a row. His dark hair was a little longer than the normal close-cropped cut he'd kept when they'd been together. And she didn't think he'd shaved in a couple days, given the stubble he was sporting. Instead of looking unkempt, however, he simply looked even more delicious. Especially with some of his tattoos peeking out at his wrists. The man was always so buttoned up and professional looking, but underneath that suit? He had a surprising amount of ink and she loved every inch of it.

She hoped he wouldn't comment on the ring. Maybe he would just let her by without one single word about it. Maybe unicorns were real too. "I've got a meeting here on the eighth floor." She took a small step away from him, finding it easier to breathe with the little bit of distance between them.

He closed the distance in one step, not letting her move even an inch. "You're getting married?" he demanded as the elevators dinged.

Okay, so he wasn't letting this go. She was aware of people heading into the elevators, clearing out the whole area, but all she could focus on was him. It was like he was a magnet, pulling her in. She wanted to run away from him, to simply jump into the cluster of people and avoid this whole conversation. But she also didn't want him to realize that she was here on a job. She needed to be polite for another minute or two before making her escape. "It would appear so." That wasn't a lie, exactly. And she hated lying to him. Even if he had broken her heart.

"But…" He cleared his throat. "We've only been broken up for two months."

He seemed absolutely shocked that she'd moved on so fast, which was a little ironic considering she'd seen a picture of him with some svelte blonde wrapped around him on a trashy blog the other day. Okay that was a lie—there had been no wrapping around him, but they had been standing next to each other and smiling pleasantly at the camera. Still, the memory of that picture and the stupid byline that had gone with it rankled Kathryn. *Sexy Bachelor and Heiress Caught Canoodling!* Ugh. Just remembering that eased her guilt. And what kind of publication used the word canoodling? Even a trashy one? Seriously.

She absolutely wasn't commenting on that. "Look, I don't want to be late for my appointment."

For the first time since she'd known him, he looked completely out of sorts, his pale eyes searching hers for something. When there was a shout from across the lobby, Daniel turned in that direction, his expression growing dark.

She knew exactly what was going on because this was part of the plan with her partner.

"What the hell!" someone shouted. "Stop that!"

She suppressed a smile when she saw a whole bunch of balloons being released. And then…bubbles came out of nowhere, being pumped throughout the lobby. Bubbles were something new and it made her giggle, despite this whole situation. "Looks like you've got your hands full," she said, moving toward an elevator that opened.

"Wait," he started, then turned back at another annoyed shout from security.

Seeing her opportunity, she slid into the elevator and quickly pressed the close door button while he was distracted. The last thing she saw was his annoyingly sexy, brooding face as he stared at her while the doors swished shut on him.

As soon as they did, she slumped against the back wall and closed her eyes for a long moment as the elevator ascended. Her stomach rolled once and it had nothing to do with the ride.

For a moment she wondered if he would figure out why she was really here today. He knew some of what she did for her contract work, but she'd never shared the details of how she worked jobs—it was confidential and she wouldn't have given away her trade secrets regardless. Getting her bonus depended on not being discovered during the actual infiltration.

She doubted he would suspect her of being here for anything other than what it appeared she was here for. She was just second-guessing herself and she needed to keep it together.

As she stepped out of the elevator and into the waiting area of White Sands Event Planning, a pretty woman with dark, corkscrew curls smiled at her from behind the reception desk. "Hello, how may I help you today?"

"Hi, I'm Kathryn and I have a meeting with Helen."

"Of course. My name is Sonya," she said, standing and smoothing down her gray pencil skirt. "Can I get you a latte, sparkling water, something to eat?"

"A latte would be great," she said as she followed Sonya down the hallway. The walls were a soft gray, with black-and-white photos from various events—mainly weddings—hanging every couple feet. All happy, smiling people. There were also a few images of clearly custom-made cakes and a couple brides in couture dresses.

Sonya showed Kathryn to a conference room that was feminine and comfortable. It was also filled with art showcasing the company's events —more happy people. This was nothing like the boring boardrooms she'd been in so many times before as part of her job.

"Make yourself comfortable. Helen is running a little bit behind, but she'll be with you within the next ten minutes. And I'll be back with your drink. Oh, we've also got petit fours and scones if you're interested. They're all from the bakery we use for weddings."

Under normal circumstances Kathryn would've said yes to all of the food, but not right now. Her stomach was knotted too tight. "I'm going to pass on the food, but would you mind telling me where your restrooms are?"

"Of course." She pointed down the hallway and gave brief directions before hurrying off in the other direction in five-inch stilettos.

Kathryn left most of her stuff on the table but slipped out her slim laptop and tucked it in the back of her skirt, then adjusted her jacket over it. She ducked out of the conference room and hurried down the hallway, her heart racing.

She'd completed almost fifty infiltrations over the last few years and had been successful with every single one of them. But it felt weird to be hacking into Daniel MacArthur's system. It was what he'd paid her boss for, but still, knowing he was in the building right now while she worked was strange. It also made her really, *really* not want to get caught. When he'd hired Tony to do this random check of security, Tony had only given him a vague week's time frame for when he should expect the hack to occur. It wouldn't do them much good if they knew exactly when to look for a hack because they would have tightened security.

The restroom was empty so she hurried into one of the stalls and unlocked the door. Then she sat on the toilet lid and got to work, her keyboard whisper quiet. A minute later when she heard someone step inside, she paused for only a moment before getting back to work.

When she heard water running and then the hand dryer, she breathed a sigh of relief as she slid her way into the building's security system.

The way his system had been created, anyone who wanted access had to be in the building to infiltrate it. And right now she was hacking into a Wi-Fi modem that hadn't been updated within the last couple days. It was how she would eventually work her way into the rest of the system. She wouldn't be able to get into his financials or anything, but she would be able to screw with his security system, which was a huge deal if someone wanted to do a specific type of job against his place.

Once she'd maneuvered through a back door and left a little message for the security team, she tucked her laptop back in her skirt and hurried out, washing her hands and drying them before booking it back to the conference room. She was just getting settled and taking a sip of her now almost cold latte when a woman with a whole lot of blonde hair and a big smile hurried into the room.

"I'm Helen, and I'm so sorry I'm late," she said.

It was hard not to smile at the woman. "Don't worry about it. I'm just relaxing in this wonderful conference room. I love the way you've set everything up." Instead of all stiff-backed chairs, there were a couple individual seating areas filled with cushy chairs in shades of purple and gray.

"Thank you. Are you hungry? Need a refill?" Helen asked as she shook Kathryn's hand and sat across from her in a matching tufted purple chair.

"No, I'm fine, but thank you."

The woman's phone buzzed a few times but she ignored it.

"Do you need to get that?"

"Normally I would say no—normally I wouldn't even have it on me, but I might need to grab this. There's been some type of breach downstairs and security is going crazy. I think they might end up doing a walk-through of each of our floors, since we rent from the MacArthur Company and their security oversees the whole building."

"Did you want to reschedule? If it would make it easier for you?" Kathryn really hoped so, because then she wouldn't have to go through a whole charade and lie to the woman. Even though this was a free consultation, Kathryn's employer would end up sending a check to Helen for wasting her time. It was the only thing that eased her guilt at taking up Helen's time under false pretenses.

"Oh, no, I don't want to do that." But Kathryn could see that the woman did want to do just that.

So she stood and smiled. "Look, I've heard great things about your company. Let's just reschedule for later in the week, okay? That way no one's rushed or stressed out."

Relief spread across the woman's face as she stood. "I think that might be better. And I will make sure my assistant reschedules you immediately."

Kathryn squashed another bit of guilt she experienced because she wouldn't be rescheduling at all, but that was just part of this job.

It didn't take long to make it down to the lobby. Kathryn couldn't fight the nerves humming through her as she descended in the elevator. Once she stepped out into the lobby, she spotted Daniel talking to two security guys forty feet away. Good, he was occupied.

The main exit had a bunch of men and women standing there, talking to her partner, Quincy. She was too far away to hear how the conversation was going, but he'd done this enough times that she knew exactly how Quincy was playing this thing off. Right now he'd be claiming that everything had just been a prank. Usually he could convince people he was harmless—he had that whole charming boyish thing about him.

She wasn't sure if it would work on Daniel's people, but as long as she got out of the building, that was all that mattered. Because they couldn't arrest Quincy for anything. He might get fined, but then of course it would get thrown out once Daniel realized they were the ones he had actually hired to scan the security here.

Moving quickly, she cursed her loud heels as she hurried toward the front door. Pulling out her phone, she stopped herself from looking in Daniel's direction even though she didn't actually pull up anything on her screen. Sooooo close. She was almost to the exit.

"Ma'am? *Ma'am?*"

Jolted out of her internal getaway pep talk, she turned to find a man in a security uniform striding toward her. "Yes?" she asked.

"We're checking the bags of everyone who leaves. I'm going to need you to come with me over to the tables we've got set up." He motioned to where they had indeed set up a handful of tables off to one side and were now checking everyone's bags like at an airport.

She stared at him, acting confused. "What? Why?"

"Henry, it's fine," Daniel said, hurrying over toward them. His gaze flicked down to her left hand, his expression darkening for an instant before he looked back at Henry again. "She's fine."

"But Mr. MacArthur, protocol says—"

"I know what the protocol says. She's fine."

The man nodded once and backed away.

Daniel looked her up and down, a quick sweep that was anything but clinical. "You're leaving so soon?"

She ignored that heated look, unsure what to even make of it. "Yeah, I guess something is going on with security?" She pointed over at the tables. "We decided to reschedule."

He nodded and kept watching her.

She shifted on her feet. Had he changed his mind about searching her stuff? "Ah, your guy can look in my purse if he wants." She held her big purse out and started to open it, but he just waved a hand at it.

"You look really good," he said quietly, his voice as intense as his gaze.

Oh. Wow. For a moment she wanted to melt under that gaze. "So do you," she said just as quietly, unable to get anything more out. And it was true. He somehow looked even better than she remembered, which just seemed unfair. She'd tried to convince herself that she'd worked him up in her mind, that of course he wasn't as sexy as she'd remembered. All lies.

"I've missed you," he blurted out, surprising her, and she was pretty sure he'd surprised himself with the admission if his expression was anything to go on.

She stared at him in shock, mainly because this was something she'd never expected from him. It was so raw and real, and for this one moment, Daniel wasn't wearing a mask. He wasn't the mysterious and closed-off man she'd shared a whole lot of orgasms with.

Oh God. She didn't know how to deal with this. "Oh, ah… I…" She didn't want to tell him she missed him too because it would give him an opening. And it would just rip her heart open all over again. Even if it was the truth.

"Mr. MacArthur." A woman wearing heels and a sharp business suit hurried over to them, nodding at Kathryn once. Then she murmured something to Daniel, so Kathryn took the opportunity to slip away. She headed straight for the security guard named Henry, who only nodded politely at her and motioned that she was okay to leave without a bag check.

She heard Daniel curse behind her but she ignored him and resisted the urge to sprint the last few feet out the door. She wanted out and it had nothing to do with the job. Nope, she just needed to get away from Daniel and his ice-blue eyes.

Daniel with the wicked grin and talented hands that had turned her to mush once upon a time.

Once she was outside in the bright sunshine, she slid her sunglasses on and sucked in a sharp breath. She felt as if the weight of the entire building had been lifted off her shoulders as she hurried to the waiting car.

They'd pulled it off.

But for reasons she understood very well, she didn't have that normal high she got after completing a job. No, she just felt…hollow and wrung out.

CHAPTER TWO

Daniel wanted to run after Kathryn, but what the hell was he going to do? Beg her to talk to him? Demand that she take off that stupid ring so he could throw it in an incinerator? The ring that was *very* definitely real. He recognized quality when he saw it.

Not that he was surprised someone had scooped her up. She was a diamond in the rough and he'd been stupid enough to let her walk away. Unfortunately he still wasn't sure what he'd done wrong. One moment they'd been on their way to a date and then she was suddenly telling him that it was over, that she'd realized she wasn't interested in a serious relationship. That what they'd had was finished.

To say he'd been blindsided was an understatement. He still hadn't recovered—or figured out what had gone wrong. Maybe all the overtime he'd been working back then? After she'd ended things he'd tried to talk to her about it—multiple times—but she'd blown him off. Seeing her today had him rattled.

She'd looked good too. No, she'd looked *stunning*. He was used to seeing her in jeans and T-shirts but today she'd been wearing a dress that showed off all her curves—and legs he was obsessed with. She wasn't tall, just average in height, but she did a lot of yoga and swimming and her legs... He had to actively stop thinking about the many times she'd had the sexiest legs ever thrown over his shoulders as he went down on her. Brought her pleasure. Gave her orgasms. Damn it— he had to stop obsessing but it was hard when she'd been here in the flesh.

He'd had to resist the urge to run his hands through her long, auburn hair, to touch what most definitely wasn't his anymore.

He was determined to finally get answers. She might be wearing a ring, but he couldn't kill that small kernel of hope inside him that maybe he still had a chance.

He walked away from his assistant, waving her off as she tried to keep talking to him, and pulled out his cell phone.

"Hey, now's not a good time," his sister Sienna whispered.

"Why not? What are you doing?"

"I'm on a job," she whispered again. "But you never call, so I answered. Is everything okay? Is it Mom and Dad?"

He ignored her questions. "Why the hell didn't you tell me that Kathryn is engaged?"

There was a moment of silence. "Kathryn's not engaged. I would know, trust me."

Hope shot through him, painful and intense. Just as quickly, he squashed it. "When was the last time you saw her?" Because that ring had been very real. And she'd been carrying bridal magazines, on her way to meet a wedding planner. Kathryn! The woman who'd once told him she thought most weddings were ostentatious, and that if she ever got married, she'd just elope.

"I've been really busy this month. I don't know... Hell, I guess it's been almost two months since you guys broke up and I haven't seen her since... Oh, shit, I'm a totally crap friend," she muttered to herself. "I've talked to her and we've texted but I haven't seen her in two months."

"I just saw her and she had a giant rock on her finger." His fingers tightened around his phone. And she'd been practically glowing, her green eyes bright and captivating.

"Well, what do you want me to do about it? Break the guy's kneecaps?" She snorted.

"Call her and find out about him."

"Are you hiring me? Because I'm not going to stalk a friend."

His sister was a PI, and even though he'd offered her a job at his company many times over, she always turned him down, preferring to make her own way instead. Something he respected.

"No, don't spy on her. I mean, maybe spy a little bit." He scrubbed a hand over his face.

"Oh my God, I'm not having this conversation and I'm not spying on my friend. I've gotta go." The line went dead.

Daniel cursed and nearly crushed his phone, but since he didn't want to have to go through the hassle of replacing it, he simply shoved it into his pocket. He had to deal with this mess here and then he would figure out what to do about Kathryn.

He'd thought he could move on, could somehow live without her. She'd made it clear she wanted nothing to do with him. But after seeing her today? The attraction burned even brighter between them and he'd seen the look in her eyes. She might be engaged to another man, but she still wanted him.

That changed everything.

If she still wanted him, he wasn't letting her go without a fight.

THREE HOURS LATER, Kathryn slid into the booth across from Quincy. "How long did they keep you?"

He grinned and waved at their server before holding up two fingers. For two drinks, she assumed.

"I hope you ordered something for me too," she said, laughing.

"Yeah, I told him what to bring when a pretty redhead got here. And to answer your first question, they just let me go half an hour ago."

She raised her eyebrows. "Dang."

"Technically I could have left at any time but I played nice since they never called the cops—and I just acted stupid. Their security had a bunch of questions and I'm pretty sure someone on their security team tried to follow me, but I lost them." His grin widened, revealing a dimple.

She snickered. "What was up with the bubbles?" He hadn't told her about that part of the distraction.

"I decided to mix things up a bit. Oh, and I saw you talking to Daniel Mac-Hottie-Arthur. I thought we were screwed when I saw that but then he let you go. What did the big man want anyway?"

She'd worked with Quincy on and off for two years. For the most part she kept her work and personal life separate—though she and Quincy had always been open about their personal lives. Until she'd started dating Daniel. She adored Quincy but Daniel had been this huge force of nature and she'd kept Daniel's name private for the three months they'd been together. Well, with the exception of her closest friends, because she had confided in her book club about him. But that was different. "Ah, well, remember that whirlwind relationship I had that ended two months ago?"

He blinked once and then his eyes widened. "Are you kidding me? You and MacArthur?"

"Yep."

"Wait, doesn't he know what you do for a living?"

"Sort of. If he guessed at why I was there, he didn't let on. And honestly, when he saw my engagement ring, I think it threw him off more than anything. He might realize the truth later. Either way, we did a good job."

"That we did." He took the beer the server dropped off and clinked the top against Kathryn's.

"We kicked ass," she added, feeling a little smug. Infiltrating his system had taken a certain amount of finesse.

"So why didn't you tell me about him before?" Quincy asked before taking another sip of his beer.

"I wasn't sure where the relationship was going." And it turned out the answer was nowhere so she was glad she'd kept it to herself.

At the time she'd liked having him all to herself—though her brothers had known because they were nosy and knew everything. But she and Daniel had managed to keep all mentions of their relationship out of any sort of society rag. He hadn't cared about the gossip stuff, but she'd wanted to be damn sure they had a future before she was publicly linked to him. She hadn't wanted any sort of media scrutiny.

Sure, it would have been on a local level, but that was too much for something that wasn't serious. Now she was glad she'd listened to her instinct and insisted on keeping things quiet. The breakup had been one of the hardest things she'd ever dealt with. If she'd had to do it while being watched by the media, it would have been a hundred times harder. "But it's all fine between us. He was perfectly polite when we ran into each other." He'd also been looking at her with that familiar hunger. Which just made the ache in her chest even worse.

Quincy snickered at that. "There's got to be some cosmic justice in that, you getting a fat bonus from this job."

She didn't bother hiding her smile. "Maybe so."

"So...you're not going to give me any juicy details? Like why y'all broke up?"

"Not unless you tell me why you and Mr. Bartender broke up last week." Unlike Kathryn, Quincy told her every single detail of his dating life. And she knew this would be the perfect distraction.

"Oh, I'll tell you. I thought he was pretty cool so I invited him to a house party—where he proceeded to pull his dick out."

She blinked. "What? I'm going to need way more details than this."

Quincy took a sip of his beer then set it down. By his expression, she knew she was in for a good story. "A bunch of us started playing poker. Then someone of course suggested strip poker. So Mr. Bartender pulls off his pants, then his boxers when he loses a couple rounds. I mean, who does that? You start with your shoes or shirt."

She snickered at the image. "So he was just sitting around with a shirt on and his dick hanging out?"

"Yep. My friends thought it was hilarious but I was a little horrified. I mean, I still slept with him, but—"

A laugh burst out of her. "Seriously?"

He shrugged, his grin widening. "I'd already seen a nice preview of what to expect."

"Impressive?"

"Oh yeah."

"But you still ended things with him?"

"Yep. He tried to get me to do CrossFit with him. I do not need that in my life."

She laughed even harder. "You're ridiculous!"

Quincy shrugged, but still grinned.

"Your dating stories are always so much better than mine."

"This is true," he said, waving off their server and declining another drink since his was still half full.

"My last date was kind of a nightmare too."

"Ooooh, are you getting personal with me?" He raised his eyebrows.

She shrugged. "There's not that much to tell. He was just a jackass. He talked the whole time, and when he would ask me a question I would start to answer it, but he'd cut me off before I could finish. Like every single time. It was all I could do not to run out of there."

Quincy shook his head. "You can't even give me a teeny bit of details about you and MacArthur? That man is seriously fine."

"No," she said quietly, and the pain must have shown on her face because his eyes widened slightly.

"Shit, I'm sorry. I didn't know you were really into him. Damn, so does that mean I need to make a voodoo doll of him tonight and set it on fire?"

She lifted a shoulder. "Maybe... No, he wasn't that bad." He'd just thought she was after him for his money.

"Well I'm guessing he wasn't that good either, if you're sitting across from me looking all sad. I'm kind of surprised you didn't destroy his life with your hacking skills."

"Hey! I only use my skills for good." Mostly anyway.

He simply lifted an eyebrow. "If in like a month or two I read about him losing millions of dollars in some freak banking error, it's not you?"

She laughed at Quincy's antics and shook her head. "I will not be getting any sort of revenge. Trust me. I just want him out of my life." It was the only way she'd get over her heartbreak. Because after two months, her heart still wasn't healed.

"Well, I'll be your alibi if you do get revenge."

She just snorted as their server returned to the table. They grabbed a couple appetizers and water. Half an hour later, she said goodbye and headed home. It was pretty late for her to be getting home anyway. Most of her jobs ended by five or six o'clock but no way would she have headed home after this one without seeing Quincy in person. She'd wanted to find out how things had gone once she'd left. And okay, she'd wanted to know if anything had happened with Daniel.

Kathryn pulled into her designated parking lot at her condominium. She loved living in the small complex, though in the last couple months she'd felt like she was missing something. Of course she knew exactly what that feeling was.

She missed Daniel.

But she had to stop thinking about him. On instinct, she pulled out her house keys and the attached pepper spray. Both her brothers were in law enforcement, and Carson—the oldest—had drilled taking protective measures into her head at a young age. He'd made it clear that she shouldn't have to protect herself—that he was pretty disappointed with the male gender in general—but that she still needed to. It wasn't like she needed him to push her; she lived in the real world.

She knew she had to be able to take care of herself.

Grabbing her purse and laptop as well, she slid out of the car and pressed the key fob to lock it. A cool January breeze rolled over her as she stepped up onto the sidewalk. The many palm trees lining the entire place rustled with the wind. Since summer was on the way—Florida just skipped spring and went straight to humid summer—she was enjoying the respite from the heat.

As she turned the corner of the building onto the connecting sidewalk, a shadow to her left caught her eye. Her breath caught in her throat as a big male figure peeled off the building.

Her instinct was to freeze up, but thanks to a whole lot of defense training from her brother, she let out a scream when she saw a masked man rushing toward her. She jerked her hand up and started spraying wildly at his covered face.

"Shit," the guy growled, clearly surprised. Then he started clawing at his eyes and screaming along with her.

Kathryn kept spraying until he fell to his knees.

As he hit the ground, she sprinted in the other direction, her shoes snapping loudly along the sidewalk. Her phone was somewhere in the depths of her giant purse and she didn't dare stop to try and find it.

Heart in her throat, she sprinted as fast as she could until she made it to the stairs to her building. She risked a glance over her shoulder as she raced up the stairs. No one was chasing after her. As she reached the top, she let out a scream as two big hands steadied her upper arms...

Wait, Daniel? She stared up at him, eyes wide.

He continued to hold on to her, his expression concerned. "Kathryn? What's wrong?"

"A man in a mask jumped out at me. I pepper-sprayed him," she managed to rasp out even though she was breathing erratically and couldn't stop trembling. She couldn't believe something like this had happened again—after being mugged a couple weeks ago, this felt like life was just taking a crap on her.

Moving into action, he grabbed her keys from her hands. "Inside, now."

She was grateful he was steady because she didn't trust herself to even open the front door because of how badly her fingers were shaking. How was that for a good getaway? She couldn't even get herself to safety she was trembling so bad.

He shut and locked the door behind them even as he held his cell phone up to his ear. "Yes, this is an emergency. My name is Daniel MacArthur and I'm at..." Daniel spoke quietly into his phone, clearly talking to emergency services.

He was calling the police, of course. Her reaction time was far too slow right now. She moved to the security pad and disarmed her security system as he continued talking, her fingers unsteady on the buttons.

Feeling almost numb, she walked into the kitchen and dropped her purse and keys onto the center island. Her place wasn't big so she could easily see him through the open bar area facing her living room, looking like emperor of the world in his expensive business suit as he spoke in clipped, efficient tones to the operator.

"I'll be waiting outside for the officer," he said before ending the call. Then he strode quickly into the kitchen.

Meanwhile she felt as if she was on autopilot, as if someone had pressed the pause button on her brain. What had just happened felt surreal, as if it had happened to someone else. And it had all gone down so fast. First she'd been thinking of the nice weather and then a monster had jumped out at her from the shadows.

Scanning her from head to toe in a clinical fashion, he frowned. "Did anything else happen?"

She shook her head, wrapping her arms around herself even as her cat, Mr. Twinkles, appeared out of nowhere, meowing up at them. "No. I...it all happened so fast. He jumped out at me like a ninja and I just reacted and started spraying. And screaming."

His frown didn't let up even as he glanced down at Mr. Twinkles. "Smart thinking, pepper-spraying him."

"I can thank my brother for that."

Daniel's mouth curved up slightly as he picked up her whining cat. "Your brothers do have some uses."

She snorted softly because he'd always butted heads with her brothers—probably because he'd been dating their little sister. Her gaze narrowed as Mr. Twinkles cuddled up to him, nuzzling his head against Daniel's chin. That little traitor!

"Did you want to call anyone? Your brother? Your...fiancé?" He practically spat out the last word even as he gently petted her cat's head.

Fiancé? It took a moment for her to realize what he meant. She looked away from him and shook her head. She still needed to return the ring to her boss and couldn't believe she'd forgotten to this afternoon. "I'll call my brother later and let him know what's going on. But not now. He's already off work and I don't want him to call up our parents and worry them." Her parents were divorced but the one thing they could agree on was that they loved their kids. And her mom would be over here in minutes, quickly followed by her father. Then it would somehow devolve into them arguing and she simply couldn't deal with that now.

Daniel nodded, still watching her closely. "It'll take the cops a few minutes to get here if you want to change into something more comfortable," he said quietly. "Or I can pour you a glass of wine?" The concern rolling off him was palpable and it shook her to her core.

Why was he even here? She wanted to ask him, but decided to wait until after she'd dealt with the cops. One problem at a time. She rubbed a hand over her face and shook her head. "No, but thank you. I'll need to make a statement and I don't want any alcohol on my breath for that. Hopefully they won't make me go down to the station for something like this. Or I don't think they will."

"Okay, then I'll head outside and wait." He gently put down a now annoyed Mr. Twinkles before he strode out the front door, looking like a warrior going into battle.

She could admit that she felt better with him being there. He'd reacted to everything so quickly and efficiently, just taking charge. Sometimes it had annoyed her when he'd just taken over when they'd been together, but in times like this, in any sort of crisis, he was definitely the man you wanted on your side. He never seemed to lose his head.

Though she didn't feel like drinking, she did decide to change out of her dress, so she hurried to her room and slipped into a comfortable pair of lounge pants and a pullover sweater. It had actually been a gift from Daniel, and she thought about taking it off when she realized that, but screw it. He'd given it to her and it was one of her favorites. Right now it made her feel better. Once she was dressed, she opened up a can of food for Mr. Twinkles—who forgot everything else existed when food was concerned—and left him to it.

As she stepped into the living room, Daniel was coming in from the front door as well, a detective with him.

One she recognized. Despite the situation, she smiled at the other man. "Mendoza, apparently I keep running into you."

The fit, very attractive Latino detective smiled at her. "Hey, Irish. I like seeing you, but I wish it was under better circumstances. I didn't call Carson about this since he's already off work. Should I call him for moral support?"

She shook her head. "No. You know he can't get involved in a case that involves me anyway. And really, I'm just making a report. I didn't even see the guy's face, and if you tell Carson…"

Mendoza snorted. "The whole Irish clan will descend on you."

Exactly. "Did you want coffee or anything?" It was late, but she also knew he would be working a later shift since he was here.

He shook his head and then motioned for her and Daniel to sit. "I'm good. Why don't you run through everything with me from the beginning?"

Daniel sat directly next to her, not holding her hand, but she felt his steady presence nonetheless as his knee pressed up against hers. As she relayed what happened, that band around her chest got even tighter.

It didn't take long for her to give her statement, while Mendoza silently took notes and only interrupted with minimal questions. Once he was finished, he looked between the two of them before focusing on her. "Look, I don't like that something has happened to you twice in the last couple weeks. I mean, this is a big city and shit happens, but is there anything going on at work? Any bad dates? Anything you can think of that could be the driving force behind this? Other than a coincidence?"

"What happened in the last couple weeks?" Daniel interjected, watching her.

"Ah, I was mugged a couple weeks ago leaving a job. It's nothing. The guy snatched my bag and got my keys and wallet. I had to cancel my credit cards and—"

"Did you change your locks?" he growled out.

"Yes. Carson changed my locks that night. And I changed my security code for good measure. Luckily my phone was on me and not in my purse."

The tension in his shoulders eased a little bit, but not by much.

"All right, Kathryn," Mendoza said as he stood. "I'll be in touch if we find anything out. I'll talk to the property management company and see if I can get a look at their security feeds. I saw a couple cameras on the way in here. They're closed now, but I'll talk to them in the morning. Just make sure you lock your doors and pay attention to your surroundings. You saved yourself a whole lot of grief by thinking so quickly and pepper-spraying him." His tone shifted slightly as he continued. "I'm just glad this story didn't have a different ending."

Yeah, she was too. She suppressed another shudder as she thought of what could have happened if the man had gotten her.

She walked Mendoza to the door, and after he left she shut and locked it. Now it was time to deal with Daniel. "Not that I don't appreciate it," she said as she turned to find Daniel standing next to her couch. He looked so huge and imposing next to the leather sofa she normally curled up on with her e-reader or paperback at night. "But what are you doing here?"

"I just wanted to see you. Today felt kind of strange between us. I... should have called," he said on a wince.

"Well, yeah, you should have." She laughed a little awkwardly. "But I'm sorry I ran out of there before. It just looked like you had a lot to deal with." Mostly the truth. She wasn't sorry she'd run. Even if she hadn't been on a job, she would have run.

He watched her closely with those pale blue eyes she'd found captivating right from the start. "Are you sure you don't want to call your fiancé?"

Ugh. She couldn't deal with this right now. "I don't want to talk about that."

"Well if you were mine, I would want to know if—"

"Well I'm not yours. And when we were together you thought I was after your money," she snapped without meaning to. The events of the night piled onto her and the pulsing headache that had started minutes ago was spreading along the back of her skull as she stepped toward him. "And I seriously can't deal with this tonight. You need to leave now."

She didn't give a crap why he'd stopped by at this point. She needed a hot shower and sleep. And she really needed to call her brother, because she didn't want him to hear about this from Detective Mendoza. She'd just make Carson promise not to call their parents before she told him what was going on.

Daniel stared at her, a scowl on his face. "What the hell are you talking about? After my money?"

She snorted in derision as she strode past him and unlocked her door. Then she gestured toward it. "I am asking you to leave now. Don't make me ask the detective to come back up here and escort you out."

His expression went thunderous at her words but he did as she said and stepped outside. "Kathryn—"

"Nope. If you want to talk, next time call me." Feeling a bit mean, she shut the door in his face and quickly locked it.

"Kathryn," he called out.

"Go away," she muttered, too low for him to hear.

"Set your security system."

Even though she rolled her eyes at his tone, she really appreciated the thoughtfulness. He'd always been like that, conscious of her security and wanting her to make sure she took care of herself and stayed safe. It was really hard to get mad at that even though she was frustrated with the sexy male in general. Why the hell had he just shown up tonight? He didn't have the right to do that anymore.

"I'm setting it now," she called out because she knew he wouldn't leave until she did exactly that.

After she did, she collapsed against the wall and rubbed a hand over her face. Was it a full moon out? Or maybe Mercury was in retrograde?

Whatever was going on, that ache in her head was nothing compared to the one in her chest. Seeing Daniel in person, especially back in her home, a place they'd gotten naked in many times, made her wish things could have been different.

But she knew they never could be. And it was something she would have to live with. When she opened her eyes, her traitorous little cat was looking up at her with judging eyes.

"Don't you start on me," she muttered.

Mr. Twinkles simply meowed before turning and giving her his swishing tail as he sauntered off to who knew where.

CHAPTER THREE

Five months ago

K athryn pressed the elevator button at the Wilson Building downtown. As she waited, a tall man who smelled really, really good slid up next to her. Without looking at him, she inhaled the citrusy, woodsy scent. Damn, whatever that was, she could get high off it. You know, if she did that sort of thing. As if drawn by a magnet she glanced over—and found herself looking up. For a moment she froze as her gaze clashed with icy blue eyes.

The man looking at her smiled politely then sort of froze as he stared at her in turn. Good Lord, this man was *sexy*. She blinked once, feeling mesmerized, and tried to force a polite smile but...she just kept staring like a lunatic. When he kept looking at her too, she wondered if she had something on her face.

Even though she had the insane urge to check her teeth, she resisted and somehow tore her gaze away to stare at the elevator doors. As they stood there, she could feel his gaze on her.

Or maybe that was just wishful thinking.

When the elevator doors swooshed open, he motioned for her to enter. And as they stepped into the elevator together, whatever that subtle, sexy masculine scent was wrapped around her. She tried not to sniff like a weirdo as she pressed the button for the top floor. "Which floor?" she asked, too nervous to meet his gaze again.

"Same one," he said in a deep, delicious voice she felt all the way to her core.

Damn, that voice should be bottled up and sold. But only to *her*. Clearly she hadn't had sex in too long because she was starting to fantasize about some stranger in an elevator. And at that thought, she started thinking about elevator sex with this particular stranger. The man with pale blue eyes, dark hair and broad shoulders. Shoulders she could easily imagine holding on to as he pinned her up against this elevator wall.

Oh my God, stop it, she ordered herself. *Get it together!* After she'd caught her asshole ex cheating on her—freaking tale as old as time—she'd sworn off men for a while. But Tall, Dark and Mouthwateringly Hot was making her rethink that. As if drawn to him, she tried to sneak a peek at his face again and found him looking directly at her.

Their gazes clashed but he averted his almost immediately and looked forward again, his posture stiff.

As the elevator dinged, he made a motion for her to step out, depriving her of that sexy voice again. And a peek at his ass.

She felt self-conscious, especially since he was in a very expensive suit and she was wearing jeans, a green T-shirt that said *Hulk Mode On* and sparkly green sneakers. She wasn't sure why she was fantasizing about this guy when she had no doubt she wasn't his type. He probably went for tall, leggy women who dressed in pencil skirts, silk tops and five-inch heels.

When they both turned left into the hallway, she said, "I take it we're going to the same place." Then she inwardly cursed herself for her nervous chatter. Clearly they were going to the same place, *Captain Obvious*.

"Looks like it." He glanced at her, his gaze sweeping over her quickly before he glanced back ahead.

Finally, blessedly, they reached the end of the hallway. As they stepped into the only office at the end of it, her friend Chloe—who she was meeting to go book shopping with over her friend's lunch break—stood suddenly.

"Mr. MacArthur, you can go on back. He's expecting you." Then she nodded once at Kathryn before picking up the phone intercom. "I'm off to lunch but Mr. MacArthur is here for you. I'll see you in an hour." Her mouth curving into a smile, she grabbed her purse. "I'm ready to do some damage on my credit card."

Kathryn grinned. "Me too," she murmured before flicking a glance at the man whose name was apparently Mr. MacArthur.

He hadn't gone very far, and instead was watching her with a sexy sort of intensity she felt all the way to her core. *Oh wow.* Heat curled inside her from just one look from him. She wondered what he could do with more than that.

Somehow she tore her gaze away and joined Chloe. They were heading to a bookstore downtown owned by one of their friends—and then probably hitting up a shoe sale Chloe had been talking about. "So who was that?" Kathryn murmured as they reached the elevators. She didn't care that they were far out of earshot, she still didn't want to talk too loud in case he somehow overheard her.

"Who was who?"

"The man you called Mr. MacArthur. What's his story?"

Her friend shot her a sly look. "Why?"

"Because I have eyes and he was sexy as hell." Her cheeks flushed even as she said the words. It wasn't like he could overhear her, but still, they were in the same building and it felt weird.

Chloe's dark eyes widened slightly. "I thought you'd sworn off men."

She lifted a shoulder as they stepped into the elevator. Things changed.

"He's single as far as I know—not that I know much. He's always very polite, not the creep type if you know what I mean."

Of course she knew.

"I'll find out more about him if you want?"

She shook her head. "No way. It's not like I'm going to see him again. I was just being nosy because he was hot and it's been far too long since

I've had sex." Besides, if she wanted to know more about him, she could find out on her own.

"Whose fault is that?" Flipping her dark hair over her shoulder, Chloe gave her a tart look as they stepped off the elevator.

"I feel like the answer you're looking for is mine."

"It *is* your fault. You get asked out all the time."

"Whatever. Let's go get some new books."

"And shoes."

"Definitely. I need some new sneakers too."

Chloe just snorted as she eyed Kathryn's sparkly ones—probably because she had like sixty pairs of sneakers—but then she grinned as they stepped out into the sunshine. "We need to get some kayak time this weekend."

Kathryn groaned slightly.

"What? The weather's gorgeous."

"You're always trying to make me get outside."

"Yeah, you need the vitamin D."

"Unlike you, I have to slather sunscreen on every inch of my body when we do." The curse of her redheaded coloring.

"We'll go early, then."

"All right." She actually didn't mind kayaking, but Chloe was way more outdoorsy than Kathryn. And she ran marathons.

That was something Kathryn would never understand—running for fun. The only time anyone would catch her running is if she was being chased by a rabid pack of dogs. She much preferred yoga and swimming.

By the time they'd made it back to Chloe's job, they were a few minutes late—so Kathryn gave her a quick hug before Chloe made a dash for the glass doors.

"This weekend, kayaking, don't forget," Chloe tossed over her shoulder before she hurried inside.

"You like kayaking?" The deep male voice made her turn around.

She recognized the voice instantly—she'd only heard it once but now it was etched into her brain. She found herself looking up into the handsome face of Mr. MacArthur. And she really wished she knew what his first name was now. "Ah, sort of."

"You sort of like kayaking?"

She glanced around, surprised this sexy god was talking to her. There was a car idling along the curb and she guessed it was waiting for him. A few people walked past them but the street was otherwise pretty quiet. Yep, he was talking to her. "Yeah, sort of. But I love my friend so I go with her. I mean, it's good exercise and she swears the vitamin D is good for me."

He chuckled slightly, giving her his full attention. Which was kind of unnerving. "What kinds of things do you like to do?"

Oh, she could think of a slew of things she'd like to do—to him. Wait, had she said that out loud? He wasn't looking at her weird so she must have kept it to herself. "Um, yoga, swimming, drinking too much chai and going on historic ghost tours." Oh God, this was like the worst dating profile description ever. What was wrong with her? Why couldn't she have given a normal answer? Yep, he was going to walk away now.

His mouth quirked up slightly as he shoved his hands into the pockets of his very expensive-looking slacks. "Historic ghost tours?"

"I've been on a lot of them, mainly along the East Coast."

"Maybe you can take me with you on one of them."

She blinked. Wait, was he asking her out? Before she could decide, his grin grew even more.

He held out a hand. A very big one. "I'm Daniel."

She held out her own, shivering at the feel of his callused palm caressing her own, at the way his hand completely engulfed hers. "Kathryn."

Something sparked between them at that moment and she knew he felt it too, because she could see the awareness flash in his blue eyes.

It mirrored the heat that rushed through her. And she realized she didn't want to take him on a historic ghost tour, she wanted to take him home right now and have her wicked way with him.

CHAPTER FOUR

K athryn nearly turned back around the second after she stepped inside her favorite bakery. It was within walking distance of her condo and she'd been craving their cranberry muffins this morning. But when she saw Daniel sitting at one of the little tables in the corner, her stomach tightened. She wanted to put her sunglasses back on as a sort of barrier.

But it was too late. He waved at her and she of course waved back, feigning a calmness she didn't feel at all. She hadn't slept well last night —every little noise had woken her. She'd already been on edge after seeing him yesterday—and the events of last night had completely screwed up her equilibrium. And now to run into him at her favorite place? What was he even doing on this side of town? He lived in a high-rise downtown, whereas she lived in a small community filled with mostly elderly people. Her grandmother had left her the condo when she passed away and it was filled with a lot of wonderful memories. Plus it was quiet and she liked it.

Daniel stood and motioned for her to come over. And...it appeared as if he already had a couple cranberry muffins. Was he a mind reader now?

Unable to stop the frown as she approached his table, she said, "Hey, I'm surprised to see you here."

"Well I can admit to ulterior motives. I was hoping to run into you this morning."

Well, at least he was being honest. Her gaze flicked down to the muffins. "How do you feel about sharing your food?"

He snickered and sat back down so she sat across from him. Then he slid the little plate across to her. "They're all yours."

She narrowed her gaze even as she snagged one of the muffins. "You don't even like cranberry."

"But you do."

"You're pretty sneaky, showing up like this." And pushing her weakness on her—carbohydrates and yummy goodness.

"I took a chance coming here. I know you used to stop by on Saturday mornings. I already ordered your favorite drink too—a cinnamon tea latte. I told the barista to start making one if a pretty redhead joined me."

"Very, very sneaky," she said, and laughed despite the tension in her shoulders. "Clearly this isn't a chance meeting. So what's going on?" she asked, only pausing as the woman from behind the counter brought her a drink and set it in front of her with a smile. "Thank you," she murmured and looked at Daniel once they were alone again. There were people in line, but almost everyone was sitting outside at the patio tables. Only one other couple sat a few tables away, giving them a decent amount of privacy.

"To start, I know I should have called, but I didn't think you'd answer." He paused, watching her.

"I might not have."

"That's what I thought. And screw it, I needed to clear the air. One day we were together and then we were just over without warning. Last night you said something that's been bothering me. You said that I thought you were after me for my money. Why would you think that?"

This was the exact conversation she didn't want to have. She could admit that money was a sore spot for her. Her parents had argued about it for most of her childhood. Her father had continuously accused her mother of only wanting to be with him for his money until finally her mother had left him and gotten full custody of Kathryn and her two brothers.

The divorce had been the best thing that had happened to her parents because they'd been able to finally start raising their kids without all the yelling and dysfunction. They'd turned into completely different people. Better people.

"Do you remember the day I ended things with you?" she asked quietly. Clearly he wasn't giving up on this conversation, so she was going to just deal with it.

He nodded, his expression darkening.

"I don't know how much you remember about that day, but I was supposed to meet you in your office before we headed out to dinner. You were running late so your assistant had me wait in your office. And…I saw something on your desk. I was *not* snooping," she added. "The paper was literally right on your desk in front of my face and the file had my name on it in big, bold print. It was a whole file about me with a little sticky note that had the words 'gold digger' underlined three times." She felt her cheeks flush in pain and anger even as a rush of ice slid through her veins. She felt exactly as she had that day when she'd seen the file with her entire life just laid out in black and white.

He stared at her in shock.

"I wasn't looking for it," she reiterated. "But it doesn't matter. It was pretty clear you'd done some research on me. And I have no idea why you thought I was a gold digger. I also hate that word, for the record, but anyway, that's why I ended things." She shrugged and tore off the top of the muffin. She wasn't hungry anymore but managed to chew and swallow it regardless.

He stared for another long moment. "I don't know what you're talking about. I did have someone look into you when we first started dating. Technically before—"

"Wait, before?" She pushed the muffin away now, unable to even pretend to eat.

He cleared his throat. "I have to be careful. Not just because of money, but because of people who try to insinuate themselves in my life for other things as well. So yeah, Jerry looked into you, but he never called you a gold digger."

"It was in your handwriting." She knew his handwriting because he'd often left her cute little notes to find in the morning when he had to get up early for work. They hadn't been living together, not technically, but they might as well have been for all the nights they'd spent together. Which had been *all* of them. They'd alternated weeks, one at her place, then the next at his. She'd even cleared out a spot in her small closet—and he'd given her half of his giant one.

"Bullshit."

Anger surged through her. "I know what I saw. It's not like I took a picture of it or anything, so I don't have proof, but it was there. I saw it with my own eyes. And I really don't want to talk about it anymore."

"That's why you ended things with me?" His jaw tightened.

She nodded. "If you'd done, like, a simple background check or something, I obviously would have understood, but that file was a thick binder. And that note..." *Ugh.* She didn't even want to think about it anymore. When she'd seen it, it had been like all their time together had been a lie, as if she hadn't known him at all.

"Did you look at the file?"

"No. I saw the top page and the sticky note and I wanted to throw up."

"I remember you bailed early that night saying you didn't feel well."

"I wasn't lying. I *didn't* feel well."

"Look, the 'file' on you is like two pages. Not a binder full of information. I feel like a dick even admitting it now, but yeah, there was some information on your financials in it. It was very basic stuff. I just...I really liked you when we met. And I've been burned in the past."

Yeah, she knew he had, which was why it wasn't necessarily the file itself but that awful note that had changed everything for her. She shifted in her seat, wanting to believe him. But she knew what she'd seen.

"I'm sorry about the file," he continued. "I'm sorry for whatever you saw. I'm sorry that you got hurt. No, that's wrong, I'm sorry I inadvertently hurt you," he clarified. "But I never, ever wrote a note calling you that. And I really miss you," he finally murmured.

Oh, God. "I miss you too," she blurted without meaning to. It was true anyway. She'd missed him for two long months and he seemed so damn sincere. Which just served to confuse her even more. She'd seen that note. Maybe…she'd jumped to conclusions? But no. That damn thing had been underlined three times.

A long, awkward pause stretched between them so she picked up her drink, sipping on it because she wasn't sure where to go from here.

"So what's going on with this whole mugging and someone trying to attack you at your condo?" he asked, shifting directions.

Inwardly she breathed out a sigh of relief. Talking about that was much better than talking about the two of them. Especially since there wasn't a "them" anymore, and she didn't think there could be after that note. "I don't really know what to say. You heard everything last night. It's just bad luck."

He frowned, and somehow he looked even more handsome, which was ridiculous. It wasn't fair that he was so effortlessly put together. "I don't like it."

Maybe the subject change wasn't the best thing after all. Daniel could go into super overprotective mode, and he was worse than her brothers. "Well, I don't like it either. But I'm being smart about it." She cleared her throat. "So how's your sister?"

"She's been really busy the last month," he said.

"Really?"

He nodded. "Yeah, why?"

"We've been texting, but she's been totally unavailable and I thought… Honestly, I thought maybe she was blowing me off because you and I broke up." And that hurt.

He snorted at that. "Sienna told me that she wanted to keep you after the breakup, and trade me in."

Kathryn let out a startled burst of laughter and took a sip of her drink. Being with him like this now brought up far too many memories, far too many emotions she wanted to ignore. Things between them had been so great, so easy. Until she'd found that stupid note and it had fed into every single one of her insecurities.

They were from two different worlds, and to learn that he thought she was a gold digger had shaken her. He denied it and she wasn't sure what to think now. "I'm sure she didn't mean it."

He snorted again. "I wouldn't bet money on that. Look, I asked her about you being engaged."

She blinked. "What?"

"Yeah. I was annoyed that she hadn't told me about it and she was surprised. So if she says anything, sorry about that."

"Oh…ah, it's not a problem." Clearly he didn't realize that she'd been behind the job at his place. And even though she wanted to tell him, she didn't want to talk about her personal life with him.

Or more specifically, her lack of one.

CHAPTER FIVE

Normally Daniel didn't go into the office on Saturdays unless it was an emergency, but he'd scheduled an appointment with the tech company that had done a sweep of security at the new building he'd recently acquired. This was the only day that had worked well for both of them.

He stepped out of his office when he heard the elevator doors ding softly. He'd told security to send this guy directly up and his assistant wasn't here today.

As Tony Domínguez stepped out of the elevators, Daniel nodded politely at him as he strode across the waiting area directly to him. "Thanks for meeting me on a Saturday."

"No problem." In khakis, a plain button-down shirt and loafers, Tony was dressed casual today.

"I've got coffee and water and can probably find some snacks if you're hungry." There should be a bunch of snacks in the kitchen for meetings.

Tony shook his head. "I'm good. But thank you anyway."

Daniel had only had coffee that morning before Kathryn had shown up at her normal café. He felt a little bit bad about ambushing her but he'd needed to see her and clear up what had happened between them.

Now that he knew *why* she'd left him, he realized that their breakup had been because of a misunderstanding. He simply couldn't understand why there had been a sticky note on the file—one he sure as hell hadn't written. Kathryn wasn't prone to making shit up either, so he believed it had been there. And he wasn't even sure why the file had been on his desk.

It didn't make sense and he intended to get to the bottom of things. He wondered if one of her brothers had somehow set him up. They'd never really warmed up to him, but...that seemed extreme. Still... Carson, her oldest brother, had stopped by to see him a couple times before Kathryn had broken up with him. Maybe... *Hell.* He was going to figure this out later.

"I assume you already looked at the email I sent," Tony said as he sat in the plush chair in front of Daniel's desk.

He rounded the desk and sat down as well. "I did, thank you." Tony had sent him a basic outline of the very few flaws in the security. But he'd wanted to talk in person about everything that had been done to break through the first firewall yesterday before giving him the full report, something Daniel appreciated.

"This is the complete file." Tony set a binder on the desk between them. "And I'll follow up with a digital copy. Everything is broken down into categories, but basically you have a few holes in the security system, and they're all very easily fixable. More than anything, it boils down to updating certain software on-site and making sure everything is automatically updated from this point forward."

"Did the whole balloons and bubbles thing have anything to do with the security breach?" A random guy had been there at the same time Kathryn— Holy shit, was Kathryn involved? She analyzed security systems for a living, exactly what he'd hired Tony to do for him. No... she went in and evaluated security programs directly with the IT and security people. But what if she had been involved?

Was that why she'd been at the building yesterday? She hadn't been wearing the ring today and had seemed almost confused by the mention of a fiancé. Had the whole wedding planner meeting thing just been a front?

KATIE REUS

When he realized that Tony was talking, he forced his mind off the sexy redhead and focused.

"Yes. He worked with a partner who got access to another floor and used a hole in their security to infiltrate yours. Since both companies are on the same intranet, it was easy enough for her. Easy is a relative term, because she's very talented. The details are all in the report."

Her? "Does Kathryn Irish by chance work for you?"

The man's eyes widened, but only for a second. "As a rule, I don't include the names of my employees in the reports—because I've had clients try to poach my contractors—but yes, she does contract work for me. And she's the one who infiltrated your system, something you must already know."

So she *wasn't* engaged. She'd been using that as a cover to get to the eighth floor. And now that he thought about it, she actually hadn't confirmed that she was engaged anyway. She'd used deflective language. Not to mention he hadn't seen any signs at her place of a man. No clothes, shoes, no pictures. And she hadn't been wearing that huge ring this morning either.

The tight band of tension eased inside him and he felt like he could finally breathe for the first time in two days. "Good to know." Somehow his voice came out calm when he felt anything but. *Kathryn is single.* There wasn't a damn reason they shouldn't be together.

"You know her?" Tony asked.

He lifted his shoulder casually. "I've tried to hire her on full-time, more than once, but she always turns me down." Which was true. When they'd been together, he'd offered her a job—at a location he didn't work at—and she'd turned him down. She'd been right to, of course.

Tony laughed at that. "She likes doing contract work. I've offered her a full-time job myself as well. I think she likes making her own schedule, and her rates are through the roof. She's worth it of course, and I think she knows she would be making less if she worked directly for me. I simply can't offer her enough incentives to come on full-time when the top companies are fighting for her attention." He shrugged.

Yep, Kathryn was incredible, in more ways than one. And as soon as this meeting was over, Daniel intended to confront her about every-

38

thing. Now that he understood why she'd left, now that he knew she was single, he wasn't wasting another day without trying to win her back. "Thank you again for all of this. I'll review it all in-depth and make sure my security team does as well. If I have any questions, I'll let you know."

They talked for a few more minutes before Tony left and Daniel flipped the binder open, scanning over the contents. What Kathryn and her partner had done had been very smart, and if he hadn't known her on a personal level and stopped to converse for those few moments, she would have been in and out of the building even more quickly than she had been.

Damn, she was good.

And now he needed to make things right with her, to win her back. He'd never stopped loving her. When people talked about the one that got away—he didn't want that to be him. He'd known from practically the first date with Kathryn that she was the one for him.

He rubbed a hand over his face, feeling off-kilter. His life was neat and organized, but then Kathryn had blown into it and tossed everything into disarray.

For the last two months he hadn't been living, he'd been going through the motions, in denial about his broken heart. He'd been going to work, making money and coming home. Sure, he went to required functions when he had to, but that was about it, and he never enjoyed them. His brother and sister had both called him out on his bullshit, but he hadn't had enough energy to do anything other than just exist.

He pulled out his cell and made a call, determined to fix things with Kathryn. Starting now.

CHAPTER SIX

K athryn scratched Mr. Twinkles under his chin, grinning at the way he cuddled up to her. She always hated leaving him because he punished her when she came back, ignoring her completely until she fed him or gave him a treat.

Typical cat.

"I promise to bring you a treat when I get home," she said as she stood, as if he understood her.

Which she was pretty certain he did.

The white, black and orange calico cat with the twinkly eyes—hence the name Mr. Twinkles—who'd stolen her heart a year ago simply sniffed imperiously at her. Then he turned his back and swished his tail as he jumped onto the floor and plopped right down in a patch of sunshine. Yeah, he would be completely fine while she was gone.

She had a meeting with a headhunter today who swore he just wanted to talk to her about a contract job, and she really wanted to believe him. But headhunters contacted her monthly, sometimes biweekly, trying to lure her away from her actual contract work to settle down with a regular nine-to-five job. But she liked the freedom of what she did and liked being her own boss. It was still very much a man's world, especially in her line of work—and she did not want to get pigeonholed into a crappy job. Maybe one day she would change her tune, but not now.

The guy had just contacted her last night, on a Sunday no less, but his credentials were good so she decided to meet up with him and see if he had anything real to offer.

She wished she'd had more time to research this new company but she'd gone out with some friends for lunch yesterday, had yoga class and then book club—which had also included some wine time—and she hadn't had time.

Twenty minutes later here she was, wearing her rainbow sparkly sneakers, dark jeans and a T-shirt that said *Book Nerd* with glasses replacing the o's. She never dressed business casual for these things, even though she was meeting in a high-rise downtown. In the beginning of her career she had, but then she'd realized that none of the security nerds like her dressed to fit in. She'd passed that point in her career and she did not have to impress anybody.

If anything, they had to impress her. And she knew it sounded arrogant, but if she'd been a dude, it would be called confidence. So she ignored the surprised look—and quick sweep of Kathryn's attire—by the administrative assistant when she approached the front desk on the fifteenth floor. The woman's demeanor instantly changed when she told her she was Kathryn Irish.

Then the pretty blonde straightened and gave her a winning smile straight out of *Dentistry Today*. "Of course, Ms. Irish, please follow me. May I offer you something to drink? Cinnamon tea latte, cucumber water?"

She frowned at the cinnamon tea latte comment, since it was her favorite. Maybe this headhunter had done his homework. "The latte would be great, thank you."

The woman briskly nodded and hurried out on heels that looked painful to walk in.

That was one of the reasons Kathryn liked working for herself. She made the dress code and she was convinced that heels had been created by a demon.

Instead of sitting down, she strode to the bank of windows overlooking downtown and smiled at the sight. She loved the Florida coast and was glad her entire family lived here—even if her middle brother was off on some assignment. The city had always seemed so big until recently. After she and Daniel had broken up, she'd found herself avoiding places they'd gone together out of fear that she'd run into him. Because apparently she was a big ole chickenshit.

When the door opened she turned, ready to politely greet Ryan Richards, and froze for all of a second when she saw Daniel striding in, wearing another custom suit and a tie she'd actually bought him.

"Oh my God, Daniel, are you that hard up for a date that you're ambushing me now?" she snapped out before she could stop herself. She was annoyed that he was surprising her like this. *Again.* "I think we're past the point of stalking now."

Annnnnnnd that was when she saw two people behind him—a man she assumed was Ryan, the headhunter, and Daniel's pretty assistant, Nicole, who was staring at Kathryn in shock. She blinked those big blue eyes at her, looking a bit like a deer in headlights.

Kathryn winced, ready to backtrack, but to her surprise Daniel threw his head back and laughed. "Why don't you guys give us a second?" he said to the other two before very politely ushering them out. He shut the door with a soft snick and turned to face her.

"What's going on?" she demanded, annoyed.

"First of all, I'm not hard up for a date, because I'm not looking. You ruined me for other women."

She stared at him, surprised by the ridiculous statement. She'd *seen* him in the society pages more than once since she'd ended things with him. Including something this morning with a brunette knockout—which was part of the reason she'd blurted out something so rude.

"Second of all, I want to offer you a job. A contract job," he said, holding up a hand when she went to interrupt him. "I know you won't work for me directly. But I just bought a new company and I trust your judgment. I knew if I called you to one of my offices, you wouldn't answer. So I set this up with an associate of mine who's letting me use this conference room."

"You can't know that for sure." Chances were, she wouldn't have answered, but still.

"Yeah, well, I was playing the odds."

She sniffed once before approaching the conference table and sitting down. "I guess now you'll never know."

He must've taken that as a good sign because he sat across from her. "I swear this is just business. But if you agree to go on a date with me, then—"

"Noooooo, no dating talk." Still, the way he looked at her got those butterflies in her stomach going. Why couldn't she be immune to him? It was so much harder because he seemed so sincere about everything.

"Okay. For now anyway." He leaned down and pulled something out of his briefcase and slid it across to her.

When she looked inside the bag and saw a toy for her cat she smiled despite herself. "What is this, bribery?"

He shrugged, a far too wicked grin playing on his too handsome face. "I've missed Mr. Twinkles."

"He's missed you too," she said grudgingly. Her traitorous cat, who didn't warm up to anybody but her—the cat who gave the cold shoulder to even her best friend and her brothers—had practically attacked Daniel with cuddles the first time they'd met. Mr. Twinkles had curled up in his lap and meowed until he'd gotten his fill of behind-the-ear scratches. That cat was shameless. "Fair warning, I'm going to give him this toy and tell him it's from me."

This brought on another laugh from Daniel. "That's fair. So...do you want to look at the job details? I know I sprung this on you, but I really do want your expertise."

It warmed her from the inside out that he respected what she did, and getting a job with him would be really good for her portfolio. Sure, she had people knocking down the door trying to get her to work for them, but doing something for Daniel MacArthur? Yeah, this would look really good. She couldn't appear too eager, however. "I'm listening."

He quickly outlined everything for her, and as he wrapped up, he said, "For the first week, you'll be located out of my main building because I want you to run distance diagnostics. But after that you'll transfer to the new building and go from there."

She nodded and then quoted him her price. It was double what she normally charged but he didn't bat an eye.

Damn, maybe she needed to raise her rates.

"I'll have my assistant draw up a contract," he continued. "I just need to know when you can start."

"Well, as I'm pretty sure you know, I just finished a contract." Tony had shot her a text this morning letting her know that Daniel MacArthur was aware of her involvement in the last job and had been impressed by her work.

He gave her a slow grin. "I didn't realize it at the time, but yeah, I did once I talked to Tony."

"Sorry about that," she murmured, feeling a little guilty. But only a little. She could have told him that she wasn't engaged but then she would have had to explain why she'd been wearing a big ring. And that hadn't been her place, not when he'd hired Tony.

"So you're not actually engaged?" he asked, even though it was clear he knew the answer.

"No. And I'm kind of surprised you thought I would be engaged two months after we broke up." The relationship had meant a whole lot more to her than that. Clearly he hadn't had any such compunction and had moved on very quickly. He'd been dating, according to what she'd seen online.

To be fair she'd gone on a couple dates too. They'd been incredibly crappy dates, but dates nonetheless. Mainly because her friends had set her up and pushed her into it. She'd thought it would help her move on from Daniel. Of course it hadn't worked.

"I..." He cleared his throat, then turned at a soft knock on the door.

After opening it, he spoke quietly to the others and as he did, the woman from before walked in with her latte. "I'm so sorry, I would've brought this sooner but the door was shut and I didn't want to interrupt."

"Don't worry about it, I really appreciate this," Kathryn said, smiling.

"Of course. Is there anything else I can get you? Some snacks? We've got anything you can imagine."

She shook her head once as Daniel popped his head back in. "I'll be right back with the contract. If there's anything in it you don't like, or if you want your attorney to look over it, it doesn't need to be signed today."

"It depends how detailed the contract is, but if it's industry-standard then we should be fine." Usually she let her attorney look at everything but deep down she knew Daniel wouldn't screw her. And she'd read enough of these things that she had a pretty good eye for what to look for. As long as there weren't eighty-four pages of fine print, they should be okay.

He simply nodded and ducked back out again. The woman did the same, leaving Kathryn alone. Suddenly the room seemed bigger without him in it. He'd always had that effect, a sort of larger-than-life thing that made people gravitate toward him. Herself included. He didn't even seem to realize it most of the time. Being around him, even in a business setting, was messing with her head. She kept thinking about how damn sincere he'd seemed when she'd told him about that note, about the file she'd seen. It was hard to believe he was that good of a liar and really, what would be the point? He could get any woman he wanted.

Needing to get her mind off him, she pulled her cell phone out of her purse and realized she had a missed call from Detective Mendoza. As she listened to his voicemail, a lead ball settled in her gut.

"What's that look for?" Daniel asked as he stepped back into the room. Alone. She guessed the headhunter wasn't needed anymore—clearly Daniel had used the guy to get her here.

She tucked her phone away. "Nothing."

"I know that look. Come on, what's going on?"

She sighed. "I got a message from Detective Mendoza. He just wants me to come down to the station."

Daniel straightened. "Did he get a break in the case?"

She shrugged, not wanting to talk about it with him. Because if she did, then he'd be even more involved in her life. She was supposed to be getting over him. At that thought, she snorted at herself. She was such a liar—if she wanted to get over him, she wouldn't have taken this job. She would have walked out of the conference room and never looked back. Ugh, she was such a fool.

Even though she told herself to keep quiet, she said, "He wants me to look at a lineup of suspects from the mugging."

"Let's go now," he said, just taking over in that way of his.

"Daniel—"

"If he called, it's got to be important."

She stared at him. "Don't I need to go over the contract stuff?"

"I'm not worried about it. We can deal with it later. I'll have Nicole email it to you. Come on." He stood, holding the door open for her, as if the situation was settled.

She wanted to argue with him, but a very small part of her liked the idea of him coming with her to the police station. Even though she knew the mugging and near attack were coincidences, the two things had really shaken her—especially the masked man at her condo complex. Her place was so quiet, and as far as she knew there had never been anything other than extremely petty crime there. As in, bikes or potted plants getting stolen.

"You're kind of a bulldozer," she muttered as she reached the door.

"And you're kind of adorable."

Her stomach flipped over at his words. What the hell was he trying to do to her today? He'd told her he wanted to go on a date with her, that she was adorable, that she'd ruined him for other women. She couldn't deal with any of this, this...blunt honesty!

Gah. She simply needed to deal with one thing at a time and right now that was apparently looking at a lineup of potential mugging suspects.

Not obsessing about her ex-boyfriend.

CHAPTER SEVEN

D aniel was in full-on overprotective mode as he and Kathryn entered the police station. To his disappointment, her brother, Carson Irish, was waiting for her right in the busy lobby.

He and the detective were pretty close in size but Carson was broader. With his buzzed haircut and tattoos peeking out from his neckline, he looked like a street brawler more than a detective. He eyed Daniel coolly, even as he pulled Kathryn into a big hug. And when he looked at his sister, his expression completely softened.

"Hey, little bit, what's the douche doing here?" he asked, even though Daniel was standing two feet away.

Kathryn gasped slightly and nudged him in the stomach. "Be nice," she ordered, but there was absolutely no heat behind her words. Once upon a time, she would've actually been annoyed at Carson, but apparently she wasn't feeling the love for Daniel right now.

That was okay. He was going to make things right. He was in this for the long run and he wasn't letting her go. Not this time.

"Good to see you too," Daniel said mildly.

Carson just grunted at him and slid an arm around his sister's shoulders before tossing Daniel a dark look.

Annoyed that he didn't have the right to touch Kathryn, not even to hold her hand, he strode after them. They moved across the lobby and through the bullpen, a cluster of desks in an open space, before stepping into a long hallway. Carson stopped them a few doors down and motioned to it.

"I can't go any farther with you, and neither can Daniel. Just take your time," he said to Kathryn, who nodded.

She glanced back at Daniel and gave him a small smile. "Thanks for coming with me." Then she nudged Carson and ordered him to be nice. Again.

As she stepped into the room, no doubt to look at the lineup, he hated that he couldn't go with her. That he couldn't support her.

"What the hell are you doing here, MacArthur?" Carson asked, practically snarling now that they were alone. The thin veneer he'd put on earlier was completely gone.

If Kathryn had told her brother about that damn note, it was no wonder Carson seemed to hate him now. "What does it look like?"

"You have no business being with my sister."

"I'm not having this conversation with you." Especially since now he was wondering if Carson had been behind that note. "So what happened? You guys find who mugged her?"

Carson's shoulders were still bunched tight, but he leaned against the wall and crossed his arms over his chest. "Kathryn went on a date with some guy a month ago and apparently he and this guy he works with target women to rob them. It's petty shit but they're fairly organized, and in my opinion it's only a matter of time before it gets more violent. Mendoza wanted her in here to look at a lineup, see if she recognized the mugger."

"She was on a date with someone?" he asked, even though he should be focusing on so many other things.

Carson's mouth lifted up ever so slightly, a dark glint in his eyes. "Yep. And it's not the only one she's been on since she tossed your sorry ass over."

He took a steadying breath so he wouldn't punch a detective in the police station. Because even as good as his lawyers were, he didn't think they'd get him out of that. "So the mugger wasn't wearing a mask, but the guy from her condo was?"

"Yeah, I know. But these guys have followed up with more muggings. Assholes." Carson frowned, then dismissed Daniel as he pulled his phone out and started texting. "They both better go away for a long time," he finally muttered, tucking his phone away.

"How sure are you that this is the guy who was harassing her?" Daniel asked.

"Four women have ID'd him so far. These guys targeted women from their gym so there's a common denominator here, which made it easy for us to track them. Dumbasses," he muttered in disgust. "If only all criminals made it this easy."

Surprised that Carson had actually told him so much, Daniel simply grunted in agreement and leaned against the opposite wall, shoving his hands in his pockets as he waited for Kathryn to exit.

He also tried not to obsess over the fact that she had apparently been on dates. As in plural. He hadn't been able to even look at another woman since her. He'd gone to a couple work functions but the women he'd brought had been friends, someone looking for a plus-one to make the night more bearable. Something he understood. It was so much easier to fend off people when you had a "date."

When Kathryn stepped out of the room minutes later, everything else fell away as he focused on her. "Are you okay?" He stepped forward, ignoring her brother completely.

"I'm good." She smiled at him and the sight of it hit him right in the solar plexus. Damn, he'd missed her smiles. Missed waking up to her every morning. He'd even missed her needy cat, Mr. Twinkles. Who, okay, he really liked. But the name Mr. Twinkles was kind of ridiculous.

"Did you recognize anyone?" Carson asked.

She nodded. "I don't think I'm supposed to talk about it with you though."

Her brother laughed lightly and kissed the top of her head. "Look, I gotta go, we just got a suspect pulled in for another case. But I'll see you at Sunday dinner." Before he left, he shot another dark look at Daniel. "Hopefully I won't be seeing you anytime soon."

"I'm sorry about him," she murmured as her brother hurried down the hallway in the opposite direction.

He lifted a shoulder. "I've got a sister myself." And if Carson thought Daniel had labeled his sister as a gold digger, then Daniel understood why the man was pissed at him. Unless he'd planted that note—then screw him.

"You're being very accommodating about all this."

"It's not about me right now and I'm sorry you're dealing with any of this at all."

She gave him a strange look but didn't respond, simply motioned that they should head out.

At that moment, walking right next to her, he'd never felt more disconnected from her. And he hated that.

But he couldn't believe it would be this way forever. If she needed time to trust him again, he'd give it to her.

~

ONCE THEY WERE in Daniel's car, Kathryn laid her head against the headrest.

"Do you want to tell me what happened in there?" There was real concern in his voice.

"The guy who mugged me worked with some guy I went on a date with. They're both scumbags apparently. And he's actually been arrested on a bench warrant from another county so he'll be going to jail and charged with crimes that have nothing to do with me or any of his other victims here. They have a ton of evidence against the guy and it doesn't look like it's going to trial at all. Not if he agrees to a slightly shorter sentence. His partner is being charged with a bunch of conspiracy stuff too. They'll go away for at least eight years, probably longer."

"Both guys, you're sure?"

"Yes. The one who did the actual mugging will serve more time but they're not cutting a real deal for either of them. If they agree to do their time without the waste of a trial, it'll shave off a few years, but not by much. Bastards," she muttered.

"Agreed." He cleared his throat and she could feel the tension rise in the vehicle. "So…you've been dating?"

She glanced out the window, looking at the cars as they passed by. "Yeah." And it was weird to talk to him about it. She sure didn't want to talk or think about *him* dating.

"How are your brothers doing?" he asked, shifting gears. "You know, besides hating me right now?"

That pulled a laugh out of her and she turned to look at him as he drove expertly through traffic. "They're good. Carson is busy as always and Colm is out of town for work now. What about your brother?"

"On vacation."

She blinked. "Seriously?"

"Yep. I'm as surprised as you," he said dryly.

She laughed lightly. Brodie was so serious, even compared to Daniel. He owned his own security firm and did a lot of work for a local billionaire. "Good for him. He deserves the break."

Daniel shot her a look.

"What?"

"Nothing. He's asked about you… He misses you too. My whole family does."

Oh…hell. Clearing her throat, she looked away again, unsure how to respond to that. Thankfully Daniel didn't push her more. Instead, he turned the radio on low as they cruised through the throng of traffic.

And by the time they made it back to her condo, she felt more at ease and was glad that he'd driven her. She was surprised, however, when she saw her vehicle in her spot already. She'd planned to grab a rideshare later and just pick it up.

"I had your vehicle delivered so you wouldn't have to deal with getting it later."

She blinked once. "How'd you even get my keys?"

"I still had that spare from before—I swear I forgot about it until now."

Well, she didn't think he was going to steal her car. Not when he had much more expensive ones than hers. "That was very thoughtful, thank you." Daniel had always been thoughtful, so it wasn't exactly a surprise.

He parked and rounded the front of the vehicle, pulling open her door before she'd even unstrapped.

"Thanks," she murmured again. If he was a giant jerk it would make all of this a whole lot easier. Now she was confused, plain and simple. "You don't have to walk me to my door."

He simply shot her a look with raised eyebrows before falling in step with her. And as they reached her door, he turned to her and said, "I think I've made it pretty clear, but I want to put it out there. I haven't been dating since you. I don't want to date anyone but you. I want another chance."

Even at the sincerity in his voice, she snorted softly.

His eyes narrowed. "What?"

"I don't like it when people lie to me."

"You mean like telling someone they're engaged when they're not?"

She felt her cheeks heat up but she lifted a shoulder. "Technically I never told you I was engaged. You made assumptions based on what you saw and I simply didn't correct you."

His lips curved up ever so slightly. "Fine, that's fair enough. Look, I never wrote a note calling you a gold digger. Yes, I had to look into you a little bit based on past experiences. I would think that was something you could understand."

"I do understand *that*." She'd seen that note in his handwriting— but he seemed so damn sincere. He also seemed sincere about not dating and she knew what she'd seen online. But she also knew that those gossip sites lied. She was too embarrassed to tell him she'd been sorta stalking him online so didn't bring up what she'd seen. "My brother looked into you a little bit too," she murmured. "Before our first date."

He blinked once before that grin was back in place. "I'm not actually surprised."

"He likes to make sure I'm not dating losers."

"So what happened with the last guy?" His tone was dry.

"I didn't tell him, but in hindsight I probably should've. It would have saved me a headache. And a mugging—and likely a lunatic trying to attack me at my condo." At that thought she wrapped her arms around herself and glanced over the balcony at the parking lot. "You really haven't been dating?" she asked, wanting to believe him.

"No. Though in full disclosure, I did take a woman to a business dinner thing recently. We both went as each other's plus-ones as a favor. She gets sick of being hit on and I do too, to be honest. It made things easy. We acted as each other's buffer. And...I think I took a friend to something last month too. Again, just as buffers. That's it."

A sharp sense of relief slid through her. "I believe you. And..." Maybe she was going to regret this, but, "I'll go on a date with you. *One* date." Until that stupid note, she'd been so secure in what she and Daniel had together. She was going with her gut right now and hoping it didn't fail her.

"Tomorrow night?" he asked immediately.

She laughed lightly. "I think I can manage that."

He watched her for a long moment, his blue eyes searching. "Why did you say yes?"

"Because I don't think you lied to me. I don't think you *intentionally* lied to me anyway. I don't know, you just seem really sincere." And she'd also missed him a whole lot. He'd always been so thoughtful—leaving sweet little notes for her every morning, not pushing her to go public with their relationship, always having her tea ready in the morning, paying attention to the little things—actually listening to her. He'd been the perfect boyfriend.

Though the word boyfriend didn't really fit him because he was all man. And if she didn't try, she knew she'd regret it. She'd ended things so abruptly and had never gotten a sense of closure.

Reaching out, he cupped her cheek, and for a long moment she thought he would kiss her. Time seemed suspended as they stood there, watching each other. But he didn't make a move. "Tomorrow, seven o'clock," he rasped out, so much need and hunger in his voice and expression.

"I'll be here," she whispered, her voice as unsteady as his. She was disappointed he hadn't made a move to kiss her, but that was most definitely for the best. Because if they started kissing, she wasn't so sure she would want to stop.

CHAPTER EIGHT

Daniel closed his laptop as his younger brother stepped into his office. He smiled, glad to see Brodie back from vacation. "Hey, how was the vacation? Catch any fish?"

Brodie raised his eyebrows. "Are you...in a good mood?" he whispered the last part like an obnoxious jackass.

Rolling his eyes, he stood and rounded his desk. "Come on, how was the vacation?"

"All right, who are you and what have you done with my brother?" Brodie grinned, his face more tanned than normal as he strode in wearing jeans and a T-shirt with a familiar surf brand on it. He looked a lot more relaxed than Daniel had seen him in a while. Normally he was in sharp suits and had a "don't mess with me" expression firmly in place.

"Ha, ha." He pulled Brodie into a tight hug.

"I'm just saying, it's the first time in a while you haven't snarled at me."

Daniel snorted. "You're full of it. And you're in a good mood too."

"So?"

"So...what? You gonna tell me about your vacation or not?" He leaned against the edge of his desk as Brodie watched him expectantly.

"I caught a bunch of fish, caught up on reading, and didn't talk to almost anyone for two weeks. It was amazing."

Daniel knew his brother had basically fallen off-grid, like he often did when he took a couple days away. But Brodie had been gone two weeks this time. Clearly it had been good for him. "Good for you."

"Now it's your turn. What's going on with you? You're not the sad sack you were a couple weeks ago."

"She's going out with me tonight," he said simply. And he didn't need to specify who she was either. He could admit that he was nervous too, which was unfamiliar territory for him. But Kathryn had always made him feel like a horny teenager with no moves.

Brodie's eyes widened slightly. "Good for you. Hope you guys get it right this time."

Yeah, so did he. He pressed his intercom. "Nicole, reschedule my four thirty and five o'clock. Sorry I didn't let you know earlier." He'd been consumed with working on contracts and had forgotten.

There was a short pause, then, "Of course, sir."

He looked at his brother again. "What are you doing here anyway? Not that I'm not happy to see you."

"I was on my way home and thought I'd see if you wanted to grab a couple beers, but I know the answer is no."

He thought about trying to squeeze it in before meeting Kathryn, but there was no way. "Why don't you call Sienna, see what she's up to?" He needed to check on his sister too. She'd been so damn cagey lately when he asked her what she was doing.

"Already tried. She answered the phone, said she just wanted to make sure it wasn't an emergency, then hung up on me." Brodie grinned slightly.

"So I'm the second choice? That's cold, man." He grabbed his laptop case off his desk and motioned that he was going to head out.

"My plan was always to ask both of you."

"Let's plan something this week, then," he said as they stepped into the outer office. He nodded once at his assistant, who was intensely focused on her computer screen. "Nicole, you can leave once you've rescheduled those meetings. I think we can afford to take off early today."

She looked surprised but then smiled. "Of course, thank you."

"Hopefully you don't screw things up with Kathryn again," Brodie bluntly said as they headed for the elevators.

"Not this time. I'm gonna put a ring on her finger." He already had the ring—had bought it a week before she'd ended things. Even when she'd broken up with him, he hadn't been able to get rid of it.

Brodie shot him a surprised look.

He simply shrugged as he pressed the down button. He knew what he wanted. And that was Kathryn. He knew they were right together and that if he didn't lock her down, it would be the greatest mistake of his life.

"That's pretty huge. Not that I'm surprised, considering the way you moon over her," Brodie said as they stepped into the elevator.

"Did you just say the word *moon?*"

His brother lifted a shoulder. "Don't change the subject."

"Anyway, I won't be screwing this up. I've got a plan."

"You and your plans," his brother muttered, shaking his head.

"I can't wait until you fall for someone."

Now Brodie just snorted. "Not gonna happen. Not in a million years."

DANIEL'S BREATH caught in his throat as Kathryn opened her door. He'd barely had time to get home, change and get over here on time after he'd seen Brodie. Now he wished he'd made it even sooner.

She had on a green summer dress that made her emerald-colored eyes seem even brighter than normal—and it hugged her curves in all the right places. She had a light tan—probably from all her forced outdoor activities with friends—bringing out the freckles across her nose and cheeks. And when she smiled at him, her expression so open, he forgot to breathe for a moment. God, he'd missed her.

"You look stunning," he managed to get out as she stepped back to let him in.

"You look pretty good yourself."

In casual jeans and a polo shirt, he didn't even compare to her. Nothing did. He held out the small bag he'd brought for her.

"A gift on a first date?" she asked, even as she took it.

He lifted a shoulder. They'd agreed to start over and treat this like a first date but that didn't mean he wasn't bringing her something. He loved the way she smiled when she opened up any sort of gift, no matter how small. She was like a kid on Christmas.

"Want to come in for a drink? I normally don't invite first dates in, but I'll make an exception." Her grin was cheeky.

He didn't like to think of her going out on dates with anyone *but* him, but he nodded and stepped inside. Her place was the same as it had been the other night, yet there was a subtle difference from the way it had been over two months ago. All traces of him had been erased and it bothered him even if he understood why.

"Ooh, fancy British tea." Her eyes lit up as she set the bag on her kitchen countertop. "And macaroons! Thank you. I'll be getting into these later for sure." Grinning, she pulled out a bottle of red wine. "I've got wine, or Carson left some beers in my fridge last time he was here. It's the kind you like too."

"Beer's good." His gaze strayed to her nearly bare shoulders. The straps of her dress didn't cover much and all he could think about was baring more of her. Of kissing her senseless, of making her climax until she was sated and exhausted.

"You can grab it," she said as she started pouring a glass for herself. "Before we head out, do you want to sit on my patio and watch my neighbors? Unless we have reservations somewhere?"

He grinned as he pulled an ice-cold bottle from her fridge. "Neighbor watching. Definitely." Back when they'd been dating, some nights they'd sit on her back patio that overlooked the condo complex pool, and people watch. She was by far the youngest person who lived here, since the place had been left to her by her grandmother. It wasn't officially a retirement complex but ninety percent of the residents were fifty-five and older. Kathryn loved people watching and he'd found that he enjoyed it too. At least when he was with her.

"You've got some catching up to do," she said as she pushed the sliding glass door open. "Mr. Diaz is now dating Miss Cooper."

A warm breeze rolled over them, reminding him that Florida summer was soon on its way. He sat next to her, stretching his legs out on a lounge chair as she did the same. Normally she would have curled up in the same lounger as him. "What happened with Ms. Lopez?"

"Apparently she caught him cheating on her with Ms. Johnson. But that was over quickly and now he's with Miss Cooper. But I saw Miss Cooper fooling around with Mr. Gomez two nights ago."

He snickered as he glanced over at the pool area where some of the residents they were talking about were lounging, drinking and playing their radio at a higher than necessary level.

A few of them waved when they saw him, including Miss Cooper. "Daniel, darling, we've missed seeing you!" she called out, yelling across the pool to be heard. "Come visit us before you leave!"

He simply held up his beer and saluted her. As he did, Mr. Twinkles slipped outside and jumped into his lap.

"He's definitely missed you," Kathryn murmured, taking a sip of her wine and watching him over the rim of her glass.

"Just Mr. Twinkles?"

"I might've missed you a little bit."

All his muscles pulled taut at her teasing tone. "A little bit, huh?"

"Maybe more than a little bit, but you already have a large enough ego, so we're going to leave it at that."

The residual tension in his chest eased. He'd been nervous on the way over here, but as always when he was around Kathryn he just felt light and free, as if he could be his real self. He wasn't rushing to make the next deal, answering a thousand emails, going from one meeting to the next or a million other things that he had to take care of during the day. No, when he was with her, he was simply *with* her and living in the moment. She always brought out the best in him.

"So I was thinking of going to Barbie's Burgers," he said. It was a local burger joint, casual, and he knew she loved the place.

"You know the way to my heart, through burgers and beer."

He did indeed.

And tonight he was going to claim her heart once and for all.

CHAPTER NINE

Kathryn Irish was with *him* again, just sitting and enjoying drinks at her place. Somehow the cute little security nerd had lured Daniel back into chasing after her like a fool.

Men were stupid when it came to women, however. So it wasn't that much of a surprise.

But Irish had to go. It wasn't personal, it was business.

Maybe it was a *little* personal.

The woman had been prepared the other night with her pepper spray, but that wouldn't happen again. Nope.

Daniel opened the passenger door for Irish before getting into the driver's side. *What a gentleman.*

It had been impossible to put a tracker on Daniel's vehicle, since security checked his truck at work, so it would be pointless—and it might get Daniel's hackles up.

Right now it was imperative that nothing tipped Daniel off.

As Daniel steered out of the parking lot with Irish riding next to him, it wasn't difficult to keep a decent way back, weaving in and out of traffic, just going with the flow. The roads were crowded for a Tuesday night but luckily the happy couple didn't go far.

It should be easy enough to keep an eye on them—on her.

It was impossible to understand what Daniel saw in the woman. Sure, she was attractive, with pert breasts and a pretty smile, but she dressed like a college-aged girl and had no style. No elegance. She was smart, however, so maybe that was the appeal?

Too bad for Irish, the time had come to eliminate her. She should have stayed away from Daniel, should have stayed broken up. If she had, she wouldn't be right in the crosshairs.

As it was, Kathryn Irish's days were numbered, so hopefully she enjoyed what little time she had left.

CHAPTER TEN

"Thanks for dinner," Kathryn murmured as she and Daniel stood. He'd somehow wrangled a table on the back deck of the restaurant, overlooking the ocean.

A cool, salt-tinged breeze rolled over them as Daniel took her hand in his. "Let's walk on the beach before we head back."

Him taking her hand felt like the most natural thing in the world and sent butterflies launching inside her. "It's a pretty night out." And she wanted to spend more time with him. Tonight had felt familiar, as if no time had passed between them at all. That in itself was a little scary, how fast she slipped back into feeling like they belonged together.

He led them across the back patio to the wooden walkway that led to the beach. She slipped off her sandals and he did the same with his shoes, leaving them by the end of the stairs as they headed toward the shore.

The sand was cool and dry against her feet.

"I don't want to wait until the end of our date to kiss you," Daniel murmured.

"Are you assuming that you'll even get a kiss on this date?" she asked, bumping him with her hip as they trekked across the sand. Chances were, he was going to get a kiss. More than one.

"I would never assume, Miss Irish," he said. "But I am very hopeful."

A grin pulled at her mouth. "We'll see." *Liar, liar.* There was no "we'll see." It was very likely going to happen. She only had so much restraint when it came to him. And it wasn't a lot.

"You kissed me on our *other* first date," he murmured, his voice dropping a few octaves.

Oh yes, she had. Just like that, a rush of heat slid through her body, curling tight in her belly as she remembered that first kiss. He'd been looking at her mouth as if he'd wanted to eat her alive and it had set something free inside her. She'd practically attacked him then—and he'd taken over in an instant, going into what she thought of as full-on dominating Daniel mode.

That kiss had led to a little *more* than kissing, and had been totally out of character for her. But she'd never been on a date with anyone like Daniel MacArthur before either. Someone who made her feel alive and sexy and who accepted her for who she was. She'd done a little bit of digging into his past social life after he first asked her out and she was *not* the type of woman he'd seemed to date before. The women he'd been linked with were all polished and elegant and had all run in the same society circles.

Her parents had been blue collar and she'd grown up as one of the boys—and she liked it that way. She had a bunch of girlfriends now, but she was always going to be a casual, jeans-wearing kind of girl at heart. And Daniel didn't seem to mind at all, he just liked her for who she was. He never made her feel less than.

"I did get kind of crazy the first night we went out," she admitted.

"So did I."

More heat flooded her as she remembered the way he'd gone down on her, brought her to orgasm with his mouth and fingers. God, he'd been frantic to make her come. And she'd replayed that first date in her mind more than once.

As they got closer to the softly crashing waves, he tugged on her hand and they both sat in a dry patch of sand, stretching their legs out. The sand between her toes felt good, the three-quarter moon shining down on the near empty beach setting a romantic tone.

"I saw Brodie today," Daniel said into the mostly quiet. Behind them music from the restaurant carried on the wind, but other than that, the waves were the only sound. "He told me not to screw things up with you."

She laughed lightly at the mention of his younger brother. "How is Brodie? I've missed him," she said, meaning it. She'd missed the whole MacArthur clan. They were fun and loud and nothing like she'd imagined a family so wealthy would be like. Parties at his parents' house had always been a riot—which ended in savage board games where one of them usually did an awful victory dance. He let out a low sort of growl that made her laugh. "You can't be jealous."

Daniel shrugged, not answering one way or another. So she rolled her eyes.

He finally spoke. "He's good, just got back from vacation. I can't believe he actually took one. He's such a workaholic."

"Do you not hear the irony in that statement? When was the last time *you* took a vacation?"

He didn't even pause. "That getaway you and I took down to the Bahamas."

At that memory, even more heat curled through her, settling low. They'd spent almost the entire time naked or with her in a bikini. Usually just bikini bottoms because she'd gone topless the majority of the time—at his request. It had been just the two of them in a private cabana on a private beach. Like something out of a fairy tale.

"You work too hard," she murmured, leaning closer to him and feeling oddly protective of him. He needed to take better care of himself.

Surprising her, he turned slightly to face her more and reached out, cupping her cheek with one big hand.

He watched her for a long moment, the sound of the crashing waves drowning out everything but the beat of her heart. He gently stroked his thumb over her cheek, just watching her with an intensity she felt to her core.

Sitting here like this, she felt exposed and vulnerable, as if Daniel could read her every thought, every want.

Going on instinct, she shifted over and straddled him, taking both of them by surprise. She hadn't planned to make a move on him but it had been two long months. And she'd missed him so much. She wasn't quite sure what this would mean for them, but this felt like more than a first date. It felt like they were together again, even if neither of them had said anything.

"Kathryn," he groaned, wrapping his arms around her and holding her tight as he crushed his mouth to hers.

She loved the feel of his tongue teasing hers, and the way he held her so close, as if he didn't want to let her go. She rolled her hips against him, wanting to get as close as possible, wanting to ease the ache between her legs. She needed way more than this though. Over the last two months she'd masturbated so many times to memories of them, even as she'd cursed him. Tonight she didn't have to imagine anymore, she had him right here in her arms.

Suddenly Daniel's fingers clenched on her hips, stilling her as he pulled back. His chest rose and fell with his ragged breathing.

She stared at him, their semi-public surroundings rushing back to her.

"We really need to stop before we...*don't* stop."

"I know," she said, even as she rolled her hips over his erection again. Oh God, she'd missed the feel of him between her legs like this. She just hated that there was clothing between them and that they weren't somewhere private.

He groaned and laid his forehead against hers. "You make me crazy."

Yeah, well, the feeling was mutual.

The sound of people laughing in the distance brought her back to reality even more. "It probably wouldn't do to get a violation out here on the beach for public indecency," she muttered as she forced herself to roll off him.

"Your brother could get you out of it—though I'm pretty sure he'd also punch me in the face."

She laughed lightly at his dry tone. "I don't think he'd punch you. Besides, you've got some moves of your own."

He grinned. "I've got moves—that I want to show you right now."

She laughed again before he stood and pulled her up with him.

It was probably for the best. Things were moving way too fast and she needed to slow things down. She'd gotten burned so badly before and now it was clear that she was just jumping right back into things with him. Before Daniel, she'd been the queen of self-control and good decisions. Whether or not getting back together with Daniel was a bad decision remained to be seen. She just knew that she didn't want to screw things up.

He wrapped his arm around her shoulders and turned back toward the restaurant. Out of the corner of her eye, she thought she saw a flash of light, but when she looked nothing was there but the sand dunes. Probably just somebody taking a selfie.

The drive back to her condo didn't take long but her stomach was doing flip-flops by the time they reached her front door. They hadn't talked much on the drive back, but the ride had been comfortable, familiar. Which scared her a little. Everything about being with him again just felt right and she was scared that it would all get screwed up again. That she'd be right back where she'd been two months ago, crying into her ice cream and Mr. Twinkles' fur. *Bah.*

As they reached the top of her stairs, she leaned back against her front door as Daniel caged her in, his big hands next to her head, his forearms and biceps flexing.

Warmth flooded between her legs at the show of power. Seriously, the man was carved from stone. It was absolutely ridiculous how he just screamed sex appeal. Arms should not be that sexy.

He stared down at her with a familiar, hungry glint in his eyes, not saying anything. But she knew where this was leading.

Even though it took self-control she didn't realize she had, she pressed a hand to the middle of his chest and gently stilled him. She couldn't let him kiss her again.

Because if she let his lips touch hers, that self-control she was barely hanging on to? Yeah, it would be completely shredded and they would be naked inside her living room within moments. Then he'd be deep inside her while they tumbled to the floor because with the way he was watching her, she was pretty sure they wouldn't make it to the bedroom. Not the first time. Maybe not even the second.

She clenched her thighs together and pushed slightly.

He groaned but he dropped his hands and stepped back.

"No more kissing for tonight." For...reasons. She was sure she had them. Right?

"Okay. When can I take you out again?"

Her brain sort of went on the fritz as she tried to think of her schedule. She blinked. "I've got plans tomorrow and then I'm free the next night."

"I'll pick you up, same time?"

She nodded, but he still didn't step back.

"I had fun tonight," he said quietly.

"Me too."

He watched her for another long moment then groaned again, softly, and stepped back, giving her room to breathe and think again. Just like that, her brain kicked into gear, all cylinders go. It was like when she was close enough to touch him, everything just slowed wayyyy down and all she had was sex on the brain.

"Good night," she murmured.

"Good night."

Somehow she managed to make her body listen to her. Sliding her key into the lock, she hurried inside. Then she locked her door, turned off the alarm, then reset it because she knew he wouldn't leave until he heard that little telltale *beep beep beep*.

Taking a deep breath, she dropped her purse onto the kitchen countertop and shoved out a sigh. Right now she could be naked and getting an orgasm, but no, she'd had to show self-control. She groaned out loud and laid her head on the countertop, berating herself as Mr. Twinkles wound his way in between her legs, meowing incessantly for her to pick him up.

As she scooped him up in her arms, her phone buzzed.

When she saw it was a text from Daniel, her heart rate kicked up about a thousand notches.

I'll be thinking of you tonight as I stroke myself off.

Her cheeks heated up even though he couldn't see her. They'd never really texted like this before. Yes, they'd sent flirty texts, but nothing overtly sexual. She bit her bottom lip as she stared at her phone. Mr. Twinkles continued to nuzzle his head under her chin, completely unconcerned about anything else.

Before she had time to obsess over her response, she quickly typed one back. *I'll be thinking of you as I tease my clit tonight.* Was that too bold? Too much? Not enough? Gah, she wasn't good at this. So she hit send before she could second-guess herself.

A moment later he sent her back an emoji of a cartoon fox with his tongue hanging out of his mouth and hearts above his head. She laughed aloud at the ridiculous emoji even as warmth filled her chest. Maybe tonight was the beginning of something new between them.

She'd missed him so damn much, had thought of him every single day that they'd been apart. Still, she didn't want to get ahead of herself. She didn't want to make the same mistakes her mom had made and fall for the wrong man.

She had to be smart about this, had to be careful. She didn't want to be humiliated and heartbroken again. Years ago she'd promised herself that she'd never let a man have complete power over her heart.

Unfortunately, being careful about matters of the heart was damn near impossible. Especially where Daniel MacArthur was concerned.

CHAPTER ELEVEN

Daniel couldn't stop the energy humming through him. Kathryn started at the office today to begin her diagnostics, and yeah, he was excited to see her. About the only reason he was excited on a Monday morning.

Instead of heading up to his floor, he went straight to the security floor.

They were supposed to have gone on a date Thursday, but her mom had been sick so she'd canceled on him. And then she'd ended up taking care of her mom all weekend, something he understood. He'd actually dropped off some chicken soup and got to see Kathryn for a few minutes but it wasn't the same as spending time with her. This morning she'd texted him that her mom was feeling better and she would see him soon.

He might have sent back a dirty text, which was probably inappropriate, but it wasn't like he was her boss. Not technically. She was an independent contractor and he could keep things professional. Mostly.

As he reached the security floor, he smiled when he saw her stepping off the other elevator. She had on dark jeans, heels—which surprised the hell out of him—and a fitted black jacket over a green camisole. "You look hot," he murmured.

She gave him a startled laugh. "Thanks. Is it the heels?" She lifted a foot, grinning.

"I wouldn't mind seeing you wearing only them."

Her cheeks flushed. "Just figured I'd mix it up today. So, this is weird timing, you showing up now. Did you plan it?"

He shook his head then glanced up and down the hallway. It was empty so he closed the distance to her and brushed his mouth over hers. He resisted the urge to tug her into his arms, to pin her up against the nearest wall.

She leaned into his kiss, flicking her tongue against his before quickly stepping back. Then she glanced up and down the hall as well. "I don't want people to think I got this contract job because...of whatever this is."

That gave him the perfect opening, the one he'd been waiting for. "So what is this?"

She blinked once, then shook her head. "No way. I've only had one chai this morning and it's far too early to have this kind of conversation."

"We're going to have this conversation soon." He fell in step with her as they headed down the hallway.

"Hmmm."

"You can hmm all you want, it's happening." He knew he should ease up, but he wanted it clear what they were—and he wanted exclusive. Always had.

Always would.

"So what does your day look like today?" she asked, completely ignoring his statement. She had on her security lanyard with her temporary pass around her neck.

"A few contracts to go over, a couple international conference calls, two off-site checks and some more boring stuff."

"You love this stuff."

He lifted a shoulder. He liked making money and he liked what he could do with that money. His company put a quarter of their revenue back into the community, into charities that truly needed it. His parents had both grown up poor and they'd instilled in him a need to give back as much as possible from the time he was young.

"Well, you clearly know where you're going, so I'll leave you to it," he said as they paused outside the security room door.

"You want to meet up for lunch, or will you be too busy taking over the world?"

Oh, he could think of something they could do over lunch. "Lunch. My office."

She lifted an eyebrow. "I recognize that look," she whispered. "So how about lunch at one of the local food trucks? There's a new Cuban one down here that I want to try."

"Food truck it is, but the offer to do lunch in my office stands if you change your mind. If not, I'll meet you downstairs at noon."

She nodded. "Works for me."

He resisted the urge to kiss her again and that was pretty much only because the door opened and the head of his security in this building stepped out.

Cora smiled as she looked between the both of them. "Mr. MacArthur, I didn't expect to see you today. Can I help you with anything?"

"Nope. Just walking Ms. Irish down here."

"It's nice to meet you officially in person," Cora said as she held out a hand to Kathryn. In a sharp black business suit, the tall, lean woman looked as she always did. Put together and intimidating. Her dark hair was pulled back in a twist and the only jewelry she wore was her wedding ring and diamond studs he knew that her husband had given her as an anniversary present. "I've heard great things about you."

Kathryn smiled back and he knew she was in good hands. He also knew she was going to help them extensively. So he murmured goodbye and hurried off.

By the time he made it back to his office, he'd already received eight texts from his assistant and six phone calls from other employees.

"Mr. MacArthur," Nicole said as he stepped into the office. She pushed back from her desk, and stepped around it wearing such thin stilettos he wasn't sure how she managed to walk in them. "I moved a couple of your meetings around today. I just sent the alerts to your phone."

He nodded. "Thank you. As long as I've got nothing between twelve and one, I'm fine." He normally skipped lunch, either eating in his office or using his lunch break to hit up the gym in the building.

She frowned down at her tablet. "Actually, I did schedule a phone conference for twelve thirty. I didn't realize you had anything on the books."

Neither had he until a minute ago. "Who's the meeting with?" he asked even though he knew he was going to cancel it. Meeting up with Kathryn was more important. When Nicole told him, he shook his head. "Reschedule it."

"Will do. Don't forget you have that gala on Thursday."

Oh, hell. "That's right."

"Did you still want me to go with you?" she asked.

Hell, he'd forgotten about that too. It was a working function and he'd needed someone to run interference. "No, take the night off." He would make sure she was still paid overtime since he'd told her to schedule the time.

She nodded. "Thank you. And I'll let the organizer know it will just be you."

"No, just leave things as they are. I'm bringing someone."

She looked surprised, but simply nodded and put something into her tablet.

Two hours later, when he received a text from Kathryn, his heart rate increased just from seeing her name on the screen. Damn, he was done for. Just absolutely done. Disappointment slid through him, however, when he read her text.

It looks like we're going over a lot of technical stuff today. Cora wants to call lunch in and since I want to make friends on my first day, I wanted to double-check with you. Rain check?

He texted back quickly. *Of course. How about dinner tonight?* Then maybe they could have that uncomfortable conversation he was dying for.

She didn't respond and he frowned.

He knew she hadn't blown him off Thursday or this weekend, but still that insecurity settled in his bones. Insecurity he'd never experienced until Kathryn. Not that she made him feel insecure in the general sense, just like he wasn't always on his game. She kept him on his toes and he liked that part, but hated being kept away from her.

Five minutes later she texted back. *I'll let you know?*

Okay, so that definitely wasn't a yes. He frowned but set his phone down and buzzed his assistant to ask if she could get the lunch meeting back on.

Hours later, and countless meetings later, Daniel had a low-grade headache by the time he shut everything down. After he checked in with security and found out that Kathryn was still on the security floor, he headed there instead of leaving.

As he reached the door to the security room, Kathryn and Cora both walked out at the same time.

Cora of course was surprised to see him, since he didn't come down here often, but Kathryn gave him a real smile he felt all the way to his core.

"Mr. MacArthur, did you need me—"

He shook his head, cutting Cora off. "No, I just wanted to talk to Ms. Irish about some things before she heads out."

She nodded. "Well, then, I'm going to leave. Night shift just got here and everything looks good. But I'm sure Kathryn will tell you everything in her end-of-the-week report." She gave Kathryn a warm smile and headed off, purse on her shoulder.

"You look exhausted," Kathryn said, then winced. "And I don't mean that in a mean way, like you look bad. Did you have a rough day?"

"Just long." A merger he was interested in had fallen through and it was the fault of no one. It was just one of those things where the timing didn't work out and he was frustrated. He liked being in control, something he could admit. And the merger would have created thousands of jobs in a community that needed it. "It's better now though." Just seeing her made everything better. "So, dinner tonight?"

She paused and he felt that knife in his gut twist.

"No pressure. I don't want you to feel like you have to have dinner with me." Especially since she was working here the next couple weeks.

She reached out and laid a hand on his forearm, her touch gentle. "I'm not blowing you off. I promise. But it was a really long day. I kind of want to go home, get into my PJs and watch Netflix. And that's not a euphemism, I really want to Netflix and chill. Literally."

He snorted. "No pressure, but if you want company, I'll join you."

She started walking down the hallway with him. "I would *love* the company. I just thought you wanted to go out. We can get takeout from that Chinese place down the street."

"Works for me. Actually, I'll pick up dinner for us on the way and meet you there so we don't even have to call it in. You know what you want?"

She grinned. "You know exactly what I want."

His mouth curved up. She never changed her order, and when he'd asked her about it she'd said that she liked what she liked, and after trying most of the menu she always kept coming back to the same thing.

"I'll pick up a bottle of wine for us, then," Kathryn said. Then she looked around at the empty hall, grabbed him by the front of his jacket and pulled him down to her for a quick, hot kiss. Breathing hard, she stepped back. "That's the last time that happens while we're at work. I just couldn't resist."

"Good, because I can barely resist you on days that end in Y." Her cheeks flushed pink and just like that his dick was hard. The weight that had been pressing on his chest all day had lifted as he headed out with her. Even though he wanted to, he resisted the urge to take her hand in his. "Oh, there's a dinner thing on Thursday night I'm supposed to go to. I know it's not your style, but if you're interested, I'd like to have you as a plus-one."

"So...that would link us publicly for sure."

"It would." He hadn't pressured her before, even though he'd wanted to. She was skittish about relationships and he'd wanted to respect that. Even if it had killed him a little inside. Now he wanted to stake a public claim.

She was silent as the elevator descended. "I'll see if Chloe has a dress I can wear," she finally said. "But yes, I'd love to go."

And just like that, he knew that things between them had changed. But he was still talking to her tonight. He wanted to know exactly where she was at, and where they stood. "Don't worry about the dress. I've got you covered."

She looked over at him, eyebrows raised. "Really?"

He nodded. He'd actually bought a dress for her for another event he'd invited her to before they'd broken up, and he hadn't been able to get rid of it. So it was hanging in his closet, a sad reminder of her.

"Should I be worried that it's low-cut and tight?"

He grinned. "You'll like it, trust me." And yeah, it was low-cut and would look sexy as hell on her.

Taking him by surprise, she grabbed his hand as they stepped out of the elevator and linked her fingers with his.

In that moment, he knew she was making a statement about them without saying a word at all. Soon he intended to claim her fully, to make sure everyone knew she was taken.

To make sure that *she* knew, without a doubt, she was the one for him. And that he wasn't letting her go.

CHAPTER TWELVE

Kathryn was so glad that Daniel had wanted to come home and relax with her. Though she knew they'd be doing more than just relaxing.

She hadn't wanted to say no to his date but she also really hadn't wanted to go out anywhere. She'd gotten information overload today at his office and was still digesting everything she'd been sifting through. When she took big jobs like this, they could be mentally draining. And she hadn't wanted to start off this new thing between them with what amounted to her lying. She wanted to start fresh—to be real and open about their relationship. First they needed to actually define their relationship, though she felt as if she'd made it clear what she wanted today.

At the sound of a knock on her door, she grinned and pulled it open.

"Did you check the peephole?" he asked as he stepped inside carrying two brown bags.

She shut and locked the door behind him. "I knew it was you."

"So that's a no."

"I'll do it next time." She should've actually checked. She knew better. It didn't matter that her mugger was in jail, there were still a whole lot of other weirdos out in the world. "Wow, that smells so good. Mainly because I didn't have to cook it."

He snickered as he set the boxes on her kitchen island top. "So how was your first day?"

She started pulling out plates and glasses for them. "Really great. There's a lot of information, more than I expected, but I know what I'm dealing with and you have a really incredible team. Something I'm sure you already know because you hired them. I'm excited to do the on-site check next week at the new building, but so far things are good. Your core security team is so sharp. Oh, and John is so adorable," she added. "I haven't seen him in ages." They'd worked together on a few jobs before he went full-time with Daniel.

Daniel frowned and she blinked.

Then she broke into a grin. "I forgot how territorial you are. What I mean is, he's adorable because his wife just had twins and he was gushing about all of them." And she was a sucker for cute baby pictures.

"I'm not territorial—just possessive of what's mine." The heated glint in his eyes, the way his voice wrapped around her, and she suddenly forgot all about the food.

Was she his? She sure felt like it. "Is there a difference between the two?"

Wordlessly he stalked around the island toward her, determination in his gaze.

"It's too soon," she whispered, even though he hadn't said a word. But she clearly read that look in his eyes.

"Why is *this* too soon?" He erased the last of the distance between them, pinning her against the countertop.

"It just is." *Wow, great response.*

"This is *our* relationship. *We* set the rules." But he stepped back, nonetheless, giving her a bit of space.

"What exactly is our relationship?" And was she being a fool by jumping straight back into something with him? She'd basically already made the decision, because after Thursday it would become common knowledge around the city that they were an item. It was a little hard to care about any sort of consequences when he was looking at her like she was the most precious thing in the world, however.

"I want to be exclusive," he said as if that was obvious.

She did too. She knew she'd agreed to start dating him but she'd never been the type of person who could date others, and she certainly couldn't date someone like Daniel *and* others at the same time. It wasn't the way she was wired. "I don't want to be with anyone else either," she whispered. "Just don't break my heart." Saying that made her feel a hundred times more vulnerable.

"Never." Reaching out he cupped her cheek, and with that small action he anchored her, made her feel more connected to him.

"How about we get dessert before dinner?" she murmured. Dessert first sounded like a great idea. The best one ever.

With that, his mouth curved up into a sexy grin before he crushed it to hers.

She was vaguely aware of her cat running off, likely to hide while they got busy. A little voice inside her told her to guard her heart, but she knew she couldn't guard it forever. She was either going to jump into this thing or she wasn't. All she knew was that she couldn't straddle the line. She had to commit or not.

Teasing her tongue against his, she molded to him, wrapping her arms around him as he pulled her close. She'd missed this, missed *him*.

For two long months, they'd been denied this.

When he grabbed her ass and started kneading it, heat flooded between her legs, hot and molten. She jumped him then, not happy with just having her arms around him. She wanted more, everything. And they needed to be naked like ten minutes ago.

He took over, lifting her up, and somehow they made it to her living room where they ended up sprawled on her much too small couch. That was okay though.

He had her clothing off in seconds, even her heels—which she'd worn today for him. "You got me naked incredibly fast."

The look he gave her was scorching. "Two months without you, Kathryn. Two. Months."

Yeah, she felt that way too. In response, she reached for the bottom button of his shirt and started working each of them free. If she was going to be naked, she wanted to feel his skin on hers. Wanted to feel him pressing her into the couch, wanted him to fill her completely as she came around him.

He let her take off his shirt but instead of letting her go for his pants he kissed her again, threading his fingers through her hair and kissing her as if he had all the time in the world.

Meanwhile she felt as if she was ready to combust underneath him. Every flick, every tease of his tongue against hers set her on fire even more.

She rolled her hips against his, the friction of his erection against her slick folds driving her crazy. She just wanted those pants gone so she could feel all of him. The stimulation wasn't quite enough even though it felt amazing.

As if he read her mind—or maybe her body language—he reached between their bodies and cupped her mound and groaned into her mouth.

"This is all for me," he growled out. A declaration, not a question.

Because yeah, her slickness was all for him. All because of him. Then he started moving down her body, kissing her slowly, tortuously so, pausing at each breast and taking his sweet time with her nipples until they were rock-hard and wet from his mouth.

Slickness flooded between her thighs as he continued downward.

Sometimes he was incredibly impatient and pounced on her, and others, like now, he slowed right down. He was getting her so damn worked up that she would come if he freaking blew on her clit softly.

"I've missed you," he said as he reached between her legs.

"I can't tell if you're talking to me or my pussy," she said, laughing.

His mouth curved up again as he looked up the length of her body and met her gaze. "Both."

She snickered, but was cut off as he dipped his head lower and flicked his tongue along her slick folds.

Then she forgot about everything but his wicked mouth and speared her fingers through his hair as she rolled her hips against his face. Oh God, he felt so good. So damn good she could barely stand it.

He teased her with his tongue and fingers, sliding two inside her, curling them up so they hit that perfect spot even as he applied pressure to her clit.

"Perfect," she managed to rasp out. It was all she could say as he sucked on her clit, finding that right pressure designed to drive her over the edge.

Something about Daniel always made her crazy like this. He'd taken the time to learn her body, and when he had—he'd played it to perfection.

She clutched onto his head as he continued stroking and teasing her, harder and faster, until a kaleidoscope of colors exploded behind her eyes, her orgasm punching through her like a shock wave designed to turn her to mush.

She'd been remembering just how good things had been between them for two lonely months and now here he was between her legs, making her crazy.

When he looked up the length of her body a long moment later his expression was positively satisfied. And it made her adore him even more. He'd always been so giving, and it made her curse herself for questioning him before. That stupid note had played on every single one of her insecurities, made her think that everything they'd shared was a lie. Looking back, she should have just talked to him about it, expressed her feelings instead of running away like she always did.

Well, she wasn't running now. Nope, she was grabbing onto him with both hands and not letting go.

"On your back," she ordered.

He lifted an eyebrow at her demanding tone but did as she said.

He stretched out on her couch, his big legs taking up all the space, and she realized they weren't going to have enough room. Not even close. "On the floor," she amended, making him grin.

Before he followed her order, he shoved his pants off and lay down on her faux Persian rug.

He looked like a god stretched out before her, all hard muscle and gorgeous thick cock jutting upward just for her. Some of his tattoos moved when he flexed and she found her gaze trailing over all of them. Most were from after his military days—he'd gone crazy covering all his gorgeous skin because he could, because he'd liked the release the temporary pain offered. There was his blue and gold family crest, other symbols of his Scottish heritage, and many more symbolizing his time in the Army. But her attention was captured by one thing right now.

"I've missed you too," she murmured, her gaze on his thick length.

He simply groaned in response, and without warning she took his thick length in her mouth.

"Shit," he rasped out as she sucked him deep.

She grinned around his cock, taking him fully in her mouth again, over and over before she finally lifted her head. "I'm still on birth control," she said quickly. They probably should have talked about this earlier—before they'd gotten turned on and completely naked.

"I haven't been with anyone else," he managed to get out as she teased his balls lightly. She knew exactly what he liked too, exactly how to get him worked up. He hissed in a breath, all those gorgeous muscles in his stomach pulling taut.

"Me neither." So they were good. Better than.

She shimmied up his body, possessed with the need to take him deep inside her. She straddled him, rubbing herself against his hard length. Her inner walls tightened in response as she got ready for him.

"You're killing me," he growled as he grasped her hips.

She thought about teasing him a little longer, but she didn't have the patience or the self-control. Moving slightly, she fully impaled herself on his cock.

He groaned, his hips jerking up to meet hers as she seated herself all the way to the hilt.

She sucked in a breath, closing her eyes as she got used to the feel of him again. Oh yeah, this was the best sensation in the world. Groaning, she let her head fall back, and so very slowly she started to ride him, rolling her hips in a deliberate, sensuous rhythm.

"You're a goddess." His words were harsh and unsteady.

And made her inner walls tighten around him even more.

When she looked down at him, his expression was dark and hungry. For her.

Then he took over, flipping her onto her back and pinning her against the rug. He'd always been like that, so desperate for her.

"You can ride me longer the next time," he said through gritted teeth. "I just need this."

She met his mouth with hers, needing to kiss him, needing that extra bond as he started thrusting inside her.

She could feel another orgasm building as he hit her G-spot, and groaned into his mouth at the sensation.

He cupped her breast with one hand and her cheek with the other, the gentle stroking of his thumb against her cheek at odds with the way he was thrusting inside her like a man possessed.

"Gonna come," he rasped against her mouth. "You need another orgasm though," he continued, his words ragged and out of control.

She reached between their bodies and started stroking her clit as he teased her breast.

That was all the stimulation she needed before she went into another free fall of pleasure. This climax was stronger since he was inside her and as soon as she let go, he did too, his thrusts even wilder as he emptied himself inside her.

As he came down from his high, he caged her in against the floor, his forearms on either side of her head as he looked down at her. His breathing was harsh, raspy. "I think we should put the food away for now."

She grinned up at him. "Yeah?"

"Yeah. We're taking a shower now and you're coming again. We've got two months to make up for."

Her nipples tightened at the thought of coming again, at his roughly spoken words. Since she couldn't find her voice, she simply nodded as he pulled out of her then lifted her into his arms.

Things felt different between them, better. As if all that time apart had solidified that they were meant to be together—that no good came of being apart.

She wasn't walking away from him again.

CHAPTER THIRTEEN

Kathryn twirled once in front of the long mirror, impressed with the transformation. She didn't dress up often but she could admit she felt incredibly feminine, and okay, kind of stunning right now. The body-hugging green dress seemed to have been tailor-made for her. It shimmered when she moved and was the perfect color for her skin tone. And while it was cut lower than she would have chosen, Daniel clearly knew what he was doing—or maybe a personal shopper had picked this out.

Either way, she felt incredible. She'd even begged Chloe to come over and help her with her hair so now she had big, soft curls hanging down her back and framing her face and she looked like a million bucks. She'd had to put Mr. Twinkles up in the guest room because she'd been too afraid that he would jump on her in this dress.

When she realized the time, she texted Daniel. *Everything okay?* He should have been there twenty minutes ago, and for Daniel anything less than twenty minutes early was late. So it was kind of weird that he hadn't contacted her.

She squashed the tension that rose up inside her. It wasn't like he was just not going to show up. After they'd spent Monday night together, they'd spent Tuesday evening in bed as well. Yesterday and today she'd been so busy that they'd only talked on the phone and she desperately missed him. She was pretty sure that Cora knew she was dating Daniel at this point, and probably part of the security team knew it too, but it was what it was. He'd let her keep their relationship quiet for months when they'd been together because of her own fears and he deserved better than that. She was proud that he was hers and wanted him to know that.

When he didn't respond, she tapped her finger against her kitchen countertop. After another ten minutes passed—and then another—real worry settled inside her. They'd planned to meet up early, to share a drink together and then head out. But at this rate the gala would be starting in...half an hour. And it would take twenty minutes to get there from her place. She wasn't supposed to meet him there, right? No, they'd made solid plans. She was just getting all up in her head.

Instead of texting again, she called this time. It rang and rang and rang—finally he picked up.

She'd started to say hey when a sultry female voice said, "Daniel's phone."

She frowned. "Hey, this is Kathryn, is Daniel there?" Maybe it was his assistant and he'd gotten stuck in a meeting.

"He's in the shower, but can I have him call you back?"

She froze for a moment. What the hell? "He's in the shower?"

"Yep," she said, giggling, the sound like shards of glass raking against a chalkboard. "I can go grab him if it's an emergency?"

Ice froze her veins at the woman's words. "Nope. Just have him call me back." With numb fingers, she set her phone on the countertop. Then she pulled out the stool and collapsed onto it, staring off into space and not seeing anything. Was he with another woman right now? No, that didn't make sense. She knew Daniel. This was...this had to be a mistake.

Suddenly her phone dinged. When she saw Daniel's name, a mix of emotions jumped inside her. But as she read through the text, she could feel all the remaining warmth drain from her.

Sorry, I meant to call you earlier but got too caught up at work. Things between us are moving too quickly. You were right to break up with me before.

83

It's not going to work out. I'll keep things professional at the office. But I'll understand if you want to end the contract now.

She stared as hot tears stung her eyes. Was he kidding her? Furiously she texted him back, hating that he'd actually texted her instead of calling. This whole situation was ridiculous. *Are you kidding me? I don't merit a phone call?*

She watched the little bubbles appear and knew he was typing. *I really am sorry, late for the gala and didn't want to deal with hysterics or tears. I know you hate stuff like this so I'm sure it's a relief not to have to go.*

He didn't want to deal with her tears? What the hell? She frowned at the phone, her gut twisting. She had no clue what to say to him at this point. It was like someone else had taken over his body. This wasn't the Daniel she knew.

God, maybe she'd never really known him at all. That was exactly how she'd felt when she'd seen that sticky note in his handwriting. And now...this? She was such a stupid fool. Feeling numb, she left her phone on the countertop, unzipped her dress, let Mr. Twinkles out of the guest room and headed back to her bedroom.

After she'd stripped and washed off all her makeup, the tears finally came. She felt like such a fool for trusting him again. It was as if she'd never known him at all. How could someone be so cruel as to break up by text? She deserved more than that and it broke her heart that this was all he'd given her.

She hadn't been able to get a hold of him today but she'd chalked it up to him just being busy. She'd been busy too, had found a few holes in his new system, but nothing major. Turned out he hadn't been too busy to talk to her, just a coward. He didn't even have the decency to let her know before she'd gotten dressed and done her makeup? Nope, he'd waited until the last minute possible. And was apparently screwing someone else.

And on that thought, another sob built in her throat. She tried to push it down, but there was no controlling emotions like this. More sobs tore free from her as she crawled into bed. Poor Mr. Twinkles jumped up next to her, meowing pitifully as she cried. At least he cared.

CHAPTER FOURTEEN

The next morning, Kathryn felt a little pathetic when she saw she had two missed texts—and secretly hoped one of them was from Daniel telling her that an alien had taken over his body and that he was sorry.

Not that it would matter at this point. He'd broken her trust again, and she was done. Hell, he'd beyond broken her trust. But just because he was a giant dick didn't mean that she wasn't going to go into work and do her job. She'd signed a contract and he could go screw himself.

Using tricks her mom had taught her she actually put on makeup to cover her puffy eyes. It helped a little bit but it didn't make her feel better. She just needed to get through today. Get through one day and then she could drown her pain in ice cream all weekend.

Once she was ready, she made sure she arrived at work early, determined to avoid him at all costs. She didn't think he would terminate her contract or anything, not unless he wanted a lawsuit on his hands, but she wasn't going to give him any excuse at this point. Clearly she'd never known the man at all. Because the Daniel she'd known wouldn't have sent her such cruel texts, wouldn't have ended things like a coward.

By the time she made it to the security floor, where she'd been doing most of her work, she'd managed to give herself exactly eighty billion pep talks. None of them worked.

As she stepped inside the room, Cora and John looked surprised to see her.

"Hey guys," she said, hoping she sounded cheerful. Or at least not like a sad sack. "I'm going to grab some coffee and then dig into some stuff in one of the conference rooms. Just let me know if you need me." She was incredibly thankful that she hadn't planned to work with any of them today, but run some of her own programs instead. At least she wouldn't have to paste on a smile all day while she was crying inside. And next week she'd be off-site so she wouldn't have to risk seeing Daniel at all. Yep, she could totally do this.

They both shared a look and then Cora approached her. She had on one of her dark, tailor-made suits that made her look fierce. Her hair was down today though, in soft waves. "Hey, I'm surprised to see you here."

"Why?" God, did Daniel actually terminate her already or something?

"Look, I know it's absolutely none of my business...but it's okay if you want to leave."

"Why would I want to leave?"

"I mean...you and Daniel."

"There is no me and Daniel." *Not anymore.*

"Oh, yeah. I mean... Look," she lowered her voice, "I saw you guys on the security feed a couple times. I know you got this job because of your skills and reputation," she rushed to add. "I swear I'm not, like, insinuating anything. I get why you want to keep things quiet, trust me. But I just meant that if you wanted to get out of here, I'm sure Mr. MacArthur would rather you be with him than here."

She blinked. "What are you talking about?"

Her frown deepening, Cora took Kathryn's arm gently and led her to a quiet area at the back of the security room. "He got a really bad case of food poisoning yesterday. He's in the hospital. I thought you knew."

She blinked again. "He got food poisoning yesterday?"

The woman stared at her. "Yeah, I assumed you knew. I mean...I saw you guys kiss on the security camera. I wasn't spying or anything. I just... Maybe I made a wrong assumption. I'm sorry—"

Kathryn's mind reeled. So he hadn't been with someone else? Who the hell had answered his phone and sent her those awful texts? "No, I... What time did he leave?"

"Right after you did, actually. The ambulance showed up maybe ten minutes later. It was a whirlwind here. Everyone was really worried about him."

A strange, sinking sensation settled in her gut. Feeling weird, Kathryn pulled her cell phone out of her purse and brought up the texts from last night. She'd told herself to delete them but now she was glad she hadn't. "So, I'm really sorry for oversharing all this, but I got some texts from Daniel yesterday. Or at least they were from his phone. He broke up with me last night after some woman answered his phone. The texts seemed weird and cruel and so unlike him, but I was so blindsided when I got them. Now... You're sure he got sick right after I left?" Because she'd left early, around three thirty.

Cora frowned. "Yeah, right around four."

She held out her phone so Cora could read the texts. The other woman's expression darkened. "Okay, this is really weird. And I can't imagine Mr. MacArthur using the word 'hysterics.'"

"Me neither." She'd thought it sounded weird last night but now... Something was wrong. It had to be. Oh God, *Daniel*.

"Hold on." Cora pulled out her own cell phone and stepped away to make a call, murmuring quietly into it for a few moments. Then she was back. "I just talked to his assistant and she said she tried to call you but you didn't answer."

"I have no missed calls. Is he okay though? I mean...are you sure it's food poisoning?" Her gut twisted as she tried to wrap her mind around whatever was going on.

Cora stared at Kathryn for a long moment. "I don't like this. Come on," she said. "We're going to the hospital."

That sinking sensation only intensified and Kathryn simply nodded before they hurried out, imagining all sorts of weird scenarios. Nothing made sense though.

Last night she'd thought the texts from Daniel were bizarre and cruel—but she'd been caught up in a wave of emotion. It hadn't even occurred to her that something might be wrong. That would have been like grasping at straws because she didn't want to admit the truth—that he'd ended things with her and broken her heart again. Hell, he'd even referenced her breaking up with him before and it wasn't common knowledge that they'd dated. But if he'd been in the hospital with food poisoning, then he couldn't have texted her.

Nothing about this was right and now fear for his safety ratcheted up inside her.

Thankfully Cora was an expert driver and they made it to the hospital in record time. "I'm just going to drop you off and park," Cora said as she pulled up to the emergency room entrance.

"Thanks. My phone is on me. I'll text you the room number." She knew his parents were out of the country, but she should probably call Sienna or Brodie.

Before she'd even made it to the front desk, she ran into Sienna, who had a small white pastry bag in her hand.

"Kathryn, you're here!" she said, pulling her into a tight hug.

"Yeah, I just found out about Daniel."

"Really?"

"Yeah. At work today, Cora told me." She thought about telling Sienna about the weird texts she'd received but decided not to. It wasn't important right now. Getting to see Daniel and making sure he was okay was all that mattered. If for some crazy reason he actually *had* sent those texts…she'd deal with it later.

"I only found out because I'm friends with a nurse here."

"How bad is it? Cora said he was fine, but…" She couldn't stop the gnawing in the pit of her stomach.

"He's okay. Just needed a lot of hydration. Brodie and I have been waiting for his discharge but the doctor disappeared, so I decided to come grab a snack."

So he really was okay. Kathryn allowed a small bit of relief to slide through her as they headed down a long hallway. "So what happened exactly?"

"He caught some kind of really bad food poisoning. They ended up putting him on an IV to hydrate him. He's fine now. Just exhausted from all the throwing up."

She hated that she wasn't with him now, that she hadn't been with him last night. "I need to call Cora. She came with me." She pulled out her cell phone and went to text the other woman but couldn't get any service. Cursing to herself, she shoved it into her pocket. Cora would just have to get the room number from the front desk.

An elevator ride and a bunch of hallways later, they made it to a small waiting room where a couple families were waiting, as well as Brodie.

Brodie shoved up from his seat when he saw her and pulled her into a tight hug. "Irish, I've missed you!"

She laughed lightly even with the tension coiled in her belly. "I've missed you too."

"Daniel's assistant said you blew her off. I knew she was lying or confused though."

She frowned as she looked between the two of them. None of this was adding up. His assistant had told Cora she hadn't been able to get a hold of Kathryn and now she'd told Brodie that she'd blown her off. She fished out her phone again and held it out. "I never would have blown Daniel off. I got these texts from him last night, but now I'm thinking they weren't from him at all."

Brodie and Sienna read the messages together, then Brodie shoved her phone back at her, his expression all kinds of pissed-off. "I know my brother. He didn't send these. I'll be back."

Before she could respond, Brodie was racing out of the room. *Hell.*

Sienna simply frowned at her. "When we went to see Daniel a few minutes ago, he wasn't in his room. I thought maybe they were in the process of discharging him..." Sienna looked around as if the walls of the room could help her.

Alarm jumped inside her. "None of this feels right." But what the hell could they do?

"No kidding. Because I guarantee Daniel didn't send you those texts. And I was really surprised when his assistant said you blew him off. I knew that wasn't like you, but..." She cleared her throat. "I never really cared for Nicole but I just figured it was a personality clash. She seemed to have a weird fixation on Daniel, almost kind of predatory—but he never noticed so I just chalked it up to me being an overprotective sister."

Before she could respond, Brodie hurried back into the room. "Apparently he's been discharged to his 'fiancée,'" he said, using air quotes. "The description of the woman is exactly like Nicole." Brodie had his cell phone out, his fingers moving quickly across the screen.

What the hell! Tension coiled inside her, pulling into a tight knot. Could his assistant...hurt him? "You guys, what are we going to do? Should we call the..." Kathryn trailed off as Brodie grunted at his phone in triumph.

"What are you doing?" Sienna asked.

"Tracking his damn phone."

"Shit, that's right. We've got that locator app on all of ours."

Kathryn knew what they were talking about because she had a "find a friend" type app on her own phone with her brothers. Carson had insisted, no surprise.

Tension hummed inside her as she waited for Brodie to pull it up. *Come on, come on,* she silently shouted.

"Let's go," he ordered as he hurried back out into the hallway, the two of them hot on his heels.

Chest tight with worry, she kept pace with him. "Where's his phone?"

"It looks like the west side, third level parking lot. Not too far from here."

"That's pretty damn specific."

"Yeah, well, this app isn't available to the public."

Heart in her throat, Kathryn tried to push back the fear bubbling up inside her as they raced down the hallway. She was glad that Brodie seemed to know his way around the hospital because all the hallways looked the exact same to her. But soon they found themselves in front of another set of elevators. They headed down two floors then hurried out and made a quick left.

"This way," he urged as they headed down the rest of the short hallway toward a set of doors that said *EXIT* above them.

The moment he pushed open the double doors into the parking garage, another wave of worry rolled over her. What if...something had already happened to Daniel? No, she refused to think like that.

"You go that way," Brodie snapped at Sienna. "You come with me," he said to Kathryn.

She wanted to argue with him that it would be better if they searched alone to cover more areas, but had to hurry to keep up with him.

Brodie had his phone out and cursed after trying to make a call. "No service in here," he muttered as Sienna peeled off to the left.

Panic punched through Kathryn as they hurried across the parking garage. She wondered if his assistant was actually dangerous or if this was just a bizarre mix-up. This whole situation was just so weird. As they raced to the right, scanning the first aisle of cars, her heart sank. No Daniel.

"There!" Brodie whispered when he spotted Daniel about thirty yards in front of them, slowly making his way down the next aisle of the parking garage.

She started to call out to him but Brodie held up a finger to his mouth.

She wasn't sure why he was silencing her but she nodded as he hurried forward, his movements economic and quick. He tugged her toward the line of cars so they had a bit of cover.

And that was when she saw a four-door sedan backing out of the parking space a few rows in front of Daniel, likely to give him more room to get inside.

Suddenly the car jerked to a halt and the front door swung open.

Before Kathryn could even slow down, Nicole was out of the vehicle and had a gun pointed at the two of them.

Kathryn froze for all of a second before Brodie tackled her, throwing her behind a parked car. Pain exploded in her knees as they hit the pavement, but it all faded as bullets pinged against a nearby car.

"Shit! Nicole, stop!" Daniel shouted.

"Don't you *Nicole* me!"

"What's going on?" Kathryn whispered. She couldn't see Daniel but she could hear the anger in his voice. He was talking so that meant he was alive. Oh God, he had to stay alive.

"You were supposed to be an easy mark! And I'm sick of waiting for you to toss over that bitch," Nicole shouted, her high-pitched voice wavering.

Kathryn and Brodie hurried around to the front of the parked car, crawling forward, trying to stay covered. Damn it, she needed service so she could call the police! At least the parked cars and concrete pillars gave them enough cover.

For now.

Clutching onto her new canister of pepper spray, she held that close. It was the only weapon she had and she would sure as hell use it.

"Come out now or I shoot your boyfriend in the stomach!" Nicole shouted.

Her gut lurched even as Brodie raced forward, weaving in between cars. He was much faster than her, already two cars ahead and so damn close to Daniel. She wasn't sure what he was going to do, but he'd been in the Marines and was now in personal security. He had to have a gun or something...right?

"Now!" Nicole shouted.

Another gunshot rang out and Kathryn flinched, crouching down behind the nearest tire.

Oh God, she couldn't do anything. The woman would kill her if she showed her face and potentially kill Daniel if she didn't. *Think, think, think.* She grabbed a small mirror from her purse and hauled her arm back, throwing it a few cars behind her. Maybe Nicole would think it was her.

Crash! A bullet smashed through the window above her. So maybe her distraction hadn't worked well. She knew if she popped her head up, she was going to get it blown off, but she needed to keep the woman talking. She needed to distract Nicole and let Brodie do whatever it was he was going to do.

"What do you think is going to happen here?" she called out. "You haven't hurt anybody yet," Kathryn added. "You can still walk away from this."

"Shut the hell up. You don't know anything about me, don't know anything about my life," Nicole spat.

"Fine, tell me about your life," she said. Oh God, she hoped there were no innocent civilians nearby. So far she hadn't seen or heard anyone else.

"Don't patronize me!" the woman screamed.

"Nicole, just put the gun down and we can talk," Daniel said quietly.

"Shut up and don't move," Nicole snarled.

Kathryn crouched down under the car and saw Nicole's high-heeled feet moving in her direction.

She inwardly cursed and squeezed in between the front of the 4Runner and the parking pillar. As she peered underneath the car again, she could see Nicole slowly rounding the vehicle—right where Kathryn had been before.

"Stay where you are," Nicole snapped, very likely talking to Daniel. She could see his feet as well, only a few yards away from Nicole.

She had no idea where Brodie or Sienna were, but Brodie had to be nearby, ready to pounce. Her heart was in her throat as she tried to figure out what to do. She needed to get help somehow.

"Over here," she shouted, wanting to get Nicole's attention. Three more shots blasted close by. Bits of concrete fell down on the vehicle next to her, setting the alarm off.

Wincing, she quickly crawled to the next parking spot, hiding on the other side of the car. How many shots could Nicole have left?

Another shot rang out, pinging against the concrete wall four feet above her head and to the left.

Was that six or seven times she'd shot? Trembling, Kathryn got down on her stomach and looked again for Nicole's feet.

Suddenly another car alarm started blaring.

"No!" Nicole screamed and then the gun went off again.

Ping. Ping.

Silence followed, then a thud.

Heart in her throat, Kathryn peered over the top of the car as both Daniel and Nicole rolled on the ground.

Daniel!

She raced around to the back of the car just as Brodie appeared from around the next vehicle, breathing hard and looking as if he'd taken a few punches.

She didn't have time to worry about him as she raced to Daniel and Nicole, her eyes widening at the sight of all the blood on the pavement. "No!"

"Stay back!" Daniel shoved up on wobbly feet, a gun in hand.

That was when Kathryn saw that the blood was pouring from Nicole's shoulder as she writhed in pain against the concrete.

"She had a partner. He's out cold and cuffed," Brodie said as he hurried forward. Ignoring the woman's groans, he flipped her over and secured her wrists behind her with flex cuffs.

Daniel held the gun on Nicole until she was secured. Kathryn threw her arms around Daniel, holding on tight. "Are you sure you're okay?" she demanded, only moving back far enough to get a good look at him. He was exhausted, his face a little hollow and like he needed to eat a few hamburgers. But he was alive!

"I am now. Oh baby, I thought—"

Just then, Sienna and three men in police uniforms stormed the parking garage.

"About time," Brodie muttered, though Kathryn knew that much time hadn't passed. But Daniel could have been killed. Any of them could have.

"She's over here!" Daniel shouted as he shifted to the side, keeping his arm tightly around Kathryn's shoulders.

"And there's another one back there," Brodie added as they approached.

Kathryn had a lot of questions—so many of them—but Daniel was okay. They were all going to be okay.

Emotion swelled inside her, tears pricking her eyes, but she managed to keep them at bay. For now. Soon, she knew she'd break. But she could be strong for a little bit longer. For Daniel.

CHAPTER FIFTEEN

Kathryn leaned into Daniel's hold, snuggling against him on his giant couch. Sienna and Brodie were sitting across from them on another couch and her brother Carson had just stopped by.

It was weird to be back at Daniel's place but she was so glad that all this insanity was behind them. Well, hopefully. It was the reason her brother had stopped by, to update them on everything from hours earlier. They'd all made their statements down at the police station, then headed back here to clean up.

"I can promise that from now on you guys have nothing to worry about. Nicole Granger, aka Nicole Vallow, aka Nicole O'Day, aka who knows how many other pseudonyms she's got, is going to be charged with a lot of crimes. And so will her brother, the man who attacked you at your condo, Kathryn." Carson's jaw tightened once, his rage clear.

Kathryn shuddered as she remembered that man running at her, and leaned closer to Daniel. "I just don't understand what she wanted."

"We don't understand everything at this point either. But apparently she thought you were an obstacle to getting to Daniel. She's milked other men out of millions over the last decade. She seduces them, takes their money, then kills them. Apparently she's very good at what she does. Until Daniel. Her brother's talking fairly freely—she was going to force Daniel to empty his bank account. She decided that working for him and trying to seduce him wasn't going to work—"

"Because he only has eyes for Kathryn," Sienna murmured, smiling softly at Kathryn.

Carson snorted. "Exactly. It sounds like she decided she wasn't walking away from this score no matter what."

"So her brother is going to jail as well? No deals?" Daniel demanded.

"Yes. They'll both do a lot of jail time. They're both wanted in five states. At this point, it might end up turning into a federal case. The team is still figuring out how much shit they have on them."

"I can't believe she got past my security," Daniel said quietly, tightening his grip on Kathryn. "We run extensive background checks."

"My guess is that the background check was fine. Everything you discovered about Nicole Granger was correct—except the fact that she's legally dead. The real Nicole Granger recently died, which is probably why it didn't flag in your system. Or maybe someone dropped the ball, I don't know." Carson lifted a shoulder. "I doubt there's a widespread problem that your company has to worry about."

"I'll look to make sure," Kathryn murmured to him, and he pulled her tighter against him.

"Thank you for stopping by to tell us," Daniel said quietly as he stood.

"Thank you for saving my sister." Carson stepped forward and, surprising Kathryn, pulled Daniel into a quick hug.

Kathryn stood as well and gave her brother a hug. While she loved him and appreciated that he'd come by, she wanted everyone gone. She didn't care that the hospital had checked him out again, she wanted Daniel in bed with his feet up. He did not need to be doing anything right now. Nicole whatever her last name was had poisoned him enough to send him to the hospital and Kathryn wasn't letting him wear himself out.

"I'm going to head out," Brodie said. "Unless you guys need anything?"

Daniel shook his head and hugged his brother too.

"I'll head out with you," Sienna said, but not before she shot Carson a strange look.

Unless Kathryn was mistaken, there was a weird kind of chemistry going on between those two, but she was so not commenting on it or worrying about it now. Nope, the only thing she was worried about was Daniel.

A few minutes later Daniel and Kathryn were finally alone and she collapsed back on the couch with him. For a long moment, she leaned her head on his shoulder and looked at the huge fireplace and mantel. He had pictures of himself and some of his buddies from the army. And there were a couple pictures of the two of them as well. She wondered if he'd just put them back up or if he'd kept them there all along. Either way, it warmed her heart to see them there right now. She could have lost him today.

Anything could have happened and she was still pretty shaken up about it.

She turned to him. "I'm so glad you're okay," she whispered. She'd only said the same words like two million times in the last few hours, but she didn't care because she meant them.

Reaching up, he gently cupped her face and rubbed a thumb over her cheek in a way that made her feel treasured. "I'm glad you're okay too. And we may never know, but I have a feeling she was behind that sticky note you saw on the file. Because I didn't write it."

"Oh hell, you're probably right. She had access to your office and your schedule and knew my comings and goings."

That lunatic had tried to split them up to make her move on Daniel —to steal millions from him. It was all too surreal.

"I love you," they both said at the same time.

She giggled slightly, the band around her chest completely snapping free. With a big smile on her face she leaned into him, wanting to get as close as possible. For the first time in months she felt so damn happy. Even with everything that had happened today, she was with the man she loved.

He tugged her into his lap and right over his thick erection.

Her eyes widened slightly when she felt that bulge. "No way, buddy.

You just got out of the hospital and are probably still a little dehydrated. The doctor said—"

"The doctor said I'm fine for physical activity."

"Pretty sure he didn't," she said, even as she shifted against him.

He groaned lightly. "Fine. How about I just lie back and you ride me?"

"I shouldn't…"

He rolled his hips once, his gaze heating. "Come on. We could have died today."

She sucked in a breath as he nipped her bottom lip. "You'll actually let me be in control?"

"Maybe," he growled. "Probably not."

"You are incorrigible."

"True," he said before he covered her mouth with his, no nipping this time but a full claiming.

She fell into that kiss, wrapping her arms around him and just settling into his warmth. She couldn't believe she'd let something come between them, that some awful people had almost ruined what they had. Never again would she doubt this man. He'd never done a thing to make her doubt him. That note had been a lie and her instinct about Daniel had been spot-on. He was one in a million.

And he was the only man she was ever going to love.

When he went for the hem of her shirt, she didn't stop him as he tugged it over her head. And when he undid her bra, she made a move for the hem of his shirt.

She trusted him to tell her if he wasn't up to this. And by the feel of his very hard erection underneath her, he was very much up to this.

Soon she had him naked—wonderfully, gloriously naked—and underneath her. And by the time they'd worked each other up and he slid inside her, his thick length filling her up, she felt as if she'd come home.

There was no other place she wanted to be and no other person she wanted to be with. Ever.

CHAPTER SIXTEEN

One month later

"What's all this?" Kathryn asked as they stepped out onto the roof pool area of Daniel's high-rise building. Lights and balloons were everywhere with little floating flowers in the pool. "It's gorgeous!"

He tightened his fingers against hers. "A little surprise for you."

She looked up at him, surprised that he seemed nervous. Oh God... She racked her brain trying to think if this was some kind of anniversary of theirs. They hadn't been back together long—though according to him those two months didn't count as a breakup. She wasn't good at keeping up with stuff like anniversaries, but she didn't think it was— Oh wait, it was Valentine's Day.

"Oh my God, I forgot to get you a Valentine's Day present." She stared up at him in horror, feeling like the worst girlfriend ever.

He laughed lightly. "That's not for another couple days."

She pushed out a sigh of relief. She'd been so busy working on her current project and of course making love to Daniel every night—and most mornings—that she'd blanked out a few things. Like forgetting to eat breakfast and pay a few bills. This last month had been a whirlwind of work and a lot of sex. Sooooo much sex. Not that she was complaining. Not even a little bit.

As they sat down at a little table that had been set up, he pointed to the edge of the building.

She looked over and all of a sudden fireworks burst across the downtown skyline. "They're beautiful." She absolutely loved fireworks, even though she hated them at the Fourth of July because she always had to combat crowds. So she ended up missing them.

A brilliant kaleidoscope of colors flashed across the night sky—reds, blues, yellows, purples. One after another. "Daniel, I can't believe you did this—" Turning back to him, she stared as he got down on one knee in front of her.

She sucked in a breath as she realized what all this was. He opened up a box to reveal a sparkly diamond ring that she was sure her mother would know the carat and cut of. But all she knew was that it was huge.

"Kathryn Irish, will you marry me?"

For a long moment she couldn't find her voice, but she nodded vigorously. "Yes," she finally rasped out, her throat thick with tears. "Yes, yes!" She didn't even get a chance to let him put the ring on her finger. Instead she threw her arms around his neck, practically tackling him.

Laughing, he scooped her up and sat on the chair, pulling her into his lap as he slid the ring on her finger. The fireworks still exploded in the distance, but they had nothing on the ring he'd just given her. "I thought for sure you knew what I was doing tonight."

Wiping away tears, she shook her head. "I had no idea. Like, not even a little bit. It's so soon," she whispered.

"So what? This is our relationship, we make the rules. And now that you've already been splashed across the stupid society pages, you're going to make an even bigger splash the next time a photographer catches you out in public with this ring."

Groaning, she brushed her lips against his. "You're probably right."

He kissed her back, deepening it for a long moment before he broke away and pointed at the sky again. "I don't want you to miss this."

She laid her head against his shoulder as she watched the fireworks, the brilliant display of colors raining over downtown and the ocean in the distance. She'd never felt more settled, more peaceful, in her entire life.

"I've got champagne on the way up too," he murmured against her hair.

The champagne sounded nice but she didn't care about any of that. She just cared about the man with his arms wrapped tightly around her. The man she'd fallen for so long ago.

He'd given her everything she ever could have wanted. But the most precious thing he'd given her was his heart.

UNINTENDED TARGET

CHAPTER ONE

Patience Carras stared at her cell phone for a long moment, deciding if she should answer. She loved her mom, but right now Patience was stretched out on a lounge chair by her pool, margarita in hand.

She just wanted to relax, maybe get a slight buzz and a tan.

It had been a long year and school had just let out yesterday, so yes, she was day drinking and enjoying her Saturday with booze and sun. She would probably do the exact same thing tomorrow as well. But if she didn't answer, her mom would just call back in ten minutes. And then she might show up.

Sighing, she slipped in her Bluetooth so she could be hands-free and still drink her margarita while talking. "Hey, Mom."

"Hey, sweetheart. How's the first day of freedom?" she asked, laughing.

Patience snorted even though she truly missed her kids already. She said it every year but she'd had a great group of kids this year. To be honest, she preferred kids to adults. They told the truth, didn't have any malicious intentions for the most part, and they said the funniest things. All that other bad crap was taught to them by their parents or the world in general. But until that happened, they were wonderful, honest little humans. "I'm currently laying out by my pool, and yes, I have on SPF 75 before you ask."

Her mom snickered lightly. "Good. So, ah… What are your plans for the summer?"

Something about her mom's tone pinged on Patience's radar. "I've got a few trips planned with friends and a whole lot of relaxing. Why?" She took a sip of her drink and smiled at the sweet-tart taste.

"Well, I have a tiny favor to ask."

Oh no. Her mom's favors were never small.

"Just hear me out," she continued when Patience didn't respond. "You know the Robinsons."

Patience winced at the name. Yeah, she knew them. Vanessa and Josh Robinson had recently died in a freak helicopter crash. "How's Trevor doing anyway?" she asked.

Trevor was Josh's older brother and a few years older than her. He ran some sort of tech empire and had become a single dad overnight when he'd become his recently orphaned young nephew's guardian. Oliver would be nine or ten months old now.

"According to his mom, not great. You know Flora and I are on a couple charity boards together. The other day she told me that his last nanny quit on him. Again. Apparently he's gone through five in the last few months."

Nooooo. Patience knew exactly where this was going now. Before she'd become a teacher, she had been a nanny throughout college. "That's a ridiculously high turnover. Especially for someone like Trevor. Unless you're leaving out a key point to this." Also, babies were pretty easy because they weren't getting into anything yet. They needed a lot of attention but they also slept a lot at that stage. It was very Groundhog Day type of stuff: eat, sleep, poop, repeat.

"He doesn't understand what's going on either because the pay is above average, he's been using a reputable agency, and the schedule isn't excessive."

"I'm sorry to hear that he's struggling." And she truly was. She didn't know Trevor well but she knew his mom and adored her. And losing his brother and becoming an overnight parent had to be tough.

"Well?"

"Well what?"

"Are you going to make me say it?" her mom asked.

"If you're asking me to nanny, I don't do that anymore. I have a full-time job." One she loved.

"He's desperate. And he would pay you double his normal salary *just* for the summer while he tries to vet people and find someone who will actually stick around this time. Apparently one of the nannies kept hitting on him and that's why he ended up letting her go."

"I thought you said they all quit."

"*Most* of them quit. One he let go because she was more interested in him than doing her job."

The beginning of a tension headache started spreading against the back of her skull. "I'm not saying yes." So that was pretty much a lie. "I'll *talk* to him and see if we can work something out very temporarily. Just to reiterate, this is for the summer only." It didn't matter that her mom was currently saying *just for the summer*. She knew what would happen if Trevor didn't find someone by summer's end. And with her mom, she sometimes needed to make things crystal clear. "I'm not quitting my job."

"I knew you would help out!"

"I'm not starting today and I'm not starting tomorrow. In fact, I won't start until Wednesday at the earliest. I've got a lot of stuff to take care of. Just send me his phone number so I can talk to him."

"Check your email. I've already sent you all the details."

Of course she had. "So how's Dad?"

"Retirement definitely suits him. He's off on some fishing charter for the week."

"I'm sure you're suffering in his absence," she said laughingly. Her mom loved her dad but occasionally they needed a break from each other.

"We'll have fun once he gets back."

"I so don't need those details." Patience loved her parents, but that was just way too much. And now…she had a new schedule to figure out this summer.

～

"I can't believe you're working all summer," her friend Rebecca said as she sat on one of the benches a few feet down from the still busy nightclub.

Music trailed out every time the front door opened and a few people stumbled out. Clubs weren't really Patience's thing but her friends had wanted to go tonight. She preferred low-key bars and occasionally karaoke. Though she wasn't a night owl at all—she liked hiking, snorkeling and spending time at the beach. So when her friends had wanted to leave at midnight she was more than happy to head home.

"You mind getting me some tacos across the street? You know what I like," Rebecca said as she pulled a twenty from her purse. "Ooh, or maybe some grilled cheese sandwiches?"

Patience snorted. "Sure. How long do you think the others will be?"

"Well, I'm pretty sure Dustin is getting that bartender's phone number, so as long as it takes him. Then we can all ride-share together."

"Sounds good to me." She waved off Rebecca's money and stood.

As she hurried across the street toward the circle of food trucks, she cursed the heels pinching her feet. She wished she was at home in her pajamas, already sleeping. Or reading.

Since the taco truck had no line she stepped up to that one first and smiled at Marco—the owner of the food truck, who was working his way through college. She'd been down here enough on weekends hitting up the local farmers market that she knew him. "Two carne asada tacos, three chicken tacos, and three with shredded spicy beef, please."

He winked at her. "No problem."

"Make that five carne asadas." She turned at the sound of a deep male voice. The man slid a couple bills onto the countertop.

Raising her eyebrows, she looked up at the guy and blinked. *Oh my.* This guy took tall, dark and handsome to a new level. His brown hair was cropped close and he had a very nice bronze tan—as if he spent a lot of time outdoors. Or maybe he'd just spent a week on the water. His eyes were a dark forest green and he had a faint white mark on his cheek, from a long-healed scar. "You don't need to buy my tacos."

"I know. I just felt like doing something nice."

"I'm not giving you my phone number."

"Pretty sure I didn't ask." His oh-so-sexy mouth quirked upward slightly, revealing a dimple as he watched her with amusement.

She laughed lightly. "Okay. Just making sure you don't think that buying me tacos means you're getting anything. Also, thank you. That's very nice."

He lifted a shoulder. "No problem." Then he glanced away, as if looking for someone.

"Were you at the club across the street?" she asked, even though he wasn't exactly dressed for it. The club wasn't fancy but he had on jeans, a plain T-shirt and boots.

He snorted softly. "No."

"So what are you doing down here at this hour?" She wasn't sure why she was being so chatty. She'd like to blame it on having too many drinks, but she'd only had one before switching to water. This guy was just sexy as hell and she was curious about him.

He grinned as he looked down at her, and damn, those eyes were captivating. "I have no idea."

"You have no idea why you're downtown?"

The man who owned the taco truck handed them two bags.

"Keep the change," Mr. Sexy said.

Marco smiled at the two of them and handed over another small bag. "Thanks. Here's some extra guacamole."

Mr. Sexy handed her the guac bag and his sexiness meter went up even higher. "My sister asked me to meet her down here and I don't know why," he said, answering her earlier question. "I think she's screwing with me."

"Is that something she normally does?" If Patience didn't love her friends so much—both of whom were now waiting across the street for her—she would think about eating all these tacos by herself.

Instead of answering, he said, "Are you good, or do you want me to call you a ride or anything?" His voice was slightly distracted as he scanned a group of guys across the street who looked like they were definitely up to no good. They were eyeing a woman walking alone and starting to follow her.

Patience started to step forward, to do something, though she wasn't sure what, when a car pulled up and picked up said woman. "I'm fine, thank you."

He nodded and fell in step with her, but he kept a decent amount of distance between them, as if he didn't want to make her uncomfortable. Something she appreciated.

"So, if I asked for your phone number, would you give it to me?" His voice was deep, sexy and intoxicating. And the way he was watching her, with a hungry intensity she felt all the way to her toes...

She was tempted to say yes. Sooooo very tempted. "I want to, but I have no time to date this summer."

He laughed lightly, the sound rich and dark, like warm honey. "I appreciate the honesty. Enjoy the tacos and get home safe." Then he headed across the street in the other direction.

For some reason she was a little disappointed that he hadn't pushed for her phone number—even though she was simultaneously glad he hadn't. Pushy guys were dicks.

"Come on girl, I'm starving!" Rebecca's voice carried from across the street, pulling her back to reality.

Soon she'd be in her own bed, full from tacos and fast asleep. And she wouldn't be regretting not giving her number to Mr. Sexy.

Probably.

CHAPTER TWO

"You should have told me you were hiring someone," Brodie said to Trevor over the phone, annoyed he wasn't there in person.

"Pretty sure that's what I'm doing right now." His boss's tone was dry.

Brodie bit back his sigh of frustration. He worked for Trevor but the man also depended on Brodie to keep his life secure. "I mean so I could have done a background check. Clearly we've been dropping the ball somewhere and I don't like the thought of a stranger in your home." Especially after the last handful of nannies—hired through an incredibly reputable company—had quit with no notice. He'd tried talking to the company, but they'd absolutely refused to let him talk to any of the women because of confidentiality. Which he understood, but damn.

"She's not a stranger. Our families are friends and have been for ages. She has an impressive résumé and it's *only* for the summer until I can find a permanent replacement. This way I'm not stressing out and hiring someone who will just quit again in a week's time." His tone was even. "And I don't get it either. Oliver is so easygoing and adorable."

Brodie nodded even though Trevor couldn't see him. He was currently at an airport, waiting for his connecting flight, so he tuned out all the background noise. "We're never using that agency again, but I've narrowed down a couple that come highly recommended."

"Good. Until then, she starts today. She nannied in college and now she's a kindergarten teacher. Once you get back, you can see for yourself that she's great."

He'd definitely be checking her out. "How can you know she's great? She hasn't even started yet." And the fact that someone Brodie knew nothing about was in Trevor's home was making the back of Brodie's neck itch. He didn't like this at all even if she was a family friend.

"I'm not having this conversation."

"At least send me her information so I can do a basic run."

"No. You need to be focusing on what you're doing right now for *me*. Not hacking her life."

He was on a job for Trevor now researching a potential new location for one of his businesses in a fairly remote area. Trevor wanted eyes on the ground and a personal report from Brodie because he trusted him. "You won't even give me her name?"

"Nope."

Brodie took a deep breath. "Is she more than a friend or something?" he finally asked. He couldn't imagine Trevor hiring someone he was involved with, but he needed to check. Trevor dated about as much as him—pretty much never at this point. Though he'd hoped to break his no-dating streak with the sexy brunette from the other night. The woman with the bright Mediterranean eyes and curvy hips he easily imagined holding on to as he tugged her close.

Trevor let out a startled burst of laughter. "My God, no. Just no. She's too young for me and just...no."

At least that was something. Romance and business did not mix. "All right, then. I'll see you Friday."

"Safe travels."

Brodie shoved his phone in his pocket and pushed his annoyance back. They had a good security team at Trevor's house. Everyone was vetted, except for whoever this mystery woman was. Trevor wouldn't even give her name because he was right, Brodie would have dug deep.

He texted the man he'd left in charge, telling him to keep an eye on the new nanny. Then he asked what her name was.

He glared at his phone when Rick texted him back, *Will do. Also I've been instructed not to tell you her name. Sorry, boss.*

Brodie snorted, his mouth curving up. Trevor was thorough, he would give him that.

~

PATIENCE STEPPED into Trevor's home office, glancing around at all the glass and sharp edges. He was seriously going to need to babyproof this space.

"What's that look?" he asked as he motioned for her to sit down in the black leather chair. He'd discarded his tie, and his jacket was tossed on the back of his chair, but he was still in slacks, a button-down shirt, and was wearing a watch she was pretty certain cost more than she made in a year as a teacher.

He really was observant. "I was just thinking you might want to babyproof in here."

He laughed lightly as he sat across from her, his dark brown eyes softening slightly. She'd interacted with him a few times over the years but he was a decade older and she didn't know him that well. But she'd always thought he was polished in that GQ sort of way. Looking at him right now, however, the man was clearly exhausted. His sandy blond hair was slightly mussed—and not in an "on purpose" type of way. He looked as if he'd been running his hands through it in agitation. "It's on my to-do list, I promise."

"So how are you doing? Seriously?" The guy had lost so much and gone from uncle to dad overnight. That was a whole lot for anyone.

"I want to lie to you and tell you I'm fine, but really I'm exhausted. *Babies* are exhausting. I love Oliver so much and I'm honored that my brother thought enough of me to make me his guardian, but...I'm running on fumes."

She'd read some business articles on him in the past and he'd seemed almost aloof and cold in them, but now he just seemed like a real man—

a very tired one at his wit's end. She nodded. "That's so normal. And I know I've said it before, but I'm really sorry about your brother and sister-in-law."

His jaw tensed slightly. "Thank you."

"So I know we went over everything on the phone, but I'm a big believer in open communication, so like I said, I'll work weekdays, have weekends off. And I'll stay on-site in the guesthouse during the week because you get up so dang early for work." It was a position she'd been in before with families.

Living on-site during the week made things easier for everyone, herself included. But there was a downside to it. She'd found that she had to draw very clear boundaries when she lived on-site. Some parents had been of the mind that because she was nearby, she was available 24/7. For the most part she'd been able to create boundaries early, but with some parents she'd had to find other employment because they simply wouldn't listen.

His mouth lifted up slightly. "All that still works. And I have a service that cleans the house and guesthouse once a week, so I'll make sure to get you their schedule. Also, I have a chef, so I don't expect you to do any cooking."

"Good, because I suck at it. And it's very unlikely I'll stay here on weekends, so if it makes it easier for your crew to clean then, that's fine with me. Also...I'll be available for evening emergencies obviously, but once I'm off the clock I'm usually going to turn my phone off." Technically she wouldn't, but she wanted it clear that she wouldn't be answering her phone for anything but emergencies.

He smiled again. "I get it. And I'm glad you're being clear with your boundaries. I wish everyone I worked with was this transparent. And I really appreciate you doing this. I know summer is the time when teachers need to recharge."

She gave him a real smile. "It's all good. So what type of sleep schedule do you have Oliver on?"

He blinked at her once. "Sleep schedule?"

Oh no. So he really didn't have anything figured out. "Okay, so he's not on a sleep schedule, but that's okay. Does he sleep through the night?"

"For the most part, yes. But lately he's been waking up crying about three a.m. He's teething."

"Oh, that's the worst."

"I've been using a cool teething ring, which seems to help."

"Perfect. I've got a couple other things to try too."

"Thank God," he breathed out. "I hate seeing him in pain."

"I know it's on my résumé, but I'm CPR certified and if you're comfortable I'd love to take him in the pool occasionally—in the early mornings or late afternoons, with sunscreen and in a floatie I'll be holding the entire time," she added. "It's been my experience that babies love water and I want to keep him stimulated as much as possible. It will help him sleep more soundly at night."

"That sounds great. My mom's taken him in a few times and he seems to love it."

For the next fifteen minutes they talked about anything she thought might be pertinent, before they both stood. "Now how about you show me that sweet baby?" she said, smiling. Flora had shown her pictures and he was the cutest thing. All chubby cheeks and big blue eyes.

"Gladly. My mom's here with him. I think they're in the kitchen now."

"I'm going to need a map to get around this place," she said as they stepped out into the hallway, only partially joking.

He snorted softly. "Oh, and my head of security is out of town but you'll meet him next week. He'll likely go over some stuff with you about the grounds here but I can't think of anything pertinent you need to know for now."

"Sounds good." Even though she'd had much different plans for the summer, she was glad to be able to help Trevor out. And Oliver. Poor thing had lost his parents and then gone through a string of nannies. Plus she'd be able to sock away some extra money, which was always a good thing.

CHAPTER THREE

Patience knocked gently on Trevor's office door, hoping she wasn't interrupting him. He'd gotten home half an hour ago and she was about to "clock out" for the day.

"Come in," he called out.

She opened the door and jerked to a halt to see Mr. Too Sexy For His Own Good standing next to Trevor's desk. What was the man who'd bought her tacos doing here? In a dark suit with no tie, just a white button-down shirt, tailored slacks and oh my God, those dark green eyes, he looked delicious.

His eyes widened slightly as he caught her gaze, clearly as surprised as she was.

"Patience, this is Brodie MacArthur, my head of security. The one I told you about."

"Oh, nice to meet you." Trevor had told her that the man was supposed to be back last week, but he'd apparently been kept away because of some business thing.

Brodie nodded politely, a mask of sorts falling into place, his expression going neutral. He sure wasn't looking at her the way he had the other night. "Nice to meet you too."

It was so weird seeing him here, sort of out of context for her brain, but she moved past it and turned back to Trevor. "I was hoping I could talk to you for a few minutes? But I can come back if you guys are busy. I was just about to head to the guesthouse."

"It's fine. Brodie was just leaving."

Brodie looked as if he wanted to disagree but he simply nodded and stepped outside, shutting the door behind him.

"I hope I didn't interrupt anything."

"No worries, trust me. Is everything okay?"

"Yep, everything's great. I just wanted to remind you that tonight is the first night I'm headed back to the guest cottage." Since Oliver hadn't been on a sleep schedule, she'd worked through all of last week and the weekend and stayed in the room next to his to get him situated and on a schedule. Now he was sleeping through the night like a dream even with his teething.

"I know, I've got it on my calendar," he said, laughing.

She was so glad he seemed to be a man of his word about respecting boundaries. So far there were no red flags and this job was easy, relatively speaking. Oliver needed a ton of attention, but he was a baby and that was to be expected. "Great, then. And just an update… There are no issues, and I'm honestly surprised you had those nannies quit so quickly. It's kind of bizarre." The place was gorgeous, with an Olympic-size pool—which she'd been in with Oliver, who loved it—a gym she had access to, and Oliver was an easy baby. He just wanted love and attention.

He looked relieved. "I'm glad to hear you say that. I've been racking my brain trying to figure out what went wrong before."

"So have you found an agency you like yet and started looking for someone permanent?" The sooner he got someone, the better it would be for everyone, especially Oliver. The fewer disruptions to his life right now, the better. Babies were so resilient, but still, he would need time to adjust to someone new. And if possible, she wanted to help out with the transition.

"Brodie has started hunting pretty seriously. He wants to do more intense background checks to make sure we don't run into the same thing as before. Though to be honest there weren't any red flags with the other women, so..." He lifted a shoulder, looking more like the man she'd known for years—well rested and put together.

"Okay, then. I'll let myself out."

"Make sure you grab something from the kitchen. Antoine said he left a casserole in the fridge and I won't be able to eat it all. Anything in there is yours. And if you have any requests, let Antoine know as well."

She hadn't actually met his chef yet, she'd been so busy with Oliver. She had tasted some of his pecan sandies and they'd been incredible. Apparently he was some sought-after French chef. "That's great, thanks. Oh, I actually did want to ask about that. Is it okay if I bake occasionally for myself in the kitchen when I'm with Oliver? I'll use my own ingredients."

"Seriously, anything you want to do is fine—and use whatever's in the pantry. Look, I trust you. And I'm grateful that you took up this position so last-minute. Are you sure you don't want a permanent job?" he asked, half-jokingly.

"I'm sure. I love what I do." Even though Oliver was sweet enough to tempt her to stay on permanently under different circumstances.

"All right, then," he said, standing with her. "I'm going to go check on Oliver."

She handed him the monitor she'd been carrying around. He was currently playing with one of the security guys in the living room, which meant he was sitting there in his Melissa & Doug turtle ball pit and gumming one of the plastic balls as he babbled to himself. "He'll go to sleep in two hours if he sticks to his schedule."

"The bouncer was a good idea," he said as they stepped into the hallway.

"I used to nanny for a baby who would bounce himself to sleep, wake up, then start all over again. That kid is now six and killing it in gymnastics." She'd stayed in touch with some of the families she'd worked for—and had a couple of the kids in her classes.

He laughed lightly and nodded once at Brodie—who she was probably going to keep thinking of as Mr. Sexy—who was standing outside the office door. The man nodded at Trevor, who kept going.

Patience stopped in front of the broad-shouldered head of security, feeling all sorts of awkward. "Hey, it's kind of weird seeing you here." She immediately winced at herself. *Way to be Captain Obvious.*

He nodded a little stiffly. "It is. So you're friends with Trevor?"

She lifted a shoulder. "Ah, our families are friends. Our moms really. We were always friendly I guess, but he's older and we went to different schools so we never ran in the same circles." And while her parents had done well for themselves, Trevor was in a different league altogether because of his tech companies.

Brodie nodded once, watching her carefully.

She felt as if she was under a microscope and not in a good way. He definitely wasn't looking at her the way he had been the other night. No, then he'd been looking at her in the way a man looks at a woman he wants to get naked with.

She had this insane need to fill silences and she hated that about herself. But she couldn't stop herself from continuing to talk. "Did you ever find your sister that night?" she asked, because he said he'd been waiting for her.

He scowled and somehow it made him look even sexier. "No."

All right then, she'd made it worse. So this was just really super freaking awkward. "I'm going to grab some food and then head back to the guesthouse. Unless you need me for something?" She wasn't sure why he was hanging out here. Had he been waiting to talk to her? If so, why wasn't he saying anything?

"Nope. I assume Trevor went over everything with you."

She shrugged. She wasn't sure if he was talking about baby stuff, but she definitely had all that under control. "Yep. I'm good."

"Okay. Let me know if you need anything."

As she headed down the hallway, she could feel his eyes on her. And for some reason she didn't think he was checking out her ass as she walked away. Which was pretty disappointing.

CHAPTER FOUR

Patience slowed her jog as she reached the gate at Flora's house and pressed the buzzer. The gate rolled open immediately and she pushed the stroller up the driveway, enjoying the cloudless day. She'd been taking Oliver out for strolls around the property and swimming with him in the pool, but today she'd decided to jog over to Trevor's mom's place for a change of scenery.

Before she'd even reached the middle of the circular driveway, Flora threw open one of the wide arched doors and strode out toward them. Her spiral-curly hair had gone gray years ago and she'd embraced it, making it work for her. She had on flowing linen pants and a matching linen shirt, both cream-colored. Wearing a single-strand diamond necklace and what were most definitely real diamonds in her ears, she was graceful and put together as always.

"You're an angel, bringing me this sweet baby today. It's only been three days and I already miss him." Patience laughed as Flora expertly unstrapped him and took him out of the stroller. He squealed in delight as she kissed his cheeks and then cuddled him close. "Want to come in for some tea?"

"Do you have coffee?" she asked as she maneuvered the stroller up the few steps.

"I sure do. I would offer you a mimosa but—"

"Ha, ha. I'm not drinking while on the clock."

"Well I'm certainly glad to hear that you're not drinking while watching my grandson." She winked at her as she shut and locked the door behind them. "So why don't you tell me all about Trevor and what I've missed with Oliver the last couple days while you make some coffee. Just make yourself at home," Flora said as they stepped into the huge kitchen.

With dark gray cabinets, a sparkling white tile backsplash, huge wood beams running across the ceiling, hanging pendant lights, double ovens, an industrial-sized refrigerator—and a full-size wine refrigerator —this place was a show kitchen for sure.

Flora sat at the oversized center island and gently set Oliver on the gray-and-white veined countertop, holding on to him tight as he bounced in place.

"Well I finally got him on a sleep schedule," Patience said as she headed for the thankfully easy to operate Keurig coffee machine. "I worked through last weekend to make sure it would stick, and according to Trevor he slept through the night for him as well. And you know that he needs to start looking harder for nannies. Especially if you want to get a good one. He's only got a couple months to go." Less than, actually, since summer break was barely two months as it was. She put a mug underneath the one-cup brewer and turned to face Flora, who was cooing at Oliver.

"I don't want to know about all that, silly girl. I want to know about *Trevor*. How is he doing? Is he coming home at a good time? Is he eating properly? Is he dating? If so, what are his dates like?"

She stared, surprised at Flora, who was never this nosy. At least not around Patience. "No way. That's not what this visit is about. I'm not your little spy."

Flora grinned, clearly not put off. "Well I had to try, didn't I? Your mom said you wouldn't tell me anything and it looks as if she was right. And now I owe her ten dollars."

Patience laughed as she pulled the full mug out from under the brewer. "Do you have creamer or sugar?"

"Both. Creamer's in the fridge and sugar is in that canister." She nodded at a plain white one next to the coffee maker before lifting up Oliver's T-shirt and blowing a raspberry on his tummy.

He giggled maniacally and patted her face.

"I just worry about him. He works so much," she said as she sat back up and nestled Oliver in her lap. "He took the loss of his brother harder than I know he's letting on."

Patience simply nodded and sat across from Flora, listening as the other woman talked. They chatted and played with Oliver for an hour and a half before Oliver started getting cranky.

"I think I need to get him back home. It's almost time for his nap and it will be good to keep naptime in the same location, at least for now." The consistency was good when she could swing it.

"Of course. I might take him a couple days next week, but I'll let you know. I'm definitely scooping him up this weekend."

"Whatever works for you. I really am enjoying taking care of him." Sure, she missed what could've been an amazing summer, but Oliver was such a sweet little baby. Being around him made her realize how much she wanted one of her own. Not now or anything, but eventually. She just needed to meet the right person before she could consider that. For some strange reason the image of tall, dark and sexy Brodie MacArthur popped into her head. Which was…beyond ridiculous. The man didn't even seem to like her now. He watched her almost warily, as if expecting her to steal the silver.

"I wish there had been a spark between you and Trevor. Then I would've gotten to call you my daughter-in-law."

She blinked in surprise as they reached the foyer. Oliver patted her face gently and made little babbling sounds as he tried to imitate their words. "That's probably the sweetest thing you've ever said to me."

"Well it's true. Then your mom and I would be related. I think of her as a sister anyway, but still, it would have been nice."

She shifted Oliver slightly on her hip and he curled up against her, all soft squishiness. "I know she thinks very highly of you. She calls you the sister of her heart."

"All right, that's enough of this. I don't want to get all teary-eyed and ruin my mascara," she said as they stepped out into the bright sunlight. "I'm surprised that Brodie allowed you to come down here without a guard." She frowned as she glanced down the driveway. "Unless they're just really good at blending in?"

Patience frowned even as her heart rate kicked up the tiniest notch at the mention of Brodie. "Allowed me?"

"Oh yeah. He's crazy about Trevor's security. And with good reason. In fact…" She pulled out her cell phone and texted somebody.

Unease stirred in her stomach. "Is there something I should know about?" Trevor had seemed pretty relaxed about everything, and she and Brodie hadn't talked much since that awkward conversation. He was kind of standoffish—and unfortunately sexy as hell so she couldn't remain completely oblivious to him. The man was impossible to ignore.

"Maybe. Trevor has had a few scares in the last couple years. It's all work stuff, not personal. But still, it's why Brodie ramped up security at Trevor's home. He doesn't go anywhere but the office and home—or work travel. He bought the giant monstrosity with all that land so he'd have space and privacy. Also…Brodie is sending someone to pick you up," she said as she looked at her phone.

She raised her eyebrows. "Is that really necessary?" Her stomach tightened that they needed to worry about security like that, and she had been clueless until now. She would have been more careful, but no one had said anything when she'd left this morning. Of course…she hadn't checked in or anything, she'd just left.

"I'll let you figure that out with Trevor or Brodie. I'm pretty sure they're going to want you to have a guard on you at all times if you're out with Oliver."

Well, if that was the deal while she was working for Trevor, then she'd just put up with it. She'd worked for wealthy clients before and a few of them had their own in-house security. Though no one had as much as Trevor. "So what do you think of Brodie?" she asked, unable to help herself. She tried to keep her voice oh so casual. Oliver mimicked her then and tried to say Brodie, but it came out in baby-babble.

Flora's eyes narrowed ever so slightly before she took Oliver from her arms and put him in his carrier. "Is that interest I hear?"

"*No.* Mere curiosity. He's kind of intense." And soooo damn sexy. "And you'd better not say anything to my mom."

"I won't say anything if you tell me if Trevor has been taking care of himself."

"Fine. Yes, he comes home fairly early, from what I understand his schedule used to be, and he takes over with Oliver immediately. Sometimes he seems worried that he'll break him, but I've seen them together a couple times playing peekaboo in the kitchen and it's crazy cute. Oliver absolutely adores him. I'll take some pictures and send them to you."

Flora's expression softened at that. "Thank you. I'd love to have some of the two of them. You know, I was a little hurt that my son left Oliver to Trevor, but he knew what he was doing. I can see it now. My husband and I enjoy being grandparents—which is a lot different than being parents."

"He's in good hands."

"Well, to answer your earlier question, Brodie MacArthur has been with Trevor for a decade now. He's good at what he does. I know his parents and like them. And as far as I know he is not a serial dater. Not... What is it that you kids say? He's not a manwhore."

Patience choked on air as Flora said the word *whore*, then she grinned. "Well I wasn't asking about that per se, but that's good to know."

She gave her a knowing look. "You were definitely asking."

Patience glanced over as the gate started to open. "Did you do that?"

Flora patted her pants pocket. "Remote control."

"Oh, right. Thank you for the coffee and company. I'll see you later."

"Sooner rather than later." Flora kissed her on the cheek and did the same to Oliver before waving at the SUV coming up the drive. Then she disappeared back inside.

Patience was surprised to find Brodie himself pulling up, aviator shades pushed onto his head as he stepped out of the driver's seat. And he looked...annoyed. Maybe even angry.

"Hey, you didn't have to come down here. It's just a short jog back," she said, smiling—and ignoring the stupid butterflies that took flight at just the sight of him.

His jaw tightened once, and oh—he was definitely angry.

"You're not supposed to leave the house without a guard." It was clear he was trying to remain polite, though his words were tight. She wondered if he was always this rigid and controlled.

She lifted the carrier out of the stroller and started securing it into the back seat. "I didn't realize. Trevor never said anything." Or if he had, she didn't remember. Crap, what if he had? No...she definitely would have remembered.

"Don't do it again," he gritted out.

Now she was starting to get annoyed. "I said okay. You don't need to tell me more than once." She wasn't a child and his anger was starting to irritate her. "If you're so worried, you could have just called me." She knew he had her number from Trevor.

"I did call you."

"Oh..." She winced. "I might've left my phone in the diaper bag."

"We were pretty damn close to calling the police."

She turned to stare at him as she shut the door on Oliver. "Seriously?"

He sighed, some of the steam leaving him but not all of it. "Yes. Trevor has had a few scares at work lately. We take his security and now Oliver's very seriously. I saw you on the security feed leaving of your own accord. I figured you'd gone to a local park so we've been out scouring. I didn't even think of Flora's place."

Okay, so now she felt bad that they'd been out looking for them. "Crap, I really am sorry. I would never do anything to put Oliver in danger."

"I know that. Get in," he said tiredly.

"Is there a serious threat? Like...should I be worried or taking precautions?" she asked as he slid into the driver's seat.

"No. There's nothing current right now. I was just...concerned."

That made her feel better at least. The drive back only took a few minutes, but they were ridiculously tense. She'd never felt so awkward in her life as she tried to think of something neutral to say. Something.

Anything! But her tongue felt too big for her mouth and her brain had completely given up on her. *Ugh. Just great.* Being around him, when he clearly didn't like her, was messing with her head. She wasn't used to people not liking her.

"What are you doing now?" he asked when they finally got inside the house.

"Oliver's already dozing so I'm going to get him down in his crib and then grab a quick bite to eat." She'd had a lot of coffee over at Flora's but hadn't eaten anything of substance and she was regretting it now.

"When you're done will you meet me in my office?"

"Sure." She knew where his office was, right next to Trevor's. Trevor had pointed it out to her, but she'd never been in there.

Fifteen minutes later, she half knocked on the already open door. Her stomach tightened slightly—she'd apologized and she clearly wouldn't leave again without a guard for Oliver, but she wondered if there was more to this threat that she should know about? He'd said no, but...his expression was impossible to read.

"Everything good?" Brodie stood as she entered, and even though the office was normal-sized, he seemed to suck up all the space with his dark appeal. He pinned her in place with those dark green eyes and she cleared her throat.

"Yep. So what's up?" She still hadn't eaten and wanted to get this over with. Mainly because being around him short-circuited her brain a bit. And that was just plain embarrassing since he didn't feel the same.

She glanced around the office and noticed immediately how spartan it was. There were bookshelves filled with some books, but mainly notebooks filled with who knew what. The furniture was high-quality, and the huge window behind his desk had gorgeous damask drapes that she guaranteed he hadn't hung up—no, a decorator had most likely done that. Brodie MacArthur didn't seem like the kind of man to pay attention to decorations.

"Normally I do all the vetting for anyone Trevor hires. Here and anyone at his office. My company is in charge of doing security checks."

She simply nodded because she wasn't sure where this was going.

"I would've done yours as well but he assured me you were a family friend."

Um...okay. "What's this about?" Clearly he was leading up to something, but she had no idea what it could be. And she wasn't going to play some weird word games with him trying to figure it out. Especially not when she was moving into hangry territory.

"I called some of your former employers and talked to a Richard Miller."

Ice coated her veins at his words even as anger simultaneously spiked inside her, all sharp, angry talons. "And?" Oh, she *really* wanted to know where he was going with this.

"And it sounds as if you had some problems with him and his wife."

She laughed then, she couldn't help it. "I kind of want to let you talk just to see what stupid thing you're going to say, but I'm going to go ahead and stop you right there. Because I can imagine where this is going. Did you happen to talk to *Alice* Miller?"

He shifted slightly in his seat, his eyes narrowing. "I called her cell phone and left a message but haven't heard back."

"Well, way to do your due diligence, jackass," she snapped at him. *Maybe* she was overreacting but she didn't care. It wasn't like Oliver was around and could hear her. And Brodie wasn't her boss. So yeah, she was angry. For being treated as a suspect when she was a good person and doing Trevor a huge favor. "Richard Miller harassed me to the point where I was close to quitting. He finally took it too far and I had to press charges against him for physical assault—which was well on its way to being a sexual assault if I hadn't stopped him. His wife left him and has full custody of their children. There is a whoooooole lot more to that story than his take. As far as I know, he's only allowed to have supervised visits—if that. *She* is my reference, not him. I don't even know if he's allowed to talk about me to anyone. I'm not sure of all the legalities, but the fact that he clearly lied to you and you just believed whatever crap he said..." She shoved up from her chair, her whole body a trembling mass of rage.

He stood with her. "Patience, I'm—"

"Don't say my name. This is bullshit. I'm working here as a favor. I had an amazing summer mapped out, but I changed my plans because of what happened to Trevor and his family. But I'm not going to put up with being around you for the next two months. So I'm officially giving my two weeks' notice now. I will help Trevor find someone, if you get that far in the interview process by two weeks, and that's it. In fact, now I have a pretty good idea why you've lost so many nannies!"

Without waiting for his response, she strode out of the room, unable to be in his presence for another second. She hadn't thought about Richard Miller in years and Brodie had just brought up one of the most traumatic memories of her life.

He called her name, but she kept going. If she looked at him again, she was afraid she might cry tears of rage. She wouldn't give that jackass the satisfaction of seeing her cry.

CHAPTER FIVE

Brodie stepped through the open doorway to Trevor's office to find his boss sitting behind his desk. Instead of his normal business suit and tie, Trevor had changed into jeans and a T-shirt. "Oliver asleep?"

Trevor nodded and leaned back in his chair, covering a yawn. "What are you still doing here? It's late. Oh hell, do we have another threat? This deal is going to kill me," he muttered, rubbing his hands over his face.

Brodie cleared his throat, for the first time in as long as he could remember feeling...not nervous, but he hated that he had to have this conversation. Because Brodie was the one who had screwed up.

Big time.

"I screwed up," he said bluntly. There was no sense in dragging this out. And Trevor was the kind of guy who appreciated when he got to the point.

Surprise flickered across Trevor's face as he shifted his laptop away slightly. "How?"

"With Patience."

Now he shut his laptop. *"How?"*

"I wanted to look into her a little more. Since we've had such bad luck with the last few nannies. I found something in her background and questioned her about it. What I found was... Well it doesn't matter. I screwed up. I didn't accuse her of anything but I might as well have." He'd been well on his way to until she'd called him out. "It was a dick move and I didn't handle things professionally—"

"Fix it," Trevor snapped as he stood. "Because if you tell me she's going to quit, I'm going to lose my mind. I'm working on a huge deal right now, and as you know, I'm not sleeping well. I love Oliver, but holy shit babies are exhausting. And I have *help*. Better than I imagined. I can't afford to lose her right now. Did she say she was going to quit?" he demanded.

Brodie cleared his throat. "Yes."

Trevor rubbed a hand over his tired face and looked over at the monitor when Oliver started fussing slightly in his sleep. "I don't care what you have to do, but fix this. Apologize, grovel, tell her I'll give her a raise, but make it right." Then he strode from the room, not waiting for a response.

Brodie winced, berating himself. He'd begun digging into Patience and he had truly screwed up this time in a way he'd never done before. Not with work-related stuff. He should have waited until he had a better picture of her, done more thorough research. Instead he'd jumped the gun and... *Damn it.* He wasn't going to wait until tomorrow to talk to her. He radioed his people and told the man patrolling near the guesthouse that he was headed that way.

It didn't take long to get to the guesthouse, which was on the other side of the expansive pool. He knocked on the navy blue door of the cottage and frowned when it opened slightly. "Patience?"

He hadn't heard a report that she'd left the grounds, but maybe she had. No, she wouldn't leave Trevor high and dry like that and he'd instructed his people to tell him about her comings and goings.

He stepped into the little cottage and called out again. "Patience?" In response he heard a slight groan.

Shutting the door behind him, he moved into action, all his training kicking in as he drew his weapon.

The groan was coming from her bedroom. No one should have been able to breach the security here. Her bedroom was clear, with the lamp on the side table turned on and the comforter slightly rumpled on one side. He twisted suddenly at another groan coming from the bathroom—and he jerked to a halt when he found her slumped over the toilet. Her long, dark hair was shoved behind her ears and her T-shirt and jeans were rumpled.

She blinked up at him, her bright Mediterranean blue eyes bleary. "What are you doing here?" she rasped out.

He'd already tucked his weapon away before he crouched down next to her. He held the back of his hand to her forehead. She was clammy, and didn't seem to have a hot temperature. "What's wrong? Do you have the flu?"

She shook her head and shifted positions, leaning back against the bathtub. "Food poisoning. I've had it before." She closed her eyes and leaned her head back as she took a few shallow breaths.

Well shit. "I'll be back." Moving quickly, he jumped to his feet.

He hurried to the kitchen, checked her cabinets and the pantry to see what she had—it wasn't much. Then he put some ice in a plastic sandwich baggie, grabbed a washcloth and a little garbage pail from the pantry and brought it to the side of the king-size bed before hurrying back into the bathroom.

She was clutching onto the countertop of the sink, struggling to her feet.

Brodie steadied her before scooping her into his arms. She was slender and soft against him, something he didn't want to be noticing.

She blinked at him, a frown pulling at her pretty mouth. Damn, her lips were full, something he didn't want to notice either. "What are you doing?"

"Helping you get to bed. Is that what you were trying to do?"

She groaned and laid her head against his shoulder as if unable to hold it up anymore. "Yeah. I need to be horizontal for a while."

Gently he carried her to the bedroom and stretched her out on her back.

She kept her eyes closed, and when he put the bag of ice on her forehead she breathed out a sigh of relief. "Feels good," she murmured. "I just want to sleep." Her voice was thready.

"You sure this is food poisoning?" She was so damn pale—her skin had a gray pallor instead of the light bronze tan and he didn't like it.

"Yeah," she mumbled. "Had this twice before. I've got…a sensitive stomach I guess."

"I've got a plastic garbage pail right next to you if you get sick and can't make it to the bathroom." Not that he planned to leave or anything. Now wasn't the time to apologize and beg her to stay, but he was sure as hell going to take care of her. He couldn't leave her when she was in this condition. He couldn't leave anyone like this.

Stepping out of the room, he radioed one of his guys, asking the man to head out to buy Pedialyte and crackers on the company card. Tomorrow morning, she would very likely want to try eating something, and saltine crackers were the way to go, in his experience. And Pedialyte was what his mom had always gotten him and his siblings when they'd been sick.

"And grab some of those fruit popsicle things." He figured they'd be good for her throat. Once he'd done that, he called Flora. He wanted to make sure Flora could watch Oliver the next day. She told him that of course she was more than happy to watch her grandson so that took care of that.

Then he called Trevor, who was concerned but also relieved that Brodie had already taken care of the childcare situation. Once he was done, he stepped back into the bedroom to find Patience exactly as he'd left her, her eyes barely open as she stared at him.

"You're still here?" she murmured, then winced and closed her eyes again.

"I'm not going anywhere. I called Trevor and he knows what's going on. Flora will be taking over for tomorrow at least. All you need to focus on is sleep and getting better."

"I don't want you to hear or see me throwing up," she muttered more to herself than him.

"It's not a big deal." It was just one of those life things. People got sick.

She made a sort of grumbling sound before she jerked upright and promptly threw up in the garbage pail next to the bed.

He moved quickly and sat next to her on the bed, holding her hair away from her face while he simultaneously rubbed her back in gentle circles with his other hand.

When she was done, he took the pail from her even though she tried to stop him. "I got this."

"Ugh," she mumbled before flopping back on the bed. It was clear she was too weak to argue as she put the ice on her forehead again.

Since she was too weak to argue, she definitely wasn't able to take care of herself. He hated seeing her like this and was surprised by the protectiveness that swelled up inside him, at the need to take care of her. It had nothing to do with wanting her to forgive him. He simply wanted to make sure she got better.

After he'd cleaned out the pail, he picked up a hair band from the countertop and stepped back into the bedroom. "You think you can sit up for a minute?" he asked.

She groaned but pushed up on shaking arms.

He set the pail down on the floor and sat next to her. "I'm going to braid your hair so it's out of your face." It was probably overly familiar since he didn't know her well—and he'd been a giant dick to her—but he wanted to help.

She made some sort of nonsensical sound, but didn't move away from him so he gathered her dark hair and braided it in the world's worst braid. It was all uneven with one side thicker than the other, but at least it was out of her face.

"Thank you," she mumbled, her eyes closed as she lay back down. "You can go now."

Yeah, he wasn't going anywhere. He moved to the armchair by the window and sat. He'd sleep here all night if needed.

CHAPTER SIX

P atience groaned as she sat up, glad that the nausea from last night and most of the early morning hours seemed to have subsided. Her stomach muscles were sore from getting sick so often and she felt disgusting.

She hurried to the bathroom and quickly stripped out of her clothes. A shower with her favorite mango-scented shampoo and coconut body wash made her feel a billion times better. Finally, brushing her teeth with a minty-fresh toothpaste made her feel human again. Instead of drying her hair, she rebraided it, mainly because she was too weak to attempt using a hair dryer for longer than a few seconds. Her entire body just felt wrung out and taking a shower had sapped most of her energy. She dressed in comfortable lounge pants and a pullover sweater that was one of her favorites because it had been washed so many times. It didn't matter that it was summer; she wasn't planning on stepping outside the cottage today and she had the air-conditioning on low.

When she stepped out of the bedroom into the kitchen, she was surprised to find sexy-as-hell Brodie MacArthur leaning against the countertop, looking at something on his phone. He wore dark slacks and a button-down shirt—sans jacket and tie—his jaw tight as he read with complete concentration.

But the moment he noticed her, he immediately tucked his cell phone away and straightened. His clothing was the same, so he must have stayed the whole night. She...didn't understand why he was still here.

"Hey, how are you feeling?" The deep rumble of his voice rolled through her and, for some reason, soothed her.

The cottage wasn't very big, with the kitchen extending into the little living room. A countertop and high-top stools were the only separation so she went to sit at the marble countertop as she answered him. "Decent. Not like I'm going to throw up again anyway."

"I've got chicken soup, Pedialyte, which I recommend to help you rehydrate, even if it is tart, and saltines."

"Saltines are good for now. And yeah, Pedialyte is..." Well, it was gross. She knew it would be good for rehydrating but the thought of actually drinking it made her gag reflex trigger. *Ugh.* "Do you have any Propel? Or even tap water is good."

"I had one of my guys get a little of everything, including Propel." He opened the refrigerator and grabbed one of the bottles.

"Not that I'm not grateful you stayed—because I am. Very much so. Thank you for staying last night and for getting me food and drinks." And for braiding her hair, something she was still in a bit of shock over. "But what are you still doing here?" she asked as he opened the bottle and slid it across the countertop to her. She was careful not to let their fingers brush—for her own sanity. She was way too attracted to this man and he'd seen her throw up multiple times. Not only that, he'd cleaned out her throw-up bucket. Just...awesome. Not to mention he'd been a giant jerk to her before all her sickness.

"Originally I came to apologize and then I couldn't leave when I saw how sick you were." The worry in his eyes was the kind you couldn't fake. Or if he was faking, he was a damn good actor.

And it completely thawed her out toward him. Yeah she'd been pretty angry at him before, but after she'd had time to settle down, she'd decided not to quit. Even if he had acted like a giant dick, she wasn't going to leave Trevor and Oliver in the lurch. They'd already lost too much. But Brodie had been taking care of her for almost...

fifteen hours. It was kind of hard to stay mad at someone who'd done that.

"Look, I'm really sorry we got off on the wrong foot," he said.

"We?" She lifted an eyebrow before bringing the bottle to her lips. The cool liquid rolled down her throat, soothing every part of her.

He snorted, his mouth curving up in a way that changed his entire countenance, making him look almost approachable. "Okay *me*. I'm sorry for, well, everything. I'm normally much better at vetting people and I jumped the gun because I didn't want Trevor to lose someone else again."

"Trevor's mom told me what happened with some of his former employees."

Brodie shook his head in frustration. "We vetted everyone thoroughly. So I don't understand what happened. I was just feeling protective of Trevor and Oliver and I completely screwed up. I'm sorry I brought up something that's clearly a painful part of your past, and that I was ready to believe the worst of you. There's no excuse for my behavior."

At least he wasn't making justifications, he was owning his bad actions. She appreciated that. "Apology accepted. And thank you for taking care of me last night. You went above and beyond what I would expect from a virtual stranger. You didn't have to stay and I appreciate it." Even if she did hate that he'd seen her throwing up. *Gah.*

He lifted a shoulder as if it was no big deal.

"Look, I'm not going to quit," she continued. "I said that in the heat of the moment because I was pretty mad at you. Rightfully so. But I'm not going to leave Trevor high and dry like that. I'll stick around until he finds someone or until the end of the summer. Whichever one comes first."

He nodded once, relief flickering in his dark green eyes. "Thank you."

When he didn't make a move to leave, she cleared her throat. "I promise I'm okay now. You don't need to stick around." She felt kind of weird with him in her personal space now that she was thinking clearly.

He was so big and seemed to sort of take up the whole room with his presence.

He frowned at her. "Do you feel up to trying some chicken soup with your saltines?" he asked instead of responding.

Since she didn't feel like making soup for herself, she nodded. "Actually that sounds good. Just a little bit anyway," she said before nibbling on another cracker.

He dumped the contents of the soup into a pan and put it on the stovetop before turning it to simmer.

"You can just nuke it if you want." She so didn't care how it was prepared.

"It'll taste better this way."

She shrugged, but smiled as she eyed his backside. It felt surreal, having this big, strong, way too sexy man taking care of her. She should probably be embarrassed that he'd seen her throw up—and she kind of was—but he hadn't made her feel weird about anything. He'd simply stepped up and helped out. Even if it had been from guilt, he'd still been there. That mattered.

"Flora said you've been with Trevor for close to a decade," she said, wanting to make conversation—and hopefully learn more about him. She couldn't even try to squash her curiosity about him.

"Yep. He was my first client. And he's still my number one priority."

She took another sip of the Propel and wondered what kind of boyfriend Brodie would be—how he would prioritize a woman. After seeing him in action last night she imagined he'd probably be pretty incredible stepping up when needed. She shelved those thoughts, however, because it didn't matter. It wasn't like there was ever going to be anything between them. Sure, there had been a little spark between them at the food truck, but that felt like a decade ago instead of weeks.

As she drank more water, she immediately felt better and took a few more huge gulps. She was definitely going to need to rest until tomorrow morning to recover. Handling a baby in this condition wouldn't be smart. "Is Trevor really going to be okay without me? I know he's working on some big project."

"Flora has taken over everything. She said to take as long as you need to rest. What did you eat, by the way? I'd like to narrow it down to make sure no one else gets sick."

"I didn't eat much yesterday. I had cereal before I got Oliver up. Coffee, of course, and then I grabbed a few cookies from the main kitchen before coming back here." They'd been fresh, warm and incredible. Now she thought they'd probably gotten her sick. *Ugh.* Probably gotten cross-contaminated with something.

He nodded thoughtfully as if he was making a mental note of everything. "I'm sorry you got sick."

"Yeah me too. I've had food poisoning before and as you saw, it's not a fun experience. Ah…I'm also sorry you had to *see* me sick," she said because she wanted to get it out there.

He shrugged one of his big shoulders as if it was absolutely no big deal. "You don't have anything to be sorry for."

"Well thank you anyway. Listen, I really am okay. I appreciate you making the soup for me. After I eat, I'm probably going to lie down for a while and just rest. But I don't feel sick anymore. Just weak." As if she'd spent the day on a deep-sea diving boat and gotten knocked around by wave after wave.

He nodded, but paused as if he didn't want to leave. Then he set his business card down on the countertop. "I wrote my cell number on the back. Just call if you need anything."

"I will. And thank you."

His sexy lips pursed once. "You don't need to thank me again. I just did what anyone would have—and I should apologize again."

She laughed lightly because not everyone would have stepped up like that. "Okay so how about you don't apologize again and I won't thank you again and we'll call it even?"

His lips curved up and oh, damn, maybe it was because she was already feeling so weak, but she felt that smile in places she had no business feeling it. He was…sexy. There really was no other word for it. And that dimple was simply adorable.

His smile had just a hint of wicked, and while he wasn't handsome in that classical sense, he had a sort of rough-and-tumble air about him. As if he knew how to handle himself—which made sense given his profession. She couldn't help but wonder if he'd be able to handle himself in the bedroom.

When he finally left, she felt the strangest sense of loss. All she wanted to do was sleep right now, but...she still liked being around Brodie. And she wanted to get to know him more. A lot more.

Considering they worked with each other—sort of—that seemed like a bad idea.

CHAPTER SEVEN

B rodie found Trevor in the kitchen, sitting at the center island in front of a chicken burrito bowl and a glass of red wine.

"How is she?" Trevor asked, setting his tablet down. He was working with various local government entities around the state on growing mini-forests in unused areas, schoolyards, smaller downtown areas where space would allow, and on the sides of roads. Brodie knew it was a project close to Trevor's heart and if it was received well in Florida, he wanted to expand nationwide in an effort to combat climate change. He was trying to better the world and Brodie liked working for someone who actually gave a shit.

"Much better. She's resting now." He hated how sick she'd been, how miserable. This morning her face hadn't had that gray pallor. Instead, her cheeks had been the same bronze as before with a slight flush of pink he found...intoxicating.

"Good. I hate that she had food poisoning. Does she have any idea what caused it? Antoine is convinced she didn't get it here."

"Not really. She had some cereal, cookies, nothing really of substance. I'm guessing the cookies, since it was the last thing she ate and no one else touched them. I had one of the guys toss them. But nothing that should have come in contact with salmonella or anything."

Though if Antoine hadn't wiped down the countertop thoroughly, it was possible. "Also, she's not quitting."

Trevor shoved out a sigh, his shoulders relaxing. "Thank God. My mom's enjoying Oliver right now but I can't put all the responsibility on her, and Patience has been incredible."

Brodie had started to respond when Antoine, Trevor's in-house chef, stepped into the kitchen, carrying a bottle of wine.

He nodded politely at the two of them as he headed for the pantry. But he paused at the door. "How is the nanny?" he asked, his French accent barely discernible.

"Patience is doing well," Brodie answered. Calling her the nanny sounded kind of dick-ish. And he didn't like it—she had a name.

Antoine simply nodded, his expression reserved as always. "Good. She's so wonderful with Oliver. Look...I've checked the expiration dates on everything and I've thoroughly cleansed the countertops—like always—and every surface in the kitchen I can think of. I also tossed any leftovers just to be certain. But I don't think she got food poisoning here." He seemed almost offended at the idea. Which Brodie could understand; the man was a master of his craft.

Brodie nodded. "That's good to hear." He'd assumed Antoine would do a deep clean, but he was glad to have it verified.

"I know she's not staying on long-term," Antoine continued, looking at Trevor. "A friend of mine knows someone who's in between jobs. I said I would pass on their information if you're interested."

Trevor nodded. "Just give the information straight to Brodie."

Antoine nodded before placing a bottle of wine in the pantry and heading out.

"I might stop by and check on Patience tonight," Brodie said. He'd texted her to check in, but he wanted to see for himself that she was okay. "Everything is quiet around the house." And he was here later than normal.

"Good. I thought about stopping by but didn't want to wake her up if she'd fallen back asleep. Any news on those threats?" Trevor asked, changing direction.

"There's nothing to them." The "threats" had more or less turned out not to be anything of substance. There were a few agitators angry about Trevor's new planting project who'd ranted on a few social media forums, but no one with enough clout or muscle to do anything other than rail about it online. Some people were simply angry about everything all the time.

"Good. Let's hope it stays that way."

Brodie nodded and let himself out. Instead of going by the cottage, he texted Patience again. *How are you feeling?*

Good, she responded almost immediately. *Had a whole bowl of soup and now I'm resting again. I'll be good to go tomorrow. I've already texted Flora to let her know.*

Glad you're feeling better, he responded. He tried to think of something else to say, but everything felt...lame. So he tucked his phone away and headed home. He'd ended up getting return calls from all of Patience's former employers and everyone loved her—had nothing but glowing things to say about her.

He really wished he could go back in time and un-fuck-up what he'd done. And he really wanted to punch Richard Miller right in his face. Repeatedly. He'd checked deeper into the guy and Patience had been right—Miller hadn't been legally allowed to talk about Patience's employment. So he'd dropped a line to Alice Miller and her attorney to let them do with that information what they could.

It wasn't much, but fuck that guy. The thought of anyone hurting any woman pissed him off, but he'd started to develop protective feelings for Patience. So the thought of someone hurting her? Hell no.

"HELLO!" Flora's voice called out from the living room area.

Patience had left the door to the main house open, knowing Flora was stopping by. "I'm in the kitchen," she said, slightly raising her voice.

The other woman strolled into the room looking elegant as ever. White linen pants, a multicolored flowing top and of course, the sparkly jewelry.

"What is my favorite little man up to?" She set her purse on the counter and made a beeline for Oliver.

"See for yourself," she said, laughing.

He was in his high chair making a big mess of the mushed plums she'd given him, eating half and throwing half over the side. She'd definitely have a mess to clean up later. And the white onesie he was in was pretty much unsalvageable at this point. But he loved the plums and the coolness of the fruit seemed to help with his teething too. She was calling that a win.

"Ooh, what are you making?" Flora sat next to Oliver, giving him kisses on his cheek and making him giggle.

Patience poured milk into her mixing bowl. "I'm making cupcakes for a friend of mine. I'm going to give one to Oliver to see how he likes it." It would be soft enough for him and he didn't seem to have any allergies so far. She was keeping a list of everything he liked for the next nanny—and for Trevor.

"Maybe you'll make an extra one for me too?"

She snickered lightly. "I think I can manage that."

"So how are you feeling, my dear?" Flora headed for the fridge and pulled out a bottle of sparkling water.

"A hundred times better—and eight pounds lighter," she said, snorting.

Flora laughed as she took a seat at the center island and kissed Oliver on the cheek again, much to his delight. He clapped his hands together, making excited sounds before trying to grab her face.

Patience tossed her a wet cloth to wipe his hands before returning to adding ingredients.

Flora started cleaning his hands as she said, "I want to ask how my son is doing, but you won't humor me with gossip."

She cracked an egg into the mixing bowl. "He's doing completely fine as far as I know. I honestly don't even see him that much. He's at work and I'm here with the cutest little guy in the world."

That got a real smile out of Flora, who turned back to Oliver, now running his favorite plastic bus through his plums. "You're right on that count."

At a slight sound, they both turned to find Brodie stepping into the kitchen. He nodded once at Flora, gave her a polite smile before he turned that intense gaze on Patience. And the look he gave her was a whole lot different. For just a moment—just a flash—there was a hunger there, bright and consuming, before he went all professional. Heat slid through her as she watched him—and her heart rate went into overtime.

"I was just stopping by to see how you're feeling." The sincerity in his voice sent a spiral of...a lot of different emotions through her.

At first she'd really hated that he'd seen her throw up—more than once. But she'd gotten over her initial embarrassment because she had nothing to feel bad for. It wasn't like she could help getting sick. "A lot better. The sight of food doesn't make me ill, so I think I'm good."

His mouth curved up slightly as he watched her, and wow, she felt that smile all the way to her toes. She was probably just projecting what she wanted, but she imagined he was amazing in the bedroom. A man who exuded so much raw sexual appeal couldn't suck in bed, right? At least he didn't in her fantasies. And yep, she'd had a couple.

"I'm glad to hear that." He cleared his throat and glanced at Flora, as if remembering she was there. "So...everything okay with you guys?" he asked a little awkwardly. Which made him that much more adorable.

"We're doing great," Flora said, giving him a big smile.

He nodded then and stepped back, disappearing from sight like a ghost who'd never been there at all. She couldn't help but wonder if she'd see him again today—then inwardly cursed herself for caring at all. Only very recently had she been cursing the man in her head and threatening to quit. Now? She really, *really* wondered what he looked like naked. Okay, she'd wondered that before too. Ever since they'd spoken by that taco truck.

"So how long are you hanging out today?" Patience asked Flora as she started adding the paw-print-covered cupcake liners for her dog-loving—aka obsessed—friend Maddie.

"I'm not sure. I have a spa afternoon planned but I might grab brunch with one of my friends before. So...if I had any hope of you and Trevor getting together, those hopes just died." Her tone was wistful.

Patience's eyes widened in surprise. "What?"

"Oh, I'm just teasing you. I love your mom so much and I had ridiculous fantasies of you and Trevor discovering that you had a spark for each other."

She snorted softly. "Trevor is perfectly handsome and kind, but he's like a decade older than me and there's no attraction there on either part."

She raised an eyebrow. "I'm pretty sure Brodie MacArthur is also a decade older than you, and I just saw some sparks fly."

Damn it. She felt her cheeks flush, but cleared her throat and focused on her mixing bowl. Trevor had one of those fancy, ridiculously expensive mixers but she was a little afraid to use it. So she was doing this with her ancient, teal-colored handheld mixer. And it gave her an excuse to *not* look at Flora.

"Nothing to say?"

"I have nothing to say because I have no idea what you're talking about."

Flora laughed softly and Oliver let out a cooing sound. "I know what I saw."

"Look, Brodie was really kind when I had food poisoning. Trust me, I guarantee he doesn't want to get together with the woman whose hair he held back while she was puking her guts up."

Flora wasn't deterred. "He held your hair back? That's so sweet."

"That's your takeaway from what I just said?"

Oliver let out a squeal and pounded his hands on the tray. Clearly he wasn't getting enough attention from the two of them.

She grinned at him. "Are we not paying enough attention to you, sweet boy?"

He babbled something that sounded a whole lot like yes and waved his hands in the air to make his point. She set her mixer down and grabbed a couple more mushed plums. When she set them in front of him, he clapped animatedly.

Flora laughed. "I'm tempted to cancel my spa afternoon and just steal him."

"You do what you want, but I promise we're fine here. So if you're worried about him—"

"Oh honey, I'm definitely not worried about him with you. You are a lifesaver. We are so grateful that you were able to step in this summer." Her expression turned serious. "It eases my mind a lot knowing that Oliver is in such good hands during the day. And I know Trevor will find someone permanent eventually, but we really appreciate you."

"You should be thankful to my mom. I can't say no to that woman."

"Not many people can. Why do you think we have her on all of our fundraising committees?"

She laughed aloud as she started pouring the batter into the cupcake liners. For a brief moment she thought about setting aside a couple extra for Brodie—just as a thank-you for being so kind when she'd been sick.

But...that seemed too weird, right? *Ugh.* She couldn't ask Flora because she knew the woman would tell her to do it. In the end she decided not to.

Even if she couldn't seem to get the man with the dark green eyes and sexy smile out of her mind.

CHAPTER EIGHT

Patience shut the sliding glass door behind her and headed to the guesthouse. The walk across the property was certainly no hardship. There was a mini-forest on the west side, and tons of lush greenery surrounded the Olympic-sized pool. At night the place was lit up with solar twinkle lights, making it seem magical.

As she walked around the pool, she could admit that she was hoping to get a peek at Brodie. Maybe even talk to him. Sometimes when she looked out the window of the guest cottage, she could pick out his silhouette among the other security guys who were patrolling. It was crazy but she knew exactly who he was even from far away. He had a specific walk. One filled with confidence—which was sexy as hell.

"Hey." Brodie's deep voice startled her as he stepped out from behind a big cluster of bird-of-paradise plants, the oranges and purple bright against the setting sun. He held up his hands, one of which had a bottle of wine in it. "I didn't mean to scare you. I was trying to let you know I was here. I was just on my way to see you."

She smiled, butterflies taking flight inside her because he'd been coming to see her specifically. But then she chastised herself. He was probably coming to see her about something work related. "No problem. You're very quiet."

He fell in step with her. "I hope this is okay, but I got you a bottle of wine." He held it out and she recognized the brand.

"Ah...it's my favorite, so it's definitely okay," she said, laughing lightly. "Are you psychic or something?" She kept her tone teasing even though she was curious how he'd known this. It seemed like too much of a coincidence.

His mouth curved up in a way that made him look boyish and charming and those butterflies were back. Okay, they'd never gone away. "I might have done some sleuthing," he admitted.

"That's a little scary."

"I asked Flora and she found out for me." He looked almost abashed, which, holy hell, this man was twisting her up inside. It should be a crime to be so handsome.

She inwardly groaned because Flora had most definitely called her mom if Brodie had contacted her. There was a teeny tiny chance that Flora had used some discretion but Patience wasn't going to hold her breath on that. "Thank you," she said as they reached the cottage. "This is really nice."

"Look—"

"I swear you don't have to apologize again. We are *totally* fine. I think it's great how protective you are of Trevor and Oliver. I do appreciate this gift though, and since I love the wine, I'm keeping it." She grinned up at him.

He gave her another one of those panty-melting smiles. "Actually, I wasn't going to apologize again."

She let out a burst of laughter. "Okay, you just had that look on your face."

He cleared his throat as they reached her door. "I was actually just going to tell you that if you change your mind about going on a date, after the summer is over, that the offer is still open." Then his eyes did that whole dark and smoldering thing.

Those butterflies were apparently taking up residence in her stomach now. They'd decided that they lived here as long as Brodie was close. She told herself to agree to a date *after* the summer, but she had absolutely no control of her mouth as she said, "We don't have to wait until after the summer."

His eyes heated up even more. "You're sure?"

"It's not like you're my boss." And she didn't want to wait two months to go out with him. Of course things could go epically wrong and then she would have to see him at work and that would be plain awkward, but...she was going to risk it. She was pretty sure he was worth it.

"How about Friday night?"

"I actually have plans with a girlfriend. It's her birthday, but I'm free Saturday."

"There's a festival down by the beach on Saturday. My sister told me about it. Would you like to go?"

She knew which one he was talking about because she'd planned to go. "I'm in."

He half grinned then, revealing that elusive dimple, and she realized his smiles should be illegal too. He looked so tough and capable when he was in "work mode," but now? *Yum.*

"Trevor said you wouldn't be staying here on weekends, so should I just pick you up from your place, or...?"

"Yeah that's fine. I'll get you all the details."

"It's a date." His voice dropped ever so slightly.

Hand on the doorknob, she said, "Did you want to come in for a glass of wine?"

He paused for only a second. "All right. I'm actually off the clock. I was about to head home, so don't feel like you have to share your wine with me."

She snickered slightly as he shut the door behind them. "I didn't say I would be sharing *this* wine."

A deep laugh rumbled out of him. "I see how it is."

She grinned at him, reveling in the chemistry arching between them. Anticipation hummed through her as she thought about their upcoming date and she couldn't remember ever feeling like this about someone. She glanced around as they moved through the living room and was glad the place was neat. Not that she was a slob or anything, but he struck her as the kind of guy who liked everything neat and tidy.

As they reached the kitchen she set the bottle down. "I think there's a bottle opener in here somewhere."

"I've got it." He was at ease in the kitchen, clearly having been in here even before the other night when she got sick.

She sat at the countertop as he moved around with a sexy efficiency, opening the bottle and pouring the glasses for them. She might have stared a little too long as his hands worked the bottle opener—and wondered how talented he was in other things with those long, callused fingers.

"Did you always want to be a teacher?" he asked as he slid a glass across to her. He leaned against the nearby countertop while she stayed sitting.

"No. I changed majors a couple times and realized I was trying to do what I thought my parents wanted me to do."

"Which was?"

"I'd assumed my parents wanted me to follow in their footsteps. My dad was an attorney and my mom managed a couple nonprofits over the last few decades. Every time I looked into business school or anything to do with law, I knew it wasn't right for me. A roommate got me my first nannying job, and after that I knew I wanted to teach. I've been teaching for six years and I love it. Kindergarten is definitely my favorite age. They're so bright and curious. I mean, they continue to be all those things, but kindergarten is that sweet spot. They want to know everything and have so many questions, and I love that wild curiosity."

He laughed lightly. "I've seen you with Oliver and you seem to have a knack with little kids. So what would you be doing this summer if you hadn't been roped into working here?"

"Well, I had a couple trips planned, which I was definitely sad to cancel. I was going to go snorkeling down in the Bahamas with some friends. I recently got my diving license so I planned to do that as well."

"I love diving," he said.

She'd love to see him in nothing but swim trunks. "Something tells me you're a pro at it. I'm definitely still a novice."

He lifted a shoulder. "I've been doing it a while."

Oh, he was definitely a pro and probably too modest to say it. She took another sip of her wine, watching him over the rim of her glass. The dry, fruity flavor burst on her tongue and she sighed in happiness. This was a really nice brand of wine, one she didn't often buy for herself. It was the kind her family usually bought her for Christmas or her birthday.

His radio made a little beeping sound and he frowned. "Sorry, just give me a second." He spoke quietly into it, and even though he was off the clock it was clear he had a small issue to take care of. She fought her disappointment as he put the radio away. "I've got to handle something. I'm sorry to run like this but I'm looking forward to Saturday."

"Me too." And she definitely was. Probably more than she should be. She hadn't been on a date in forever and she couldn't ever remember being so attracted to someone as she was to Brodie MacArthur. There was something about his eyes and smile that drew her in. He had just a hint of wicked about him that made her wonder what was going on in his head.

Saturday couldn't come quick enough.

CHAPTER NINE

"This festival is different than I thought," Brodie said as they strode down the roped-off street.

"How so?" Patience asked, surprised he'd never been. Or at least it sounded as if he hadn't.

A couple blocks along the beach had been completely roped and barricaded off so vendors could set up down the middle of the street. There were tons of food trucks, kites for rent, face painting for all age groups, and in a couple hours a live band would start at one end of the street. The scent of deep-fried goodness filled the air, intermixed with the salty tinge of the ocean nearby. It reminded her of her childhood, so she savored it.

"I've never seen so many people flying kites in one place. Hell, I've never seen so many different types of kites." He glanced over toward the beach as they walked, looking at the kaleidoscope of colors.

Dragons, peacocks, rockets, anything you could think of—the kites were blanketed against the pale blue sky. Thankfully a steady breeze had kicked up all day, making her almost forget the summer heat. Not completely, because that was impossible in Florida.

She snickered softly and took a bite of her churro. "First, I can't believe you've never come, since you've lived here your whole life."

"I don't know how it happened but my parents always took vacations during this festival when we were kids. My sister went for the first time last year and hasn't stopped talking about it. She said something about a kite competition?"

"The kites were originally just for the kids—they used to have competitions to see who made the best one. Now the competition is open to everyone, but it won't be until tomorrow. The ones you're seeing now are just for fun. They've even got rentals for those who don't feel like making one or bringing their own. It's turned into this whole big thing. I think it's pretty cool." They passed a tent filled with different wood carvings of various sea life. She smiled at the artist, recognizing him from all her years coming here.

"Did you ever enter?" Brodie asked.

"Oh yeah. A couple years in a row, but it was pretty clear I lacked any real creativity early on. I never placed or anything."

"So…are you ever going to share your churro bites?" he asked mildly, a grin tugging at his mouth—giving her a glimpse of his dimple. Today he was dressed casually in shorts, a T-shirt with the name of a local fishing charter company and Nikes. It was nice seeing him laid-back like this as opposed to the sexy business suit. She liked both versions of him.

In response, she shot him a sideways glance and grinned.

"Is that a yes?"

She made a biting motion with her teeth then shook her head.

He looked almost startled but then he let out a burst of laughter that took years off his face. "Okay, so Patience doesn't share food. *Noted.*"

"I feel like I should just be up-front about who I am on our first date." And she really hoped there would be a second date. He was so much fun and had been so easygoing and relaxing today. "But I'm in a good mood, so…" She held out the little funnel holding the churro bites.

He snagged one quickly and tossed it into his mouth. Then he groaned. "No wonder you don't want to share. I should have grabbed one myself."

"To be fair, I told you that you were going to want some," she said as they reached an empty bench facing the beach. She motioned, asking if he wanted to sit down.

Thankfully he did, and she practically collapsed on the bench, glad to give her feet a break. She'd definitely worn the wrong shoes today.

"Are you tired?"

"No I'm good." She held out the funnel again. She'd been teasing him about not sharing. Mostly. "I just shouldn't have worn my new sandals today." But they were so pretty and she'd wanted to wear them for their date. Sparkly little gold straps crisscrossed over her feet and wrapped up around her lower ankle. Pretty, yes. But they had no cushion and no heel—no support. So she might as well be walking around in bare feet.

"If you want to head back to the parking lot, we can."

"I'm good, I promise. Besides, we haven't even finished seeing all the vendors. And there's one at the end who sells cute Christmas ornaments. I buy one every year." They were all hand-painted with incredible details.

"You can't have been coming here that long, so how many years is every year?"

"Is that your not-so-subtle way of asking how old I am?"

His mouth curved up and she had all sorts of wicked thoughts. "I know how old you are from your file."

Dammit. She'd forgotten about that thing. "I've been coming here since I was ten and I've been collecting ornaments that long."

"A Christmas fan, are you?"

"Of course. I should probably say something like 'giving gifts is so heartwarming,' and okay, it totally is. I *love* giving gifts—now. But when I was ten, all I cared about was getting stuff. I was such a greedy little thing. I thought if I showed my support for Christmas, Santa would hook me up. And my mom had no idea, she just thought I was this big Christmas fan like her and she loved that I wanted to start collecting Christmas ornaments. Now it's sort of like this bonding thing between us. We buy each other ornaments every year."

"I've actually met your mom—when I stopped by Flora's. She's a trip." Again with the half-smile that did crazy things to her insides.

She blinked. He'd met her mom? And her mom hadn't said anything to her? That was…interesting. She didn't know how to feel about that. "That's certainly one way to put it. What about you? I know you've got a sister but I don't know much of anything else." Flora had mentioned something about him having siblings but she hadn't wanted to be nosy. That was a lie—she *had* wanted to be nosy, but had decided not to be.

"I've got one brother who just got married. Took us all by surprise. Sort of."

"How did he sort of take you by surprise?"

"Well the woman he married, they'd broken up for a while. But it was all a misunderstanding and then as soon as they were back together, he proposed about a minute later, and then two months after that he was rushing her down the aisle."

"Sounds intense." She ate another churro bite, savored the sugary goodness.

"When my brother wants something, he goes for it." He looked at her then, his gaze smoldering and intense. God, what was he thinking right now?

She felt that look all the way to her toes and had the urge to lean over and kiss him. She'd never been one to make the first move on a date, but she was really, *really* tempted. She cleared her throat. "So what about your sister? The one who called you downtown that night we first sort of met."

His expression darkened slightly. "My sister is always in…intense situations. She drives me crazy."

"Why?" She offered him another churro bite, and when he declined she popped one in her mouth. These things were like little bites of heaven.

"Because she's my little sister and I'm probably way too overprotective. She's a PI and always seems to be in danger."

"If she was a man, would you feel as worried about her?"

"I'm going to be honest and say no. And not because Sienna can't take care of herself, because she absolutely can. But the world is not kind to women. And I hate that. I hate that she has to worry about more things simply because men can be assholes."

She nodded in approval. "True enough." She knew that firsthand.

"Can I ask you something?" There was a hint of...some emotion she couldn't define in his voice.

"Yeah."

"If it's too personal, tell me to screw right off."

Oh, she thought she knew where this was going. "Is this about Richard Miller?"

"I...kind of. I found out a little more, and for the record, he wasn't allowed to talk about you. I let his wife and her attorney know."

She raised her eyebrows slightly. "Wow. Thank you. Long story short, he always gave me a creepy vibe. But he was gone all the time, traveling for work, so I took the job. I loved his wife and honestly didn't understand why she put up with him. She had a blind spot where he was concerned. I think we all have them."

He nodded, quiet as she continued.

"Anyway, he lost his job and was supposed to be job hunting but instead spent all of his time trying to talk to me—in front of his kids. I mean, if he wasn't going to be working, I don't even know why I was there at all. I was getting ready to put in my notice because it had gotten to be unbearable to be in the same house as him." He'd been like this lurking shadow. Always there. *Ugh.* "All I wanted to do was work and it was like he wanted all my attention on him. The only reason I stayed was because of the kids. He didn't pay any attention to them, treated them as if they were an inconvenience... You sure you want to hear all this?" It felt heavy for a first date.

As the waves crashed in the background and people milled down the sidewalk behind them, he nodded. "Yes, but only if you want to talk about it. I probably shouldn't have asked."

"It's okay that you did." She was glad to be able to tell him this part of her past. She'd moved on from it and didn't have nightmares anymore. People were passing by them so quickly she wasn't worried about people eavesdropping either. Everyone was caught up in their own world, herself included. "One day the kids were napping and I was doing dishes. He cornered me in the kitchen and made a pass at me. A blatant one. I told him to back off and he tried to act like I was overreacting and reading into things. That he was just being friendly."

She rolled her eyes as she remembered how offended he'd acted.

"I snorted and told him that would be my last day. He looked almost panicked and just attacked. I wasn't prepared for it but I managed to get him off me and bash him in the head with a pan I'd just washed. Then one of his kids woke up, which seemed to startle him even more. He ran out of the house, I called the cops and..." She shrugged. "There's more to it than that, but luckily his wife believed me and left him. And the cops handled everything professionally, so I call that a win too. It was easy for her to get full custody—he actually didn't even fight it, from what I understand."

"I think I know, but why isn't he in jail?" Brodie's jaw was tight and she could see the anger simmering under the surface—at Miller, not her.

"He attacked me but he didn't do any real physical harm. I mean, I have no doubt he planned to rape me. He was absolutely crazed. But it never got that far and it was a 'first-time offense.' So." She lifted a shoulder. "It's not okay what happened, but I can't change the outcome so I made the decision to move forward and not let anger consume me that he's out walking around like he did nothing wrong. If he hurts someone else, it's on him—and our crappy justice system."

He watched her for a long moment, then reached up and surprised her by cupping her cheek gently. "You're incredible."

She blinked even as she flushed at his soft touch. "I don't know about that."

"You are. Thank you for sharing all that with me. And I know I'm not supposed to apologize again—"

"Then don't." She'd enjoyed today and didn't want any more apologies, didn't want to dwell on the past anymore. She wanted to live in the moment with him.

Brodie's mouth quirked up slightly. "All right." He still cupped her cheek, watching her for a long moment before he cleared his throat and dropped his hand. "Hey, do you mind sitting tight for a couple minutes? I wanted to grab some more of those churro bites. I'll grab you another funnel too?"

She grinned slightly, the weird band around her chest easing a bit. She was glad she'd told him all that, felt almost relieved to get it out there. "I'm actually good, but thanks." She crumpled up her little funnel cake holder and handed it to him as he stood. "I wouldn't mind some water though."

He nodded and hurried off—and she totally checked out his ass as he walked away. Because the man had a seriously fine one. A nice, perfect bubble butt she wanted to grab onto. *Gah.* She'd never felt such an intense reaction to someone and it had her off-kilter. Brodie had her off-kilter in general.

Tearing her gaze away from the fine man, she stared out at the kites and felt more relaxed than she had in ages. She wasn't sure how much time passed but eventually he returned and she frowned when she saw he was carrying a brown bag and the food. "What's this?" she asked as he sat and handed her the plain bag.

"It's those wind chimes I saw you admiring earlier. I passed them on the way to grab the food." He shrugged as if it was no big deal.

But that vendor wasn't anywhere near the food carts so he'd gone out of his way to get this for her. Her eyes widened slightly as she peered inside. "Brodie, that's incredibly thoughtful. Thank you." She wanted to tell him that they had been way too expensive, which was why she hadn't even thought of buying them when she'd seen the price tag. But she didn't want to insult his gift either. And...they were gorgeous. "Seriously, this is so generous, thank you."

He lifted a shoulder but she could tell he was pleased by the small grin that played across his face. Wicked, wicked smile. "I'm glad you like it."

Patience stared at him for a long moment, then suddenly they both moved into action. She wasn't sure who leaned forward first, her or Brodie. But they were staring at each other and then suddenly they were kissing, his mouth on hers, dominating and teasing at the same time.

She leaned closer, the bag crinkling between them as she grabbed onto his shirt and tugged him closer.

He tasted sweet like the sugar from the churro, and when he gently bit her bottom lip she moaned into his mouth. The way his tongue flicked against hers sent spirals of pleasure rolling through her as she wondered if he'd be talented with that tongue in other ways.

God, she could straddle him right here, just move and slide her legs over his, roll her hips against his. And at *that* thought, she slightly straightened and pulled back at the same time he did. Heat pooled low in her belly and it took a moment to get her breathing under control.

His breathing was as uneven as hers as he watched her with hungry eyes. "We'll probably get written up on indecency charges if we keep doing this," he murmured.

That pulled a laugh out of her, easing all the tightly coiled sexual energy inside her. Sort of. "Probably. I'm also debating whether I care or not."

He let out a startled laugh then and grinned at her before popping another sugary bite into his mouth. "I had fun today," he said a few moments later.

"Me too. The day's not over though." She definitely wanted a repeat of that kiss, only a much longer one in private. "I still want to check out the Christmas vendor if you're up to it."

He gathered their bags, carrying all of them, and took her hand in his as if it was the most natural thing in the world.

Surprise flickered through her, but she liked the feel of his callused fingers holding hers. Liked being with him in general.

It almost felt like they were a real couple. Yes, she knew she was getting ahead of herself, so she stopped that train of thought right then and there. She liked Brodie. Way too much. But she'd been wrong about men in the past, so for now, she was just going to enjoy the day and not focus on the future or anything else.

CHAPTER TEN

Patience realized she was humming to herself as she slid the cupcakes into the oven. She felt like some kind of cartoon princess, making cupcakes and singing to herself, and it was ridiculous. *She* was ridiculous. But she couldn't stop smiling and had been since Saturday. Brodie had taken her back home, kissed her again—and made it clear he'd wanted more, but had respected her decision not to take it further than a kiss—and even though she hadn't seen him since then, they had been texting. He'd been working at Trevor's office all day and she could admit she missed seeing him.

And kissing him.

It was probably better that she wasn't distracted by him at work though. So here she was on Monday, making cupcakes for another friend—it was her specialty and her friends always begged her to make her special cream cheese cupcakes—while Oliver was sleeping.

"What are you doing?" a male voice demanded.

She glanced over her shoulder as she set one of the mixing bowls in the sink to find Antoine the chef looming in the doorway. "Making cupcakes." Seemed pretty obvious what she was doing.

He frowned as he stepped into the room. He had on linen slacks, a loose linen tunic, and his blond hair was thick and sun-kissed, making him look more like a surfer than a chef. He was only a few inches taller than her, but had a presence that made him seem bigger than he was. "You have a kitchen in the guesthouse," he said tartly.

Surprised by his rudeness—but not going to feed into it—she looked away from him and turned the water on hot to start cleaning the dishes. As she did, she glanced at the monitor. Oliver was still sleeping soundly.

"Excuse me, did you hear what I said?" She could feel him moving up behind her and on instinct she tensed.

But she wasn't going to flinch and let her fears based on the past take over. This guy was harmless and clearly wanted to argue with her. But she worked with kindergarteners on a daily basis. She was so not getting into anything with him. She added soap to the sponge. "I heard you, but I'm not sure what response you want. I'm making cupcakes while Oliver is sleeping, and I'm not in your way." What was with this guy?

"Must be nice having a job where you can slack off," he grumbled as he stalked toward the pantry door.

Holy hell. Something had crawled up this guy's ass, apparently. Or maybe he was always a dick. She chose silence instead of engaging in dialogue with him. She'd learned that was sometimes the best way to defuse any situation. She started washing the dishes she'd used and setting them onto the drying rack next to the sink.

"You better not have used any of *my* ingredients."

Okay, enough was enough. She shut off the water and turned to face him as she wiped her hands on the gray-and-white checkered dish towel. "Trevor said I could use this kitchen anytime I want. He even said I could use *any* ingredients in here—but I used my own. Oliver is very clearly sleeping," she said, jerking her finger over her shoulder at the monitor. "If you have a problem with me being in here, take it up with Trevor. Otherwise, you better back off."

His eyes widened slightly and it was clear she'd surprised him. Maybe he was just a big bully, and while she didn't want to buy into stereotypes, on all those chef shows the chefs were always kind of jerks. Always yelling at people.

He let out a huffing sound. "Just stay out of my way," he snapped before he turned on his heel and literally stomped from the room. Like a toddler.

Well, then. She would definitely be staying out of his way. He must be really good at what he did for Trevor to put up with that kind of attitude. Though something told her that he didn't act like that to his boss. No, she'd learned that some people showed their true colors to those they assumed couldn't do anything for them.

When she heard a rustling sound on the monitor, she turned to find Oliver waking up and rubbing his eyes.

She glanced at the oven timer and hung the dish towel over the lip of the sink before hurrying from the kitchen. Time to get back to work.

HOURS later and finally off the clock, Patience realized she was humming to herself yet again as she pulled into the parking spot of the specialty lingerie shop. "Cut it out, girl," she muttered to herself.

She'd never been here before but several friends had mentioned the place, and something told her that if she and Brodie continued down their current path, she was going to want to have some sexy undergarments on hand. Though he was a guy and probably wouldn't care about her plain black bra and underwear. But screw it, she wanted to feel sexy and feminine for herself. Okay, for him too. She wanted him to like what he saw if and when they got naked. At this point she was pretty sure it was a "when." At least on her end.

An hour later, after spending way too much money, she deposited the two black-and-white striped bags into her back seat. They joined the bag of specialty coffee she'd bought for Brodie. She'd been sneaky and asked Flora what he liked, and to her surprise the woman had told her. And Flora also hadn't teased her or anything about her interest in Brodie.

She was still annoyed by the way Antoine had acted toward her today in the kitchen earlier, even though she'd tried to brush it off. She'd had a great day with Oliver—playing in the pool with him, and Flora had dropped by for another visit—and then Trevor had gotten home early so she'd taken off to run some errands, including dropping off those cupcakes to her friend.

And now she needed to take her bags back to her house instead of the guesthouse. Because if anything was going to happen with her and Brodie, it certainly wasn't going to be at the guesthouse. That felt waaaaay too weird. Technically it was her private quarters but it was still where she worked, and she wasn't going to be hooking up with the head of security there.

If she even hooked up with him at all. *Dammit*. She had to stop getting ahead of herself. They'd been on *one* date—one really fun date. And they'd shared a couple kisses. And a lot of texts. Even though she tried to tell herself that she needed to slow down, it was hard to when she was extremely curious what the sexy man looked like naked. Because the man could kiss. She'd always thought that kissing was an extension of other things. He'd taken his time, been teasing and sweet, but she'd been able to feel raw energy humming through him as she'd clutched onto his arms. He'd been as amped up as she was.

Yep, she had to stop this train of thought now before she worked herself up.

As she turned onto the next street, she frowned when she saw the same car behind her that she'd seen back at that coffee place. She swore it was the same black sedan because it had a yellow sticker in the same place. Whoever the driver was could just be going to the same place as her, but it felt weird because she remembered seeing the same vehicle hours ago. It was after dark...and maybe she was letting her imagination run away with her. She watched a lot of true crime shows, and the truth was, after what had happened with Miller, she was more vigilant about her surroundings.

As she came to a four-way stop, she started to slow. The car behind her sped up, ramming into her.

Her head snapped forward as her car flew into the middle of the intersection.

Heart in her throat she pressed the gas, wanting to get away from this lunatic. She'd sped forward, flying through the intersection, when flashing blue lights came out of nowhere. She started to pull over when the car behind her reversed and raced off in the other direction.

The blue lights got brighter, obscuring her vision, so she flipped her rearview mirror up even as her heart rate increased. Why wasn't the cop chasing after that driver?

Feeling disoriented, she rolled down the window as a female officer approached her vehicle.

"Ma'am, are you okay?"

"Yeah... Shouldn't you go after him?"

"I've already called it in," she said, crouching down by Patience's open window. The woman's blonde hair was pulled back in a tight bun, highlighting sharp cheekbones. Her name tag said *Officer Kaminski*. "My partner is a few blocks back and he'll pick the guy up. Are you sure you're okay? Do you think you can step out of your car?"

With trembling fingers, she unstrapped as the officer opened the door for her.

"It looks like your bumper is demolished," the officer said, wincing slightly as they reached the back of Patience's car.

Sighing, she rubbed a hand over her face. She was going to have to make a report, call her insurance and deal with a bunch of stuff she didn't want to. She was grateful to be okay, but this still sucked. Who the hell had that asshole been, and why had they hit her? For the briefest moment, she thought of Miller getting word about who she was working for. Was it possible he'd come after her when Brodie tipped off Alice about what he'd said? No... She wasn't going to read into this and there wasn't remotely any proof that this had been him. Still, the thought lingered in her mind. "It definitely looks like it. So what do you need from me?"

"I'll help you fill out a report, and if you want, I'll call you a tow truck? I think you could probably drive with this, but it won't be safe driving around with no lights at night."

She looked at the back of her car and winced again when the whole bumper fell off. Yep, she was calling a tow truck. "I'll call my insurance first. I have a towing plan."

The woman nodded, and as she headed back to her patrol car,

Patience grabbed her cell phone from her purse and started making calls. She contemplated calling Brodie, but he wasn't her boyfriend or anything and they weren't at that level yet. She did text Trevor to let him know she'd be arriving back at the property later and potentially in a rental. She seriously doubted he would be worried about her coming back late, but she still wanted to let him know that she would be a while. Because she was going to need to get a rental. She had that service in her insurance but it was already seven o'clock and she wasn't sure how late rental car companies were open.

The officer walked back up to her as Patience started to call her insurance company. Looked like tonight was going to be a long one.

Part of her almost gave in to the fear clawing her up inside that she had been an intentional target. She was sure that it had been—whoever had hit her had done it on purpose. But it could have just been road rage at some perceived slight she'd committed. It could be anything at all.

Still, she swallowed back the bubble of fear that dug in and started to take root.

CHAPTER ELEVEN

Patience frowned when she saw Brodie's phone number on her screen. Without pause, she answered even as those familiar butterflies started up their dance once more. "Hey."

"You were in an accident?" he asked immediately.

"Yeah, sort of. I'm dealing with it right now. I just let Trevor know in case I came back to his place in a different vehicle. I didn't want to surprise your security team rolling up in something else."

There was a pause. "You could've called me."

"I didn't want to bother you. I know you were at the office all day." And okay, they were in a very new stage of their relationship—they weren't even really defined as anything. They'd been on one date.

Another pause. "Where are you now?" After she told him, he continued. "I'll be there in ten minutes."

Before she could respond, he'd already hung up. *Okay, then.* She would be waiting for him.

She rubbed her temple as the tow truck guy strode up to her. "Did you get everything you need out of your car?"

"Yes, thanks." She had her shopping bags, purse, and a few things from her glove box she hadn't wanted to leave. "And you're going to take it to the auto body repair shop on Loch Ness Road, right?"

"Yep. I know the owner. I've been there a few times."

Good, one less thing she had to worry about. She knew the owner too and it was where she normally got her car serviced. Thankfully her insurance company had been fine with her using his company for the repair. They were closed but he was going to leave it in the parking lot and she'd stop by tomorrow with her keys so he could work on it.

"So did you catch the guy?" she asked as Officer Kaminski approached. "Do I need to press charges or anything?"

The tow truck driver had already jumped up into his vehicle and had the engine running. Patience stepped away, walking along the side of the road toward the officer as the driver pulled out, her sad car in tow.

This was a residential area and fairly quiet. She was really close to her home, could probably walk home if she wanted. And right about now she was thinking about doing just that. She wouldn't because Brodie had told her he would be here soon. The rental car company hadn't gotten back to her so she was just going to head to her house instead of Trevor's and Uber to work early in the morning.

"No," the woman said, her expression clearly frustrated. "I don't know how he slipped us but it's like he disappeared. I ran the plate but it's coming back as not in existence."

That...wasn't good. "I'm just glad no one was hurt, myself included." The road had been nearly deserted when he'd hit her. The cop had been idling underneath a cluster of bushes by the stop sign, very well hidden. For that she was very grateful, because if that jerk had targeted her because she was a single woman alone in a quiet area, things could have gone very differently.

"So what's going on with your insurance company? Do you need a ride? I thought you'd leave with the tow truck driver."

"I have a friend on his way to pick me up. He should be here soon." Or she hoped he would take her home. If not, she'd be Ubering for sure. But something told her no way in hell would Brodie leave her here. Not the man who'd held her hair back as she got sick.

"Well, I'm going to stick around until you get picked up." Her radio sounded so she stepped away and started speaking into it quietly.

Patience pulled out her cell phone and texted her mom to let her know what had happened. Moments later she received a flurry of texts wanting to know if she was okay, even though she'd very clearly said that she was perfectly fine and uninjured. Her mom drove her crazy sometimes but there were certainly worse things than a parent who actually cared.

In the midst of her texting, headlights from the opposite direction of the police car flashed and she instinctively knew it was Brodie when she saw the outline of the SUV.

He pulled off onto the side of the road as she approached the vehicle, and when he jumped out his expression was tight. He scanned her from head to toe in a completely clinical fashion.

"I'm fine," she said, feeling ridiculously better now that he was there. "Promise."

"You're sure?" He ran his hands over her shoulders and up and down her arms as if making sure for himself. And okay, she found that incredibly sweet.

She waved at the officer and motioned that she was heading out. "I'm so ready to get away from here."

He nodded. Moving incredibly fast, he picked up her bags and had the passenger door open for her. She inhaled his masculine, sort of woodsy scent as she brushed against him. Surprising her, he actually strapped her in and she had to resist the urge to inhale deeply.

It was pretty clear that he was the overprotective type, something she'd never thought she'd like. But right now she definitely didn't mind —she kind of liked it. Maybe more than liked it. Years ago she'd gotten into a fender bender and called her boyfriend at the time—definitely an ex now—thinking he would come pick her up. Nope. He'd chosen to stay with his friends because he hadn't wanted to miss the ending of a football game. She'd realized her priority in that moment.

"So what exactly happened?" Brodie asked as he pulled away. "Trevor didn't have many details."

She hadn't wanted to worry anyone. "Some guy ran into me from behind. Seriously, just some giant jackass decided to run me off the road. I thought I'd seen the same car earlier when I was out running errands but there's no way to be sure. The police had someone looking for him but he slipped them somehow. Maybe he lives nearby or something."

"Are you sure it was a man?"

She paused. "Actually, no. I never saw the driver. It was too dark out to see anything. I'm just assuming it was a man." She was fighting the worry building inside her, that maybe this hadn't been a case of road rage. Glad she didn't have to tell him where to go since he'd picked her up for their date on Saturday, she settled back against the leather seat. "I'm sorry I pulled you away from work."

He glanced at her. "It's not a problem. Normally I don't work this late anyway. But regardless, you can call me if you ever have an issue with anything. Even if we're not..." He cleared his throat. "Just, no matter what. Any time of day or night."

Wow. "Thank you." She'd never dated anyone who'd been so...nice. They might have gotten off on the wrong foot, but he was showing her who he was more and more through his actions.

"Did anything weird happen today while you were out? Anyone who you had a difficult interaction with?"

Her heart rate kicked up a bit. "No. And...this feels stupid, but I kept thinking of Richard Miller. I doubt this was him or anything, but I don't know. He was on my mind because of..." She cleared her throat.

Jaw tight, he simply nodded as he pulled into her driveway. Before she'd gathered up her bags, he'd already rounded the vehicle and opened her door. As she slid out, he plucked her bags from her hand—and she was glad that lingerie was wrapped in soft paper so he couldn't see what was inside. The first time he saw it—if he ever did—she wanted to be wearing it.

"I'm going to look into Miller a bit," he said as they approached her front door.

She blinked at him. "What?"

"Did you tell the cops about him or..."

She flushed. "No. Maybe I should have but..." She hadn't wanted them talking to him, hadn't wanted anything to do with that asshole.

Brodie nodded again. "Okay, then I'm going to dig into his where-abouts. I want to know where he was tonight."

"Thanks." A weight she hadn't realized had been pressing on her chest lifted.

Once they were inside, he set all her bags on the kitchen island while she disarmed her security system. She felt tense, her neck and shoulders a bit sore, and she wondered if it would be worse tomorrow.

"I love this place," he said, pointing to the logo on the outside of the coffee company bag he set on the countertop. "I buy all my coffee there."

"I know," she said, flushing. "You're not the only one who can be a sleuth. I found out what your favorite type of coffee was and I was going to surprise you with it. It's for you. I hope that's okay?" It felt kind of weird to be getting him a gift because she wasn't sure what stage they were at. But he'd gotten her those wind chimes, so whatever this was, she'd decided to throw out most of her rules where he was concerned. She'd wanted to do something nice for him, so she had, simple as that.

"That's really thoughtful. So can I have it now, or..." He grinned and she felt it all the way to her toes. He should definitely smile more often.

She snickered. "Go ahead. I was going to give it to you for our next date, but now is just as good a time as any."

"What's in the other bags?"

Heat infused her cheeks as she thought of the silky, skimpy bralette and thong set she'd bought. The pale blue bralette gave absolutely no support and was definitely just for looks. It had ties at her shoulders and the thong had ties at her hips—and she'd definitely bought them with him in mind. Yep, she'd imagined him slowly unwrapping her.

"What's going on in your head?" His voice dropped an octave as he watched her with intensity. "Because I really want to know what's in those bags now."

She cleared her throat. "Just girl stuff."

He eyed the striped bag. "Like, dirty stuff?"

"Put it this way, if you're lucky, you'll get to see me wearing what's inside."

His dark green eyes practically went electric at her words. "I hope I'm a lucky man."

Oh, she had a feeling that he was definitely going to be lucky. And that meant she would get lucky too if he was the giving type of lover.

Something told her that he would be. She really, really wanted to find out. She felt like she knew him so well already, but had to remind herself that they'd only been on one date—and she didn't want to jump into anything too soon and ruin what they could have.

CHAPTER TWELVE

"Boss, I think you need to get to the kitchen." Angelique's voice came over the radio comm line, her words clipped. The petite martial arts expert was one of his best security contractors.

Brodie recognized that tone. "On my way." He'd been checking out a potential disturbance along one of the hedge lines, but it only took him a couple minutes to make it inside the house.

"I know she took it!" Antoine shouted.

Before he stepped into the kitchen he heard Angelique calmly speaking to Antoine, and Oliver fussing. His heart rate increased as he entered the kitchen to find Patience holding Oliver against her chest, rubbing his back as a red-faced Antoine glared at her.

"What's going on?" Brodie asked as he looked between them.

"She took it," Antoine shouted again. "I know she did." His whole body was vibrating with rage.

It was very clear to Brodie that Patience was fighting back tears. Her Mediterranean blue eyes shone with them as she looked at him, rocking Oliver now. It took everything in him not to snap at Antoine for upsetting her. She'd already been through enough after that asshole hitting her last night—at least Miller didn't seem to be a threat. He'd been logged flying out of the state a week ago for work and hadn't returned.

Jaw tight, he strode fully into the room, putting his body between hers and Antoine's as he faced the chef. "I'm only going to tell you this once." His words were clipped and even. "You need to stop yelling. You are very clearly upsetting Oliver—*Trevor's* baby. If you raise your voice again, I will escort you off the property. What the hell is wrong with you?"

Antoine took a deep breath and nodded, but his cheeks were still flushed an angry red.

Brodie turned around and looked at Patience, who seemed to have blinked away the tears. God, he wanted to comfort her. "Are you guys okay? Do you need to take Oliver somewhere else?"

Oliver was now sucking on his thumb and had his head curled up against her neck, clearly having calmed down. "He's fine now," she said quietly, continuing to rub his back.

"Let's start at the beginning. What's going on? What do you think she took?" Brodie turned back to Antoine.

For a moment, Antoine looked as if he was going to yell, but took another deep breath. "She's in here all the time, messing with my stuff. I had some very expensive truffles I was saving for a recipe for Trevor on Friday. Now they're missing. And so is a *very* expensive bottle of wine." He sniffed once. "I brought it up here from the wine cellar a couple hours ago and now all of a sudden it's gone." He glared over Brodie's shoulder at Patience.

"I didn't take anything," Patience said tiredly as if she'd already told the man more than once. "Look, just go check the guesthouse and my car... Ah, never mind. My car's not here." Her expression was one of exhaustion as she continued. "I have nothing to hide."

Brodie knew she hadn't taken anything and didn't want to check at all. But he nodded once, keeping his professional expression in place. Then he looked over at Angelique, who had a grim expression as she watched Antoine carefully. "Keep an eye on him."

Angelique nodded and he had no doubt she would. An Air Force vet, she was exceptionally trained in defusing situations and had a ridiculous amount of martial arts training. But she was small in stature and had a soft look about her—with big eyes and long dark hair she often wore in a braid that made her look younger than she was. People never saw her coming when she took them down.

He'd been trying to keep his distance from Patience all day, not wanting to invade her personal space while she was at work. He wasn't sure what they were at this point and it was too soon to ask her. He gave her a small smile he hoped was reassuring before he hurried out of the room.

Once he was inside the guesthouse, he started in the kitchen since it seemed the most likely place. But when he found the bottle of wine and truffles sitting neatly on a pantry shelf—just out in the open—he frowned.

This was ridiculous. There was no way she'd taken this and then told him to come check the guesthouse when it was in the most obvious place ever. It wasn't even hidden, not really. If she wanted to hide it, she would've put it under the bed or under her mattress, or hell, anywhere but the dumbest hiding place in the world.

He grabbed the bottle of wine and truffles and tucked them into a box of oversize garbage bags. Then he closed the pantry door and started timing himself. He figured he'd give it ten minutes before returning to the kitchen.

Once the time passed, he stepped back into the kitchen.

Patience was leaning against the countertop farthest from Antoine and the monitor next to her showed Oliver sleeping in his crib. Good, he didn't want this jackass anywhere near Oliver at this point. Didn't want him near Patience either.

"Well?" Antoine stepped forward.

"Well what? There's nothing there. She didn't take it."

The man's eyes flared in true shock. And *that* pinged on Brodie's radar. He was way too shocked that Brodie hadn't found anything—because he'd been expecting him to find it.

"You're a liar!"

"Excuse me?"

"I know you're sleeping with her. I see the looks you two share. You're just covering for her!"

Patience let out an angry growl. "He is not!" She stepped forward, hands on hips. "I didn't take anything, you big bully. I don't know what's wrong with you, if you're always this miserable or—"

"Patience," Brodie said quietly.

Her jaw tense, she looked at him, eyes flared with indignation.

"Why don't you head out of here? Go wait in the living room?"

It was clear she wanted to argue with him but she snagged the monitor and left.

Once they were alone, he turned to Antoine. "You're going to take the next two days off and calm down," he said. And in that time Brodie was going to dig into Antoine a bit more. Something was clearly going on with him, and planting stuff at her place was flat-out malicious. It also made him wonder if there was more to the other nannies quitting now. Maybe he'd been bullying them.

Antoine's dark eyes widened, his chest puffing out like a freaking peacock. "You're not my boss."

"No, I'm not. But I handle all of the security here. And it's pretty clear that you are becoming a threat. You need to go home and calm down. Trevor isn't here and you don't need to be here anyway. Enjoy the paid time off."

It was clear that Antoine wanted to argue, but he sniffed and went to one of the drawers. He pulled out a rack of knives and looked at Brodie, as if daring him to argue with him. "These are my *personal* knives. I'm taking them with me so she doesn't steal them too."

Brodie simply sighed and nodded. He knew they were the chef's knives. Everyone did. The man was obsessed with them.

He subtly nodded at Angelique to make sure she followed Antoine off the property. Moments later he found Patience sitting in the living room by herself, her shoulders tense.

She sprang to her feet when she saw him, clutching the monitor in her hand. "Brodie, I didn't—"

"I know. Take a deep breath. He's gone for the next two days. You're not going to have to deal with him. I'll get all this sorted out."

At his words, she let out a huge breath. "He's such a bully," she muttered even as she sat back down on the couch.

"Are you okay? Can I get you anything?"

She shook her head. "No. Just thank you for believing me."

He nodded once even though he wanted to say more. He wanted to talk to her about what he'd found—to pull her into his arms and comfort her—but first he needed to tighten up security and figure out how Antoine had gotten into the guesthouse unseen. "We're going to talk about this soon, but for now just hang tight in the house with Oliver. No one will bother you the rest of the afternoon."

She looked up at him from the couch, watching him with trust and a whole mix of emotions that punched right through him. He'd fallen for Patience faster than he'd ever thought possible. She was sweet and funny, and when he thought of the future, she was in it. Hell, she consumed his every waking thought. He'd never seen her coming.

And he was going to figure out what the hell was going on and why Antoine had clearly tried to set her up. She was his to protect.

HOURS LATER, Brodie found Patience in the kitchen, making a grilled cheese sandwich. A woman after his own heart. Trevor was out of town for a couple days so Patience was staying in the house at night in the room next to Oliver's.

"You got a couple minutes?" he asked.

"I have a lot of minutes," she said, smiling. Her long, dark hair was pulled up into a ponytail and she had on small studs in her ears—he'd noticed she wore those with Oliver but on Saturday she'd worn big, sparkly hoops. "Oliver is asleep and it's likely he'll sleep all the way through the night. Since Trevor's gone, I'm about to binge-watch some bad television on that big-screen in his living room." She slid the sandwich onto a plate with a spatula. "You want one? I can make another."

She was much more relaxed compared to earlier and he was glad to see it. In her bare feet, she looked happy and comfortable—and he wondered how she'd look in his house. In his bed.

He cleared his throat. "I'm good, but thanks. I wanted to talk to you about everything from earlier." Brodie didn't like any of it—was now concerned that Antoine was the reason the other nannies had quit. He'd put in a call to the agency he'd hired them from and was waiting on a call back. Hopefully they could give him more insight.

"Okay, I figured this was coming."

"Look, I found that wine and truffles in the pantry of the guest-house," he said quietly. No one else was in the house right now. His people were all patrolling the grounds like normal, but he'd wanted to wait to talk to her when Oliver was asleep and she was alone. He hadn't wanted to overwhelm her.

Her eyes widened and she nearly dropped the plate. "What?" She set it back down on the countertop, turning fully to face him. "I didn't take those stupid truffles! I wouldn't even know what to do with them. I certainly didn't take his precious wine—"

"I know you didn't take anything. The hiding spot," he said, using air quotes, "was too stupid. I know you're smarter than that."

She blinked once at him. "You think I would be smarter if I stole stuff?"

He lifted a shoulder and motioned for her to sit at the center island. "Go ahead and eat. And yes, I do. Antoine's surprise was far too shocked when I told him that I didn't find the wine and truffles."

"I don't know what's wrong with him. Freaking psycho probably just wanted to get me fired. He's been pretty rude to me a few times," she said as she went to the refrigerator and grabbed a sports drink. "I brushed it off because I assumed it was just his personality."

"He has?" This was news to him. And his security guys kept him apprised of everything that went on here. So that meant Antoine had been sneaky about his actions. This...was not good. And it backed up his hypothesis about Antoine and the women who'd quit.

Nodding, she sat back down and opened the bottle. "Yeah. He didn't seem to like me using the kitchen even though Trevor said it was totally fine. I used the utensils and stuff in here but I used my own ingredients and made sure to wash everything. I've worked with his type before. He's just a bully, seriously. Maybe it's short man syndrome," she said, rolling her eyes.

"What kinds of things has he done?" Brodie asked.

He listened as she went over the couple times Antoine had gotten in her face—every single one she'd been alone with no security around. It didn't surprise him—no way would his people have let that slide.

"The night you got sick, what did you eat again?" he asked as she set the partially eaten sandwich back on the plate.

She froze, her eyes widening. "Antoine gave me a cookie. Personally. Actually, he was kind of nice to me then, which is why when he was rude to me later I was surprised. It was like a Jekyll and Hyde type of situation."

Brodie tightened his jaw, running through different scenarios in his mind. His security team still hadn't figured out for sure how anyone had gotten into the guesthouse without being seen, but the door had been unlocked. And so had one window. Antoine could have timed it. He worked here so it would be easy to watch everyone's security shifts— even if they were often random patrols. But he would have been very careful to avoid the cameras.

Patience stared at him. "You think he targeted me or something? That doesn't even make sense. Why would he want me to get sick?"

Brodie had some thoughts about that but he kept them to himself for now. "Possibly to make you quit—why, I'm not totally sure. Yet. You're staying inside the house tonight, right?" He wanted it confirmed.

"Yeah, until Trevor gets back I'm staying in the room next to Oliver's. His house is huge though. I might get lost." Her lips quirked up and he resisted the urge to close the distance between them and kiss her senseless. He loved her full lips, the way she smiled, how kind she was. Damn, he really was falling hard.

"I'm going to take care of something tonight. I want you to stay inside the house. But I'll be available by phone if you need anything."

"Anything?" she asked, a hint of heat in her words as she cocked an eyebrow.

Oh, she was going to kill him. "I'm on the clock," he murmured. "And technically so are you."

"I know," she said on a laugh, her expression mischievous. "I was just curious what your answer would be."

"What if my answer had been yes to whatever 'anything' is?"

"I guess you'll never know." Grinning, she took another bite of her sandwich.

Yes she was definitely going to kill him, but in the best way possible. Now he had to shelve thoughts of that, because he had some digging to do. He was going to figure out this mystery and make sure Antoine didn't bother Patience again. And if he was a threat, Brodie would take care of that.

CHAPTER THIRTEEN

A couple hours later, Patience slipped out of bed at the soft knock on her bedroom door. Brodie had told her that the place was locked down for the night so she guessed this was him. Still, when she reached the door she said, "Who is it?"

"It's me."

Her stomach muscles tightened at the mere sound of his deep voice. "Is everything okay?" she asked as she opened the door. She had the monitor next to her bed and Oliver hadn't stirred, but maybe something else had happened.

He nodded once, his expression intense in that hungry way that made her toes curl. "I just wanted to say good night," he rasped out.

Oh. "Good night," she whispered.

He watched her for a long moment, his green eyes seeming darker in the dim hallway. When he moved toward her, she stepped forward on instinct, leaning her body into his as he cupped the back of her neck and slanted his mouth over hers.

She arched into him as their mouths collided, savoring the way he took complete control. Heat flooded her entire body from just that one electric kiss—and it took all of her self-control not to climb his body the way she wanted.

Okay, so she barely had any self-control at this point. When he teased his tongue against hers and backed her up against the wall, she hooked her leg around his hip, her foot digging into his back upper thigh. He rolled his hips against her and now she was the one moaning into his mouth. Everything about Brodie turned her on but when he pinned her against the wall like this? The slightly dominant display, the show of strength… She was definitely into this. Into him.

He clutched onto one of her hips even as he kept his other hand firmly in place behind her neck. She wasn't sure why that was so hot, but she loved the feel of him holding her like this. Her nipples beaded tightly as his tongue delved into her mouth, tasting, teasing, taking.

She dug her fingers into his shoulders, never wanting this to stop. But thankfully one of them was thinking clearly.

Him. *Not me.*

Breathing hard, he tore his mouth from hers and stared down at her. "I really did just come to say good night. And I need to leave now."

She let her leg drop from around him even though she *really* didn't want to. Heat was pooled low in her belly—and other places. Just a kiss and she was about to combust. "I'm glad you've got self-control," she murmured.

His mouth curved up the slightest bit. "Barely. But I'm already regretting walking away from you."

"Just for tonight though." She wanted that spelled out clearly. Because this could not be all they had together. Hell no. She wanted to experience all of Brodie MacArthur.

"Just for tonight," he said in agreement, his eyes smoldering.

As he took another step down the hallway, then another, she slipped back into the bedroom and shut the door. Sighing, she collapsed against the bed, her entire body tingling with anticipation of what was to come.

They'd only been on one date and shared a couple kisses, but they had been the most incredible kisses of her life. Where on earth had this man come from? He'd completely disrupted her whole life with that talented mouth and tongue. And his sexy voice.

And his sweetness, thoughtfulness and protectiveness. The texts he randomly sent her throughout the day were cute and seemingly at odds with the man she viewed as so tough and capable.

Her clit pulsed between her legs and yep, she was definitely going to have to take care of business tonight. Otherwise she was going to toss and turn the next few hours in discomfort.

She just wished that Brodie was here with her, and they were both getting each other off. But her hand would have to do for now.

~

PATIENCE JOGGED down the stairs the next morning, feeling ridiculously energized even as worry hummed through her. The events of yesterday still lingered in her mind, but she was still excited about where things were headed with her and Brodie. She shouldn't be, considering she'd gone to bed sexually frustrated last night instead of getting a taste of the real thing—and it had felt way too weird to take care of herself in someone else's bed.

But she was still excited nonetheless, knowing that this weekend she and Brodie were going on another date. And since Flora had texted her, telling her she was coming by early to grab Oliver, she'd let Flora in the house then showered, taken a couple extra minutes under those wonderful jets, dressed in summer shorts and a tank top, and was ready for the day.

When she stepped into the kitchen, she was surprised to find Brodie there with Flora and Oliver. Brodie had on what she'd come to think of as his standard issue "uniform." Black slacks, a white button-down, with no tie. He didn't have on his jacket this morning, however, and his sleeves were rolled up, showcasing the roped muscles of his forearms. *Good morning, indeed.*

Oliver's little face lit up when he saw her and that definitely made her heart squeeze. She was totally going to miss the little guy but at least she knew she'd see him in the future since their families ran in the same circles. He made grabby hands for her so she headed straight for him and lifted him out of his high chair. "Hey, guys."

"Aren't you looking refreshed this morning," Flora said, a twinkle in her eye as she took a sip of her coffee.

Patience was sure there was more to *that* comment but she chose to pretend there wasn't. "It's no wonder. This house is incredible and the beds are like clouds. It's like five-star hotel quality," she said as she kissed Oliver's cheek.

"It's true," Brodie said, a smile tugging at his mouth. "I've stayed over a few nights and I'm always sad to return to my own bed."

"So what's up?" she asked, looking between the two of them. There was something hanging in the air, some sort of weird tension suspended and ready to pop.

"Well, we have a bit of a change of plans this week. I went to Antoine's house last night and the place was empty," Brodie said.

"Like he moved or something?" she asked as Flora took a wiggling Oliver from her. He was apparently done with her and wanted his Nana now.

"As in, I don't think anyone has lived there for a while." Brodie's expression was grim as she moved toward the coffee maker.

"So what does that mean?" She poured herself a cup in what she was coming to think of as "her mug," a blue-and-white striped mug that was the size of her face—perfect for coffee.

"His phone has been disconnected, but I've done some digging into him. When we hired him, he came highly recommended. And until the incident with you, we've never had an issue with him. He's been here years. But I looked into his finances, and over the last few months it seems as if something weird is going on—and I'm worried it might have to do with Oliver."

She froze, coffee mug in hand. "Oliver?"

"Antoine gets paid very well. But he also has a gambling addiction that's just showed up on our radar. As in yesterday. He's apparently been able to pay off his debts—until recently. Which is why nothing pinged on our radar. I can't say for sure, but with all those nannies quitting so suddenly... Something isn't adding up. Especially since he recommended a nanny to Trevor. Which in itself is fine, but the résumé he gave me is too good. The woman doesn't have much of an online presence, and the references... I'm not buying them. There's a lot of things that are triggering some red flags. So I want to be cautious, especially since Trevor is out of town and Antoine has spent a whole lot of time in this house. And somehow he was able to get into the guest cottage unseen. For now we're going to relocate Oliver to Flora's lake house."

Her heart rate increased as she digested all he was saying. It sounded a whole lot like Antoine wanted to kidnap Oliver—or at the very least he was working with people who did. This was all too surreal. She'd worked for some wealthy clients before but no one on the level that Trevor was so she shouldn't be surprised that someone might try to kidnap Oliver. Still, the thought that someone could take a sweet, innocent—helpless—baby and use him for ransom was terrifying. "What do you need me to do?"

"Honestly, I want you to pack up and go somewhere you feel safe. Flora tells me your parents' house should be safe, but if not, I'll set you up somewhere myself. It's just for a few days. I've already called a friend at the FBI and he's looking into everything. Antoine owes money to some shady guys and if they had plans to kidnap Oliver or rob Trevor's place, we'll find out."

Holy crap, the FBI.

"That's no problem. I'll stay with my parents. But are you sure you don't want me to stay with you?" she asked, looking at Flora.

Flora shook her head. "No. Frank and I will have things under control. I'll feel better knowing he's with me, to be honest," she said as she cuddled Oliver close. "And Brodie is going to have some of his security at our vacation place as well. It's pretty hard to reach, so if anyone manages to track us down there, we'll have plenty of notice and be able to get out."

"Well I'll be a phone call away. You're sure the security will be enough for Oliver?" she asked, looking at Brodie.

He looked amused for a moment and cleared his throat. "Yes, of course."

"Sorry, I'm not questioning your ability to do your job. I just... Now I'm really worried for Oliver." She looked over at him, at his sweet, smiling face.

"It's all good. I understand. We're getting ahead of this to make sure nothing happens to him. I've also set up an SUV for you to use for right now. I don't like that you were in that 'accident' the other night and the driver still hasn't been found. It could be a coincidence, but I don't believe in those."

She went still inside. "Do you think I'm...a target?"

His jaw was tight. "I'm not ruling out the possibility. Do I think you're a real target for kidnapping? No. But I think that you might have been targeted yesterday in an effort to take you out and make room for a new nanny. But all that's shot to shit now so there's no reason for Antoine or anyone else to come after you. Still, I want you holed up and out of sight. It's why I want you in a company vehicle and...I'm going to have someone on you."

"On me?"

"You're going to have security. At least to follow you to your parents' place and...to look after you there."

"I...okay. Obviously I want to be smart about everything." She wished he was going to be coming with her, but knew that would be impossible. He had a whole lot of security issues to deal with now, that much was clear. "Okay then, I guess I'll just pack my bag and head to my parents' now?" She lifted an eyebrow at Brodie, who nodded.

"I'll walk you to the guest cottage."

She gave Oliver kisses and Flora a brief hug before heading out.

"I didn't want to offer in front of Flora, but you are more than welcome to stay at my place," he murmured as they moved around the pool.

Oh that sounded so good. *Way* too good. "I really want to say yes, trust me. But I have a feeling you're going to be working around the clock trying to make sure Oliver is safe, so it's probably better that I stay at my parents'." And she didn't want the first time she stayed at his place to be because of a threat. She wanted to be there because he'd asked her —just because.

"The offer is there. And you can stay in a guest room—I'm not trying to pressure you for anything."

185

"I know. And fair warning, I'm probably going to pressure *you* if I stay over," she said.

He grinned down at her. "I swear I never know what's going to come out of your mouth."

"Is that a good thing?"

"It's a great thing."

He did some sort of sexy security guy thing and swept the entire guest cottage before allowing her inside to pack her small bag and toiletries. Then, after a very brief kiss in the living room, she was gone, with one of his security guys following after her.

And she was really glad to be driving one of Brodie's company vehicles. The thing was like a tank—and he'd mentioned that it had bullet-resistant windows—so she felt secure inside it in case some other weirdo tried to run her off the road. But she hated what was going on, hated that Oliver might be in any sort of danger. She trusted Brodie to take care of things and understood why he couldn't be with her.

Even if she wished he was.

CHAPTER FOURTEEN

Patience glanced at her cell phone as she headed to her mom's house. When she saw her neighbor Marcy's name on the caller ID, she frowned. Using the vehicle's OnStar system, she answered. "Hey, what's up?"

"Hey, look, I know you're doing that nanny gig for the summer," she said. "I'm sorry to bother you."

Patience had told her neighbors because she wanted them to look out for her house. And Marcy had been wonderful enough to check her mailbox during the week. But at her neighbor's tone, a lead ball settled in her gut. Oh God, had something happened?

"One of the boys knocked a baseball into your back window. It's completely broken. We're totally going to fix it, but I wanted to let you know."

The tension in her belly eased. She was actually surprised her security system hadn't gone off, but...she couldn't remember if she'd set it when she left with Brodie the other night. She'd been so distracted after dealing with the police and her insurance company. And then Brodie's larger-than-life presence in general. "It's totally fine. Actually, I'm only a couple minutes away. I'll meet you out front."

"All right, see you then."

She knew she was supposed to go to her parents', but this should only take a few minutes. She glanced in the rearview mirror and saw the SUV trailing her a few vehicles behind. She figured he'd just follow her.

As she reached her driveway, she saw him park across the street at the curb. *Good.*

She waved at him as she got out. The man, Mac, was as big as Brodie, but he had a head full of red hair and a beard to match it. Plus she'd seen more than a couple tattoos when he'd pushed his sleeves up. He definitely had the intimidating look of what she imagined security people looked like.

She hurried across her yard, ready to get this taken care of. She had tons of boards saved in her backyard shed that she put up during hurricane season to protect her windows. It was just Florida life.

Marcy and Bradley were waiting in their yard as she hurried across the grass. Poor Bradley looked so dejected, his little face turned down as he glanced at his scuffed black-and-gray sneakers.

"Hey guys," she said, smiling at Marcy.

"I'm sorry I broke your window, Miss Patience," he murmured.

"It's okay. Accidents happen. I promise I'm not mad."

He glanced up at her, his expression hopeful. He was only nine and she'd watched him and his brother grow up over the years. She couldn't believe he was so worried about this, but he was still a little kid. "Really?"

"Really. Unless you did it intentionally?"

He shook his head vehemently. "I would never do that!"

"Then it's totally fine. I promise, accidents are no big deal."

"Head inside," his mom murmured.

"So it sounds like you've had a morning," Patience said as she headed around the side of the house, Marcy walking with her.

"I love summer but I also hate summer," she said, laughing. "I told them so *many* times to play ball in the backyard and not here. But they only listen half the time."

She snorted because she understood. It took a long time for kids to grow out of that phase and actually start listening to instructions. She hated it when adults thought kids should act like adults—because they weren't. They were little humans still trying to navigate and figure out the world. And it was a long process. She stopped in front of the broken window and hid a wince. "You weren't kidding, this is pretty bad." A huge hole was in the middle with the glass spidering out in all directions.

"Yeah, he got it good. Ugh. I'm so sorry."

"It's no big deal. I'm just going to grab the board and put it in place for now. But I don't think it's supposed to rain this week anyway." She would deal with the glass shards later too. Right now she just wanted to take care of this and then get to her parents' house.

"I've already called someone and they said they can be out this afternoon."

"Okay, that works. I'm actually not going to stay, but text or call me with the information of whoever is fixing it. And can you make sure you're with the repair person?" Marcy had a key to her house so she could let herself in.

"I will. And again, I'm really sorry."

"Please don't worry about it. And I'm going to pay for this myself. You're collecting my mail for me during the week over the whole summer, which I really appreciate. As long as you can be here when it gets fixed, let's just call this a neighbor tax, okay?" Marcy shook her head but Patience held up a hand. "I'm serious, just accept the invoice and I'll pay it. I promise I'm not worried about this." After the day she'd had, a broken window was no big deal.

"I'm so glad you're our neighbor. I swear, you better never move."

She laughed lightly as she unlocked the fence and headed for her shed. She glanced over her shoulder and waved at the driver of the SUV again. As she turned back around, she shot a quick text to Brodie, telling him what she was doing. She planned to stay only long enough to get the board put in, check her security system, then text Marcy with the code too. She wanted to at least clear the zone for the window and set the rest of the house.

After she had the board securely in place, she headed around the back to make sure the shed was locked up. Once she was done, she hurried around her pool and across her backyard. As she reached the other side of it, her back door opened.

She froze to find Antoine standing there, a small gun in his hand.

She stared in horror as he took a menacing step forward, the gun pointed right at her. "Where's the baby?"

She blinked, completely paralyzed. Oh no. *No, no, no.*

He stepped closer, his face red and mottled. "Don't make me ask again. Where is that brat?"

"I..." she rasped out, rooted to the spot. She tried to find her voice, cleared her throat. "What are you doing here?"

"I'm pretty sure it's clear what I'm doing here, you stupid bitch. You screwed up my payday."

"You want Oliver?" she asked, trying to play dumb and stall for time. The security guy would come eventually. Right? He had to!

"I'm not going to hurt him," he snapped. "Not as long as Trevor pays me what I need." With a trembling hand, he wiped his sweaty brow and glanced around her yard before motioning her toward her back door. "This way!"

She really, really hated that she had a privacy fence right about now. No one could see what was happening. "I don't know where he is. I was sent home. They told me to take the rest of the week off. I'm just a nanny," she said as she slowly stepped toward him and that gun. She should be running from it, but he would just shoot her.

So she went against her instinctive flight nature and trudged across her yard, her feet dragging like sandbags. She didn't know if she was playing this right at all. Because what if he decided she was useless to him now? Then he'd just shoot her. She fought a shudder, but an icy chill settled into her bones, and she started trembling.

Antoine grabbed her upper arm as she reached him and yanked her hard toward him.

Surprised by the sudden show of force, she stumbled, nearly tripping into the doorframe.

"Watch where you're walking," he snarled before slamming the gun against her temple.

She cried out as pain ricocheted through her head. Blinking, she tried to focus, but blood rushed in her ears, terror forking to all her nerve endings. She had to get away from this lunatic.

Antoine grabbed her arm again, yanking her up. She blinked, spots flashing in front of her eyes. "You're coming with me." He propelled her through her house, heading down the hallway and straight for the front door.

Blood streamed into her eyes and she tried to wipe it away but winced in pain.

He was oblivious to anything as he continued hauling her along the wood floors. "I won't be able to get as much for you as that kid, but I will get something."

She wished she had any sort of defensive training but she wasn't sure it would have mattered since he had that gun.

Unable to see well and blinded by the pain, she stumbled forward as he threw open the front door.

Heart racing as they stepped out onto her porch, she was just glad that Marcy was nowhere to be seen. Neither her nor her kids, because that would be an absolute nightmare. But...where was Brodie's driver? She could see the SUV but he wasn't visible. Oh God. Had he been hurt? She'd been depending on him to see Antoine, to help or call in backup.

No, no, no. Sweat poured down her spine and on instinct she tried to yank away from him.

His grip tightened on her arm.

She sucked in a breath as his nails dug into her skin. Everything was happening so fast. Too fast.

"Make a move and I'll just shoot you and take the loss," he growled quietly as they descended the short set of porch stairs.

Nausea welled inside her even as her emotions fractured in all directions. He was doing this in broad daylight, near the street where anyone could see. He had to be insanely desperate, and desperate men did terrible things. Where was he taking her? She was parked in the driveway but she didn't see any other vehicles.

God, why had she stopped at all? She should have just gone straight to her parents' place.

Damn it, where was that guard? If he wasn't going to help her, she had to help herself. She couldn't get into whatever vehicle Antoine had. That was certain death.

Think, think, think.

She had to do something. She knew that when being kidnapped at gunpoint or knifepoint, you needed to escape within the first ten minutes—or something like that. If she didn't, the chances of her dying went up by a whole lot. But she was terrified of being shot if she tried.

As they reached the sidewalk, she saw a four-door green car with tinted windows across the street, parked in front of a neighbor's house. It didn't look familiar.

"Where's your car?" she asked as he tightened his grip again. Then she winced and cried out instinctively at the bruising hold.

"Shut up," he snarled, dragging her across the street.

She looked around wildly, hoping that someone saw, called the police or...something. The sun beat down on her face and even though sweat trailed down her spine, ice still clung to her bones.

She saw movement out of the corner of her eye, but before she could turn, Brodie slammed into Antoine.

The man flew forward. The gun fired. Glass shattered, the car window exploding.

She screamed briefly at the ear-piercing gunshot, but Brodie tackled Antoine against the car with a thud. The weapon flew across the asphalt, skittering into the gutter.

"Get off me!" Antoine screamed as he tried to take a swing at Brodie.

Brodie grabbed his arm and twisted it behind his back as he slammed Antoine against the truck again.

Patience moved into action, racing around the front of the car to pick up the gun. Before she could make it, the broad-shouldered security guy who'd been following her came seemingly out of nowhere and scooped it up with efficiency. Mac quickly tucked it away and started to say something to her, but she turned back to find that Brodie had Antoine on the ground, hands behind his back as he secured Antoine's wrists expertly and efficiently.

"Mac, get over here," Brodie snapped.

The other man took over as Brodie jumped up and pulled her into his arms. "I've already called the police and they're on the way."

She had so many questions— So. Many. But she buried her face against his chest as stupid tears leaked out of her eyes. She didn't even mind the pain from her head as she held on to him tight. She could have died. Been tortured. Oh God. Anything could have happened.

Having Brodie's arms around her grounded her even as she allowed the leash on her emotions to slip. She didn't want to break down here, but she was damn close as he murmured soothing words to her. The only thing keeping her from having a total meltdown was Brodie's strong embrace.

He'd come for her, had been there when she needed him most. Brodie had saved her.

And she wasn't letting him go anytime soon.

CHAPTER FIFTEEN

"This is ridiculous," Patience said as she got off the hospital bed. "I don't need to be here."

Brodie stepped forward, his expression as intense as it had been all afternoon as he gently placed his hands on her shoulders. "You *do* need to be here. They're almost done. The doctor said all she needed to do was get your prescription and then you'd be discharged. I know this sucks."

Yeah, she knew all that. Crossing her arms over her chest—and knowing she was being churlish—she sat back down. And winced at the pulsing pain in her head. Thankfully she hadn't needed stitches and she didn't have a concussion, but they had put a few Steri-Strips on her forehead.

She'd been here for hours since she wasn't considered an emergency and she just wanted to go home and sleep in her own bed. The police and EMTs had asked some questions, she'd filed a police report and had been taken to the hospital for further examination. "Have you heard anything else?" She'd seen Brodie glance at his phone a few times.

Brodie took one of her hands in his, squeezed softly. "Antoine is being officially booked. And the Feds are involved now too. It's a mess, especially since this involves Trevor. For now, it's out of the media, but that might change."

Sighing, she simply nodded and squeezed his hand back. This was definitely a mess. But she was grateful to be alive and relatively unharmed.

She'd also found out in the previous hours that the security guy Mac had seen movement in her house and hurried to try and warn her—after a quick text to Brodie. He hadn't been able to get to her in time before Antoine had pulled that gun on her. By then Brodie had arrived and they'd worked together to bring the lunatic down. Apparently Antoine owed the wrong type of people a lot of money and had the bright idea to kidnap Oliver to get what he needed from Trevor. Sighing, she rolled her shoulders once, trying to ease some of the tension. Until she got out of here, she knew that it wasn't going away.

"You want me to find out what's taking so long?" he murmured when she didn't respond.

She nodded and smiled. He was such a steady rock right now. "Yeah. Sorry I'm being kind of grumpy." She hated hospitals and she kept reliving how helpless she'd felt at the end of that gun. It had been an eye-opening, horrifying experience that had torn a strip in the fabric of her reality. She knew that no one was ever truly safe, but it was as if her bubble hadn't just been popped, but smashed to bits. Somehow she'd managed to convince her mom not to rush down to the hospital, but only because she'd promised her she would call as soon as she left—and told her that Brodie was with her.

With care, he took her face in his hands and softly kissed her mouth. Just a barely there brush that curled through her, sending little waves of pleasure throughout. It was almost enough to make her forget every-thing. Almost. "I think you're allowed to be grumpy after all you've been through," he murmured as he pulled back.

She went all mushy at the softness in his voice and in his expression. She covered his hands with hers and smiled up at him. There was a lot she wanted to say, but she would wait until they were out of here.

After he left, she went to look at herself in the bathroom mirror and winced. The doctors had done a good job, but she was definitely going to have a big bruise. And of course it was right on her face for the world to see. Though she couldn't complain. Not since things could have ended up a whole lot worse.

When she heard the door open, she stepped out of the bathroom and found Dr. Shimko stepping inside, a smile on her face. "You're officially good to go. I'm sorry about the wait."

"It's no problem. I know how busy you are." After signing some paperwork—all electronic, thankfully—she tucked her prescription into her purse and tried to text Brodie.

She didn't have service though, so she headed to the nurses' station down the hallway. When she reached the end of it, she froze to find him with his arms around a stunningly beautiful, tall woman. He was smiling down at her with pure adoration and had his arms loosely around her, and the woman—who looked like a freaking model—had her arms thrown around his neck. She gave him a big hug, and when she went in for a kiss, Patience jerked back.

Feeling raw and vulnerable, as if she'd just been sucker punched, she headed toward the elevators. She told herself she was being stupid. It wasn't like he was her boyfriend. They had no official title. They'd just gone on one date.

But...she'd been stupid enough to think there might be something real there. Since she didn't understand how someone could be so caring and sweet and still be seeing other people, kiss someone else when she was right down the hallway... *Ugh.*

A tight ball settled in her gut as she reached the elevators. No way was she going to stay and talk to him. She was just going to go home and text him on her way. She did *not* have the mental fortitude to deal with any of this right now. And stupid tears started pricking her eyes, making her suck in a breath. She would not break down at the hospital.

Nope. Not happening. She wasn't a crier, but right now the accumulation of everything was pushing her down until it was hard to breathe. And she couldn't help but feel betrayed by Brodie even if he hadn't technically done anything wrong. But she couldn't do something casual with him. She wasn't wired that way. When she was with someone, she was with only that person. She didn't do casual dating. She never had. And if that was what he wanted, she wished he'd told her.

Thankfully there was a Lyft driver only a block away and he picked her up in barely two minutes. As the guy pulled away, she texted Brodie as a courtesy, telling him that she was exhausted and had decided to catch a ride home.

He'd probably feel relieved because now he could spend the evening with the stunning model. *Ugh.*

She let her head fall back against the seat and closed her eyes. Soon she would be in her bed and she was going to forget this whole day had ever happened. And probably cry herself to sleep.

CHAPTER SIXTEEN

"What the heck are you doing here?" Brodie asked his sister after she kissed him on the cheek and stepped back.

"It's a long story. Has to do with one of my jobs." Sienna's brown hair was pulled back into a ponytail and she had on jeans, despite the hot weather, and a much too big Ramones T-shirt that was hanging off her shoulder. She'd tied it at her hip, presumably so it didn't hang down to her thighs. It kind of looked like it might belong to a man, because as far as he knew she wasn't a fan of the Ramones.

"Do I want to know?" he asked, eyeing the T-shirt and debating if he should ask if she was dating someone. Because she'd been kind of cagey lately in general.

"Probably not. So why are you here? You look fine."

"You would tell me I looked fine if I had a broken leg." Which she'd actually done before when he'd broken his ankle. Her exact words had been "rub some dirt on it" before she'd taken him to the hospital.

She grinned. "It happened one time and you never let me forget it."

He snorted softly. "I'm here with one of Trevor's employees." Even if he wanted to, he couldn't tell her more than that. Not since it was an open investigation and involved people under his purview.

But his sister didn't miss anything. She narrowed her dark green gaze ever so slightly. "Does this employee happen to be a woman? Because your face just did a really weird thing."

"My face did nothing," he said dryly. "You really need to work on those PI skills."

Completely undeterred, she continued. "Oh my God, have you finally fallen for someone?"

He lifted a shoulder as he felt his phone buzz in his pocket. Thankfully Trevor had been able to catch a flight out and was headed straight to see his parents and Oliver, so he knew it couldn't be him. But it might be his Fed friend with more updates.

His sister started going on about "how the mighty have finally fallen" but everything funneled out as he read Patience's text. He shoved his phone in his pocket. "I've gotta go."

Sienna grabbed his forearm, worry clear in her gaze. "What's wrong?"

"My girl just left."

Sienna blinked. "Oh my God, you really have fallen for someone. Go get her, then."

Heart and mind racing, he hurried out of the hospital and to his vehicle. What the hell had happened? He'd *just* gone to see about her discharge and then she'd...left?

None of this made sense.

The drive to her house took far too long—and she didn't answer his calls, making time stretch to eternity. In reality, the drive was more like twenty minutes. By the time he'd made it there, he'd worked himself up, the fear inside him growing each second that ticked by. Had something happened to her? According to the app he'd installed on her phone— with her permission—she was definitely at her house.

The neighborhood was quiet, and sunset would be here soon, so everything was cast in shadows as he pulled into the driveway.

He knocked on the door once. Then twice. Now real fear settled in and he was feeling irrational enough to kick the door in when it suddenly swung open.

Patience's beautiful blue eyes widened as she stared up at him. "Brodie."

He took a moment to scan her from head to toe, to make sure she was fine—well, as good as could be expected. He hated to see the bruise darkening on her forehead and wanted to pummel Antoine all over again. "Why did you leave the hospital? Is everything okay?"

She rubbed the uninjured side of her head. "I don't want to do this right now."

"Do what? Is something wrong?" For the first time in as long as he could remember he felt unsure of himself. Something had clearly happened to upset her, but he couldn't imagine what he could have done. "Your feelings about wanting to leave the hospital were valid." Maybe she'd thought he'd been dismissive of her need to leave? He didn't think he had been, but he was covering all bases now.

She sighed and he couldn't read her expression at all. "You didn't do anything."

"Then why'd you leave?" He shoved his hands in his pockets.

She wrapped her arms around herself, looking vulnerable and small. "Look, it's not a big deal. I just saw you with that gorgeous woman, and her kissing you. And...I feel stupid saying this, but I thought maybe I meant more to you. But I mean, of course you're free to date other people. We've only been on one date and I don't own you. It was just sort of like a sucker punch and I didn't feel like talking to you or looking at you, to be honest. I just wanted to come home and sleep. So... yeah. I know it was lame to leave like that but..." She shrugged, the action jerky.

"A woman kissing me?" His mind blanked. "Wait, tall, dark hair, smart mouth?"

She narrowed her gaze at him. "I don't know if she has a smart mouth."

"The only woman who kissed me was my little sister. She also patted my head like I'm a puppy. She was at the hospital, something to do with her job. We were both surprised to see each other." Hell, if this was the only issue, then there was no issue. Because he wasn't letting her be alone tonight. Or any other night. Maybe he should be annoyed that she'd jumped to conclusions but she'd just been held up at gunpoint, attacked and almost kidnapped. He wasn't going to pile on because she was a human with human reactions. Her emotions had to be raw right now.

Her arms dropped from around her middle and her expression thawed. "Really?"

"Really," he said, stepping forward to close the rest of the distance between them. He didn't like having this conversation out on her front porch.

"I'm sorry I jumped to conclusions," she murmured, looking sheepish.

"Can we talk about this inside?"

"Of course." Stepping back, she closed the door behind them.

"For the record, I'm not dating anyone," he said. It was definitely time to have this conversation. "I have no desire to date anyone but you. I'm not into dating, for the most part. I mean yeah, occasionally I do, but work usually consumes me. I met you and now thoughts of *you* consume me. You're all I can think about day and night. Honestly I think I have a problem." God, he wanted to touch her so bad right now, to hold her close.

"I'm not into casual dating either," she murmured. "I felt stupidly hurt when I saw you with her. I should have been a freaking grown-up and just talked to you but I was feeling way too vulnerable." She groaned. "And now I feel *really* stupid knowing that she's your sister."

He gently cupped her cheek, was glad when she turned into his hold. "You should never feel stupid. I'm glad you cared enough, but I hate that you left without talking to me about what you saw. You need to be resting right now. I'm going to be taking care of you."

"I see the bossy Brodie is back." Her smile met her eyes now as she looked up at him and he found himself getting lost in the Mediterranean blue.

"I'm not even going to deny it. I like to take control of situations, especially when people I care about are concerned. So I prescribe that you get in bed, and we'll put on whatever TV show you want, and relax for the rest of the night. But only if that's what you want."

"Are you inviting yourself to stay over tonight?"

"Absolutely."

She gave him a full smile then and it was like a punch to his solar plexus. "Okay, then. But you're sleeping without a shirt."

He blinked. "Now who's the bossy one?"

She grinned slightly and stepped forward, wrapping her arms around him.

He gathered her into his arms and savored the feel of her close to him. He'd almost lost her today, almost lost her before they even had a chance to start. He wasn't going to let that happen again. The very thought of it terrified him—she'd come to mean so much to him in such a short time. "If I can't sleep in a shirt, then you're not gonna either."

"We'll see." She laughed lightly but that wasn't a no.

He would take what he could get. And he didn't care if they simply slept tonight with all their clothes on. He just wanted to be with her, to take care of her. To know that she was safe.

He'd fallen so damn hard for her and today had only proved that point beyond a shadow of a doubt.

CHAPTER SEVENTEEN

Patience walked into the kitchen the next morning to the heavenly scent of coffee. Brodie was leaning against her countertop, shirtless, wearing only boxer briefs and looking *very* good in her kitchen. Like he belonged. He had a smattering of hair on his chest and his abs were deliciously cut.

She was so damn grateful he'd been able to stay with her and he didn't seem to be leaving anytime soon. Which was fine with her. Apparently Trevor had told him to take care of her after everything had happened, and he'd agreed. He'd told her last night that he hired capable people and that they could do their jobs while he took care of her.

She'd slept practically plastered to him the entire night, barely making it through fifteen minutes of the movie they'd chosen. She vaguely remembered him turning it off but then she'd crashed hard.

"Morning." His gaze fell to her mouth as she strode farther into her country cottage kitchen.

"Morning. How long have you been awake?"

"Just about half an hour. I tried to be quiet so I wouldn't wake you."

"You didn't." Of course he was thoughtful enough to be quiet. The man had shown her exactly who he was in little ways every time they were together. She walked straight up to him and wrapped her arms around his middle.

He leaned down, hunger sparking in his gaze as he brushed his lips over hers.

There was a minty freshness combined with the coffee. He'd clearly found one of her extra toothbrushes—she'd seen it next to her toothbrush this morning before she'd brushed her own teeth. It had felt...nice to see another toothbrush next to hers. But only because of him.

She smiled against his mouth. "I like seeing you in my kitchen," she said, feeling kind of vulnerable admitting that. Even though he'd told her that all he wanted was her, she was still reeling from yesterday and felt out of sorts in general. Her entire world had shifted yesterday.

"I like being here. So how are you this morning?" He lifted her up onto the countertop with ease, eyeing her bruised head.

Spreading her legs, she pulled him to her and stroked her fingers up his muscled forearms and biceps. The man really was beautiful.

"Much better now." Leaning forward, she tugged him down to her.

When his mouth met hers, she groaned against him. God, she loved waking up to him. Her head ached a bit but she didn't care. Basically nothing separated them now. Certainly not his boxers or her little tank top and sleep shorts.

She was wide-awake and wanted more of Brodie. She wanted *all* of him. They'd had the whole sex talk and both of them were clean and she was on the pill, so if he was ready for more she definitely was. So. Much. More.

He kissed her softly at first, his tongue teasing hers oh so gently until she reached between their bodies. She didn't want soft or gentle. She wanted the dominating, take-charge Brodie this morning.

She rubbed her hand over his hardening length, not dipping underneath his boxers, but cupping him over them. He shuddered, letting out a sort of growl as she wrapped her fingers around his cock—and the man was thick.

He deepened the kiss and reached for her tank top. Cool air rushed over her as he managed to get it over her head and toss it behind them.

He barely gave her time to register her state of undress before he cupped one of her breasts.

Then he pulled back and looked down at her, his gaze landing on her breasts. Her nipples tightened under his scrutiny and she couldn't help but love the way he was watching her—as if he wanted to worship her. She'd never had anyone look at her like this, as if she was impossibly precious.

"You're so fucking gorgeous," He teased one nipple, his callused thumb sending out little shocks of pleasure to all her nerve endings as he stroked. "And I've definitely fantasized about you. Ever since that night at the taco stand."

Hearing the truth in his voice, all her little insecurities disappeared. She shoved at his boxers, wanting to see all of him. "I've been fantasizing about you too." Soooo much.

He helped her get the rest of his briefs down his legs and she sucked in a breath as he was fully revealed to her.

Hot damn. "Wow." It was out before she could stop herself. But come on, the man was thick and perfect and needed to be inside her like ten minutes ago. Her inner walls tightened as she imagined how he would feel, thrusting into her.

"You're really good for my ego," he murmured as he tugged her shorts off. Then, taking her by surprise, he slid her to the edge of the countertop and bent between her legs.

Oh, double wow. She moaned as he flicked his tongue up her already slick folds.

He just got right down to it and she was definitely ready for all of him. She slid her fingers through his short hair, holding his scalp as he ran his tongue along her folds, making her mindless with pleasure.

Her stomach muscles pulled taut and heat rushed between her legs as he focused on her clit. She jerked against his face, enjoying how giving he was. And she wondered where he'd been all her adult life.

"Fuck, you taste good," he growled against her.

The reverberations of his words—and his words—sent more spirals of pleasure through her.

He slid a finger inside her, groaned again when he found how wet she was—which turned her on even more. Her inner walls tightened around him as he increased his pressure on her clit, teasing and sucking until she was writhing against his face, about to come apart at the seams.

He shouldn't have been able to learn her body so fast, but he wasn't taking any prisoners. As he worked his fingers inside her, her climax started building, that delicious pressure inside her pushing, pushing. But she wanted him inside her when she came the first time with him. It felt important.

She clutched onto his shoulders, barely able to rasp out, "In me now."

Breathing hard, he lifted her off the countertop and pinned her against the nearest wall as he guided himself to her entrance.

The shocking display of his strength as he held her up was insanely hot. Hell, *he* was insanely hot. His biceps flexed with his movements, his jaw was clenched tight in concentration—and all of it was on her. *For her.*

As he slowly pushed inside her, his neck muscles tightened as he kept his pace slow, steady.

She sucked in a breath as he pushed all the way to the hilt. She'd never felt so full, so turned on. So…connected to someone.

"Are you good?" He brushed his mouth over hers as her inner walls pulsed around his thick cock.

"Just need a second," she rasped out. Because she definitely needed to adjust to his size.

As he kissed her, he reached between their bodies and started teasing her clit with his thumb.

Oh, hell. It was too much.

And that sent her over the edge. Her orgasm, which had already been right on the brink when he'd just been using that wicked, talented tongue, hit fast and hard as he kept up the pressure.

She clutched onto his shoulders, kissing him as she came around him. "Move," she rasped out against his mouth. Her orgasm was a live thing, pulsing through her, wave after wave of pleasure racking her body.

It was like she'd unleashed him with her soft order. He didn't hold back then, started thrusting, over and over, his big body and upper arm strength keeping her in place as he took all of her.

She rolled her hips against him, meeting him stroke for stroke, her own climax fading as he found his.

When he came inside her, it was with a growl of pleasure that was way too sexy. Her body felt like a live wire as his grip on her shifted, as he slowly pulled out of her.

She felt the loss of him immediately, but he cupped her ass, holding her close to him as he stepped away from her kitchen wall—a wall she would never look at the same again.

He started moving through her house, carrying her to her bathroom. She was still coming down from her high and barely knew her own name at this point. She simply clung to him, enjoying the friction of her still-hard nipples grazing against his chest.

"Hold on," he murmured, and she realized he was starting the shower.

She let her legs fall as they stepped inside. He moved under the jets, taking the brunt of the coldness as the water heated up, and she knew in that moment that she was pretty much over the moon for this guy. She wasn't going to say the L word yet but… She was headed that way fast. Like, "rollercoaster with no brakes" fast.

"That was amazing," she murmured as he finally stepped out of the way so they could both get under the warm, pulsing water.

"We're just getting started," he murmured before kissing her again, this time soft and slow.

The promise in his gaze and in his kiss set a new blaze inside her. One that gave her hope for the future. One that definitely involved him.

CHAPTER EIGHTEEN

One month later

"Do you mind if we stop by Trevor's before we head out?" Brodie asked from the driver's seat of his SUV.

"Of course not. Hopefully I'll get to snuggle Oliver if he's awake." A couple weeks ago they'd found the perfect replacement for Patience. A friend of Flora's named Marcela. She was in her late forties and her kids had gone off to college recently. She was looking for a new chapter in her life. Oliver was already in love with her. Since Trevor liked her and Brodie found nothing bad in her history, it was a good match. "Is everything okay?"

"Yeah. I just promised I'd drop something off before we left."

"Two weeks of sun, sex, and sand sounds incredible," she murmured, leaning her head back against the headrest. She started teaching school in a couple weeks, so Brodie had taken off work so they could spend a couple weeks doing absolutely nothing but relaxing together.

Her summer had ended up very differently than she'd originally planned but she wouldn't have it any other way.

"Oh, I got a call from the detective this morning. Antoine took a deal but he's going away for a solid twelve years at least."

She breathed out a sigh of relief. *Thank God.* She'd known that he was going to jail but at least they were avoiding a stupid trial. And twelve years was a long time with him locked up and unable to hurt anyone. Brodie had also spoken at length with the nanny agency and it turned out that one of the men Antoine had been involved with had harassed them into quitting. They'd been too scared to say anything to anyone. And thankfully Brodie had also figured out how Antoine had gotten into her guest cottage unseen. There had been a couple small holes in the camera security setup around the cottage itself and he'd used those spots to his advantage to sneak in. An outsider wouldn't have been able to make it that far, and everything had since been fixed.

"So, what kind of bathing suits did you pack?" Brodie's grin turned sly as he took another turn.

They were practically living together at this point, with him spending most of his time at her place, mainly because his condo was downtown and was kind of cold. But he hadn't seen anything she'd packed.

She grinned at him. "Who says I packed one at all?"

His fingers tightened around the wheel, his knuckles turning white. "You're determined to kill me, aren't you?"

She simply grinned at him, excited for this adventure. And something told her that this was only the beginning.

"I love you," he murmured, his voice turning serious all of a sudden as he reached out and gently brushed his knuckles over her cheeks.

It wasn't the first time he'd said it, and she didn't get tired of hearing it. She didn't think she ever would. "I love you too."

EPILOGUE

Four months later

"So what's the special occasion?" Patience asked as she sank down onto the quilt Brodie had laid out on the beach. It was way too cold for anyone to be out today, but he'd said he wanted a picnic. Which was kind of nice since Christmas break was coming up and there was no one here right now.

He lifted an eyebrow at her. "Do I need an excuse to take out the woman I love?"

"Good point." She grinned as he pulled out her favorite brand of champagne.

The last few months they'd both been busy with work but he'd officially moved in with her and she loved waking up to him every morning. Well, most mornings, because he did some out-of-town stuff, but they now shared a closet and everything. And his clothes were definitely nicer than hers, considering his custom-made suits. He kept buying her gifts and random things that just made her heart sing with joy. She wasn't used to a man spoiling her and she could admit that she loved it —loved *him* even without the gifts. But she knew it was one of the ways he showed her that he cared.

He pointed the bottle away from them to pop the cork, and once he'd poured their glasses, handed her one. "Oh, look at that." He pointed to where a plane was doing loops of skywriting.

She laughed as she watched the plane dipping up and down. "Who on earth is out here to even see this?" She froze when she realized that...*they were*. Patience shot him a sideways glance, only to find him watching her with an intense gaze.

Gently, he tipped her chin back up.

She stared at the sky, and with each word that was revealed, her heart rate increased. Holy cannoli.

Will you marry me? was spelled out in giant white clouds.

When she turned to look at him, Brodie was kneeling in front of her, a ring box open. "The last few months with you have been the best of my life. I love you so much it hurts, so much that it surprises me every damn morning that I get to wake up to you. Will you marry me, Patience?"

Tears stung her eyes as she set her glass down. "Yes," she managed to rasp out through her emotion. "Yes!"

Keeping his eyes pinned to hers, he slid the diamond onto her finger.

"You're a very sneaky man," she murmured as he brushed his mouth over hers.

He tugged her into his lap. "I tried to figure out a way to do it with kites, but figured this was just as good since it's at the beach—near where we had our first date. I love you so much, Patience." He captured her mouth with his again before she could answer.

But that was okay. He knew how much she loved him. Soon she was going to get to be Patience MacArthur. And she couldn't wait.

SAVING SIENNA

PROLOGUE

Four months ago

Carson held on to Sienna's hips, holding her closer than necessary as they swayed to the music. This woman was pure fire in his arms, sensual, funny, and gorgeous.

His sister Kathryn had just gotten married and she and her new husband—Sienna's brother—had already left.

But the reception was in full swing and even though he'd planned on leaving early, he'd decided to stay as long as Sienna did. Because he couldn't seem to get enough of her.

"I've never seen you look so relaxed," Sienna said. She had a bunch of little flower things in her hair and had curled it so that it was around her face in waves, making her look like a fairy princess.

And the fact that he was thinking those words told him he'd probably had too much to drink. "I know how to have a good time," he murmured, his gaze falling to her mouth. Damn, he wanted to show *her* a good time. Wanted to get her off with his mouth, his fingers, hear her moan his name as she came...

She snorted softly.

He frowned. "What?"

"Nothing. You just always seem so serious."

For the most part he was. No use denying that. In the last couple weeks he'd learned that Sienna was most definitely not. They'd both been involved in the wedding—Daniel had surprisingly asked Carson to be a groomsman, and his sister had asked Sienna to be a bridesmaid, which was not a surprise. Those two were thick as thieves. And everyone seemed to like Sienna.

Himself included.

She always had a mischievous gleam in her eyes though, as if she was up to something. And he found himself ridiculously intrigued by her. He wanted to know every little thing about her, which disturbed him.

As the music stopped, she grabbed his hand and tugged him along with her without even asking.

Later, he would realize he hadn't even thought to protest, he'd just gone along. Because why wouldn't he? "Where are we going?" he asked as she continued off the dance floor and through the throng of tables. It was like the bride and groom had invited the whole town.

She flashed him a quick grin that lit up her whole face. "You'll see."

For a brief moment he wondered if she was going to drag them up to her hotel room. Even though it would likely be a mistake since they were sort of related now, he found he didn't care in the least. But no, she was taking them to the kitchen.

"Pretty sure you're not allowed in here," he said as she pushed through the swinging door to where the catering crew was moving about.

To his surprise, one of the servers smiled and gave her a little wave. "Hey, Sienna, you need anything?"

"No. Daniel said he left something for me."

The woman smiled and nodded and didn't question their presence at all.

Carson followed her to one of the walk-in refrigerators and couldn't help but stare as she bent over, her already tight-fitting dress pulling taut against the most perfect ass in the world as she bent down and grabbed...

She made a sound of pleasure as she pulled out a very expensive bottle of champagne and held it up. "Success!"

Carson lifted an eyebrow. He recognized the brand and it was like a month's salary for him. Probably more. "Your brother left that for you?"

She lifted a shoulder, that mischievous glint firmly in place. "Maybe not for me *exactly*, but he's already gone, so this is ours."

He shook his head slightly and, moving on instinct, he grabbed for her hip, tugging her to him. God, he wanted this woman more than he'd ever wanted anyone. She called to him on the most basic level.

She moved immediately against him, wrapping her arms around his neck, the bottle lying against his back as their mouths collided.

They'd been flirting on and off over the last week through all the wedding stuff, and deep down he knew they'd been building to this. Hopefully to more. Because she was the kind of woman you held on to and never let go.

She tasted sweet, like the cake they'd had earlier. And she felt like heaven in his arms, tall and lean, and she fit perfectly against him.

Suddenly the door opened and Sienna pulled back.

One of the servers he recognized from the kitchen stared at them wide-eyed. "Oh, ah, I'm sorry."

"No, we're sorry. We'll get out of your way." Then Sienna was moving again, tugging him along with her.

He wasn't used to being manhandled but he found he liked it when Sienna did it. He realized he was simply following her anywhere she dragged him and... He was surprisingly okay with that. She could manhandle him straight to the bedroom. Or shower. Or any flat surface really. He wanted her hands all over him.

As they hurried back into the kitchen, he grabbed two glasses from a drying rack.

She arched an eyebrow, her grin pure wicked. "You think I'm sharing with you?"

"I think if you drink a whole bottle by yourself, I'll be carrying you to your room."

She laughed as they exited the kitchen, the pure music of it wrapping around him, warming him from the inside out.

217

In that moment, he realized he could fall really hard and really fast for this woman.

CHAPTER ONE

S ienna snapped another picture of the interior of the expensively furnished stateroom on this ridiculous yacht. With each picture, her smile grew a little bit wider.

Some jerk thought he could hide his assets from his wife? That was where Sienna came in.

Snap. She snagged another picture of the paneled ceiling and track lighting. The wood was quality, a nice pale color that made the room seem even bigger. With four oversized windows, whoever stayed in this room would have a gorgeous ocean view from most angles.

She flipped to panorama mode and got everything in one swoop.

Snap.

Another one of the bathroom—which was nicer than hers at home. Two pedestal bowls over a white-and-gray marble countertop. The backsplash was intricate, the white and grays of the tile changing with each step she took, as if they were liquid. Whoever had designed this had an incredible eye—and money to burn. She took another panorama of this room too, wanting to get all of its glory.

As she stepped out into the wood-paneled passageway, she scrolled back through her pictures. Triumph surged through her as she scanned the gorgeous colors popping in each image. The sunlight really had been in her favor today and these images were going to help her client get everything she deserved in her divorce.

Sienna uploaded the photos to the cloud, then tucked her phone away, as well as her backup camera. Because she *always* had a backup.

As she headed in the direction of the aft deck, ready to disembark as soon as she could, she froze when she heard male voices.

Hell. She'd had to pay off someone at the marina to get access to this particular boat. The woman running the desk for some of the rental charters also headed up access for the cleaning crews. All it had taken was a hundred bucks and a bit of the truth about what she was doing and the woman had told her she had an hour to get in and out.

Sienna had only been here for twenty minutes, so clearly something had gone wrong.

Unfortunately she knew what she had to do.

Pulling her phone back out, she turned the volume down and tucked it and the small camera into her plastic waterproof case hooked around her neck by a sturdy lanyard. She'd brought this just in case, because as a private investigator, she *always* liked to be prepared.

And this wasn't the first time she'd had to find an alternate escape— by means of jumping over the side of a boat.

She picked up her pace as she hurried in the opposite direction along the wood-paneled passageway with wide, tinted windows overlooking the marina. Her heart skipped a beat as she spotted three men walking along the outer passageway, likely going in the direction of the flybridge. One of the men looked at her and... *Oh God!* Wait, he couldn't see her. Not with the tint. Still, her adrenaline surged.

Feeling bold, she pulled out her phone and snapped a few pictures of all three men without the flash. Actual images of her client's husband on this boat that he was pretending he didn't own? That was gold!

But now she had to hurry. She ducked out of sight and on silent feet she hurried through the kitchen. The voices got louder as she eased the other galley door open. It silently closed behind her, but her heart was an erratic drumbeat in her ears.

It wasn't like there were cameras here, and the owner was hiding that he even owned this yacht—in an attempt to screw his wife over in their divorce. Sienna didn't think he'd call the cops if he found her. If he did, he'd have to admit he owned it on the record.

Still, she did not relish getting caught. Because from everything she'd found out about this guy, he was not a nice person. He might try to hurt her as opposed to calling the authorities.

As she stepped into the open living area, she raced across it and opened the door that led to one of the outside decks. A blast of summer air hit her as she stepped outside. Just as quickly she shut the door behind her, trying to force her heartbeat to slow down.

The deck chairs were all stacked together, not set out as if they were about to be used. She glanced around the marina, saw everything was mostly quiet, though a few fishing boats were heading in.

These yachts were owned by people who rarely used their expensive toys—people who had more money than sense. Or common decency, in her experience.

She glanced around and knew she only had a minute or two max to escape without being discovered. Since she was on the bottom level, she didn't have far to go. Sighing, she hoisted herself over the edge of the railing and dropped down into the water.

She made a splash, there was no way around it.

Kicking off the side of the boat, she swam away from the bow toward another row of smaller boats—cruising sailboats. Her arms and legs burned as she swam, her shoes weighing her down. She risked a glance over her shoulder as she reached the next occupied boat slip. No one was shouting at her at least so maybe no one had seen her.

Of course there could be any number of people watching her from one of the yacht's interior rooms. Oh well, she couldn't help it now.

She just needed to get onto dry land—and get out of here fast.

Heart racing as she swam around the nearest sailboat and toward a sturdy-looking ladder, she kicked harder. As she reached the top, two strong hands grabbed her under the armpits, hauling her up.

She started to struggle, going into pure fight mode until she realized who it was. "Crap," she muttered. What the hell was *he* doing here?

Carson Irish, brother to her new sister-in-law. A sexy detective she'd fooled around with once. Or twice... Gah, three times! A man she couldn't get out of her head. His gaze swept the length of her dripping wet body, then he looked up and down the dock and sighed.

Across from them a shrimper eyed them for about a second, then went back to work untangling his net. Clearly he didn't care what they were up to, which was good for her.

"Can we get the hell out of here?" she finally said, her adrenaline still pumping. The sailboat blocked them from view of the yacht, but she needed to get out of these wet clothes, check her phone and camera, and she really, *really* wanted to put as much distance as possible between her and the men on the yacht.

Jaw tight, Carson simply held on to her elbow as if he thought she'd run from him and they hurried down the dock toward the parking lot.

"Why are you here anyway? Are you following me?" she muttered as they reached the gravel parking lot, her sneakers making squishing sounds with each step.

"Where are you parked?" he asked instead of actually answering as they reached his truck.

"Over there," she said, jerking her chin and trying to hold on to some sliver of dignity even as water pooled around her feet and her clothes stuck to her in odd places. She really hated that she was wearing a white T-shirt and a bralette right about now.

"Follow me to my place," he said—basically ordered. "You can dry off there."

She had a change of clothes and a towel in her trunk, but she wanted to grill him more about what he was doing here. "Thanks," she murmured before jogging off to her Jeep. As her clothing made weird sucking sounds against her body, she realized that she'd been a fool for hoping for any sort of dignity at this point.

Sienna had been to Carson's place before—once—so she knew exactly how to get there. He lived in a low-rise, two-bedroom condo two blocks from the beach. It was nice, with more than decent security, and since she knew where his assigned parking spot was, she parked there instead of in guest parking. By the time she grabbed her duffel bag out of the back of her Jeep and made it to his front door, he'd joined her on the front step.

"You mind stripping off before you come inside?" There was a hint of challenge in his voice, and in those pale blue eyes she wanted to drown in.

If he thought she wasn't up to it, he was very wrong. As he headed inside, she left her shoes outside on his mat and stripped off everything except her bralette, panties and the lanyard around her neck. She'd checked on her phone and camera and they had come through her adventure perfectly fine.

When he returned a few moments later, his eyes widened slightly as his gaze swept over her shivering body, but he handed her a towel and, to her surprise, glanced away as if trying not to stare.

Which was just as well. They'd tried to make something work a few months ago and it simply hadn't happened. Okay, that was a huge lie. She'd run away when he'd tried to get serious, because that was what she always did. Men were more hassle than anything. Except...that wasn't true with Carson.

"Think I could grab a quick shower?" she asked through chattering teeth as she tightened the towel around her.

"Yes." He looked at her, his expression unreadable. "Then you and I are going to talk."

That sounded ominous so she chose to ignore his words. She plucked her bag up and headed to the guest bathroom instead of his. It would feel too intimate, too weird to take a shower in his.

She didn't want to see where he kept all his personal things or know if he hung his towel up after showering. *Nope, nope, nope.* That was more information than she needed in her head. Especially since she knew exactly how he sounded and looked when he climaxed. She'd been doing her best to ignore that she still wanted him with a hungry desperation bordering on stupid. It was like she couldn't just shut her brain off, couldn't completely forget about him—about his wicked kisses and all the dirty things he'd murmured in her ear.

By the time she'd washed the ocean out of her hair and gotten dressed, she felt like a new person. She even had mascara in her duffel bag so she swiped some on for good measure. And that was going to be the only makeup she had for the rest of the day, which was just as well.

She had jeans, a T-shirt and flip-flops in her duffel bag, which was perfect for today. After braiding her damp hair, she found Carson in his kitchen, leaning against one of the countertops, his phone in hand as he looked at something.

His hair was cropped close to his head, showing off perfect bone structure. Even the bit of dark scruff on his face looked sexy instead of unkempt. His T-shirt molded to all of his muscles, particularly his biceps, which she'd had fantasies about. At five feet eleven, she was used to being taller than a lot of men, but with Carson she actually had to look up. He had to be at least six feet four inches. Maybe five. And he was built like...well, like someone she wanted to wrap her legs around.

He immediately tucked his phone into his back pocket when he spotted her. His eyes heated for a moment as he took in her appearance. "I wondered what happened to that T-shirt."

She was wearing one of his faded black and white Ramones T-shirts, had tied it at her waist because it was way too big. "I'm not giving it back."

"I didn't ask for it."

She sniffed once and looked away, glancing around his kitchen. Everything was all neat and tidy, no surprise. This man liked order in his life. And she was like a wrecking ball.

"I tossed your sneakers and your clothes into the washer."

Surprised, she looked back at him. "Thanks. So were you following me?" she asked bluntly, wanting to get that out of the way now.

"Not exactly. But I saw you sneaking around so I decided to hang out and see what you were up to. Then I watched you break into a multimillion-dollar yacht."

"I didn't break into anything." The sliding door had been unlocked.

He lifted a dark eyebrow. "Fine, I watched you bribe someone and then get onto the boat."

"So you're kind of stalking me, then? Pretty sure that's against the law."

Carson's mouth curved up slightly at the corners, making him look ridiculously adorable. Such a big, bulky guy should not be adorable. "So is breaking and entering."

"I already told you, there was no breaking. Just entering. And technically, that yacht should be part of my clients' asset list. Her husband just forgot to add it to their divorce proceedings."

"I figured as much," he said mildly.

"Did you happen to see who got on the yacht while I was on it?" She'd seen three men, but wondered if there had been more.

"Just three guys. I was more concerned with making sure you got off safely than who they were. I was pretty close to making an excuse and going aboard."

She blinked in surprise. "Seriously?"

"*Seriously*. Trouble seems to find you."

She made a scoffing sound and pulled her thankfully dry phone out of her pocket. Her entire life was in her phone. "I've gotta go," she said as she read her incoming text message.

"Everything okay?" He pushed off the countertop, going into what she thought of as sexy mode. He had on a T-shirt and jeans, and his badge and gun weren't visible. Maybe he'd left them in his car or put them away. He didn't look anything like a detective right now. No, he looked more like a street brawler with his tattoos and scruff.

"Everything's fine. I just need to go see a client about something."

"You need to be more careful," he said as she headed for the door, duffel bag tossed over her shoulder.

"Last time I checked, I don't answer to you."

His gaze fell on her mouth, lingered too long as he met her at the door. He stood in front of it for a long moment, blocking her way. "You drive me crazy and I still want to kiss you right now," he murmured.

Why, oh why, did he always just say whatever was on his mind? It simultaneously drove her crazy and was also sort of hot. Well, not sort of. It was super hot. Just like the man himself.

She let out a growl of frustration and nudged him out of the way.

But he decided to follow her outside, carrying another towel with him. "Take this to dry off your seat."

Dang it, why was he so thoughtful? Because her seat was definitely still wet even with the towel she'd sat on.

"Thanks...ah, I can pick my clothes up later, I guess?"

"I'll get them to you. I can drop them off at your place."

"Okay, thanks. Just text me," she said as she slid into the front seat and rolled down her window, glad for a bit of a barrier between them.

"Are you actually going to text me back this time?" He leaned on the top of the frame, looking at her through the open window.

She tried not to obsess over the way his forearms and biceps flexed, or stare at the plethora of tattoos winding around said biceps and disappearing under the sleeves of his T-shirt. Some had to do with his military days, others were Celtic designs linked to his Irish heritage. Each one meant something, she knew. "I'll text you back about my clothes."

"But not about anything else, huh?" Again, his tone was dry.

"Not if you're going to ask me out on another date."

His gaze landed on her mouth again and heat rushed through her, wild and hungry. For him. It took all of her self-control not to whip her door open and devour him. Just climb him like a tree and have her way with him.

This man was her kryptonite and she was determined to stay away from him. She knew how good he tasted, how talented he was with that mouth, and she had so little control right now. So she started rolling the window up, which just made him laugh as he stood up. For some reason she always seemed to amuse him.

Meanwhile he drove her absolutely insane. Whenever she was around him, she wanted to crawl out of her skin he had her wound so tight.

Because getting involved with Carson Irish again? Absolutely no way in hell. That way would lead to heartbreak.

CHAPTER TWO

S ienna sat down in front of Eileen Bentley's desk and spread out the blown-up pictures of the yacht. She'd already sent them directly to her client, but she could admit that she liked to be a bit of a showman on occasion. Especially when she'd taken such gorgeous pictures.

After leaving Carson this morning, she'd stopped by the hospital to see a client—and had run into her brother Brodie, who was apparently smitten with someone—and she'd been running around all day ever since.

"These are incredible," Eileen said, touching the photos. She shook her head slightly. "I can't believe he thought he could hide this from me. That he thought I'd be so stupid."

"That's not all he's hiding," she said. Because Sienna hadn't set up this meeting just to show her client the printed pictures. She pulled out another file and set it on the desk. "He's hiding money in various accounts as well. A hundred thousand here, another hundred thousand there."

Eileen's expression darkened as she flipped open the file and briefly scanned the first page. The woman had given up her career for her husband, and they didn't have kids. But her husband had wanted her to be a stay-at-home wife, to take care of everything for him, set up busi-

227

ness dinners, organize his multiple businesses in an admin capacity. She'd basically been working for him for free as an executive assistant. And Eileen had been very good at her job. She'd saved her husband from a couple lawsuits and had organized two of his restaurants so much they'd nearly doubled earnings in one year.

Sienna saw that a lot, wives giving away all their labor for free and then, in the end, their husbands tossed them over as if they meant nothing. She could admit that it enraged her and she liked helping all these women get what they deserved.

Because that kind of shit would affect Eileen's Social Security down the line, or make her less hirable, something that a lot of people, especially women, didn't think about.

Sienna kept those thoughts to herself, however. Because at this point, Eileen was going to come out of the other side of this divorce in very good shape.

"If he's smart, he'll skip court altogether so none of this becomes public, and you guys should be able to work out an agreement," Sienna added.

Eileen's expression was still dark and when she smiled it was more of a baring of teeth. "Oh, he'll come to an agreement."

It seemed her work here was done. Sienna stood and held out a hand. "Sorry you're dealing with all this, but I hope you're able to settle quickly and move on with your life."

"Thank you," Eileen said as she stood as well, offering a perfectly manicured hand. "Hiring you was the best thing my lawyer ever advised me to do."

After leaving, Sienna decided to stop and grab a beer and a bunch of fried food before going home. She didn't have anything in her refrigerator, and after the day she'd had, she was starving.

As she slid onto a barstool at a local burger joint she'd only recently discovered, she nodded once at the bartender. Thankfully they weren't too busy tonight. "Cheeseburger with fried onion rings and a Guinness," she said.

"Make it two." Carson freaking Irish, like a ghost who came out of nowhere, sat next to her.

She was secure in her observational skills, but damn, she hadn't even seen him come in. She blinked at him. "Seriously, stalk much?"

"I swear I didn't know you were going to be here. I was back at that booth and saw you walk in. Besides, I'm the one who introduced you to this place."

Sienna bit back a reply because Carson was right. Maybe she'd subconsciously come here because she'd wanted to see him? No, she refused to believe that. She was simply hungry. *For food.* "Did you just get off work?"

He nodded and she realized he looked exhausted, so she decided not to needle him. Much.

"Rough day?" she continued.

He scrubbed a hand over his face and took the beer placed in front of him with a nod of appreciation. "You could say that."

"Want to talk about it?" She wrapped her fingers around her Guinness, letting it settle in its frosted mug as she traced her finger from the top of the glass to the bottom.

"Not really. How about you? Did your day get better?" There was definitely a hint of amusement in his tone now.

"Well, I didn't have to jump into any more bodies of water, so I call that a win. Plus...I'm pretty sure my brother has fallen for someone." Seeing Brodie all smitten had been a surprise.

Carson shot her a sharp glance.

"Not Daniel—he's obsessed with your sister. Something you know. You were at the freaking wedding."

He grinned then and it softened all of his hard features, making her panties melt just a little bit. She'd never understood the phrase panty-melting before Carson Irish.

"True," he said. "It's the only reason he's alive."

"I'm going to pretend you're just joking."

"I am. But there was a time when I wanted to punch his face in." Carson's expression went all surly for a moment.

"You and me both, but at least he got it together and married Kathryn." And now Sienna had a new sister. Another reason she wasn't going to play with fire, aka Carson. She didn't want to screw up their family dynamics.

"So what are you doing after this?"

"Going home, maybe a hot bath, then bed. I've got a lot of paperwork to do tomorrow. I never realized how much paperwork would be involved with being a PI."

He grinned and she really liked that look on him. "It's a lot more sitting in cars and waiting on stuff to happen than you thought, huh?"

She laughed lightly. "Yes. But I still love it. I like puzzles, mysteries— and I really like helping spouses uncover when their significant others are trying to hide stuff from them. It's just so shady and gross."

He nodded, watching her thoughtfully. "Did you have a bad breakup?"

She blinked at the abrupt personal question. "Why?"

"Not that I think I'm God's gift to women or anything, but you and I have chemistry. And don't deny it," he said when she opened her mouth to do just that. "Because I know you weren't faking with me. But you refuse to see if we can take it any further. Plus you take a whole lot of joy in 'sticking it to,' and I'm only quoting you, 'asshole men.'"

She took a sip of her beer, mulled over her response as a mournful Irish ballad played in the background. Finally she cleared her throat. "First, yes we have chemistry." So much. And no, she hadn't been faking her orgasms. So many orgasms. "Second...you're my sister-in-law's brother. That's way too messy and complicated." And those were two things Sienna did not deal with. They'd had sex, sure, but...yikes. More would not work. Nope.

There was more to it than that but she was so not going to give Carson the real reason.

Instead she continued, "And yes, I do enjoy sticking it to assholes. They deserve it. I like to believe I'm helping deal out a little cosmic karmic justice. It has nothing to do with any particular man or...whatever. I love my brothers. They're amazing. So is my dad. And so are a ton of other guys I know. I'm not a man-hater."

His gaze narrowed slightly. "What guys?"

She snorted softly as their burgers were placed in front of them.

"Please tell me you're not jealous."

He lifted a shoulder. "Well, I'm certainly not going to lie to you."

She blinked at his words. "Are you always so honest?"

"With you." Carson watched her intently, his blue eyes vivid in the dim bar.

Damn it. He really did always say the right thing.

She looked away from him and down at her burger. It looked as if they'd added an extra slice of cheese. Her mouth watered. "I'm about to show you a good time," she said to her food, which made him throw his head back and laugh.

"I love that I never know what's going to come out of your sexy mouth," he murmured. Then he took a bite of his own burger.

She...didn't know how to respond to that. She did, however, like sitting there with him with the quiet buzz of the bar around them.

When she was with him, the silence was never uncomfortable. No, it was more companionable. He was content with just being with her too.

She swore he was like the perfect man for her.

Except...he didn't like her job. Didn't like that she got put in dangerous situations. And she wasn't going to change who she was for anyone.

Not even the sexiest man she'd ever known.

"Damn it," he muttered, breaking into her thoughts.

She looked over and saw him reading a message on his phone. "What's up?"

"We're shorthanded now, just got called out on something."

Sienna fought the disappointment that he had to leave. It wasn't like she'd planned to see him tonight anyway. That had just been a bonus she wouldn't admit to. "Stay safe," she murmured.

Giving her a look she couldn't even begin to describe, he tossed a few bills on the bar, more than covering both their meals. She wanted to protest, but knew it would be pointless.

As he headed out, an unexpected pang slid through her rib cage, hitting her right in the heart. Oh, who was she kidding? It wasn't unexpected. She already missed Carson and that spelled trouble with a capital T.

CHAPTER THREE

S ienna pulled into her driveway, exhausted from the day she'd had. And completely wired at the same time, all because she'd seen Carson. Twice.

Sighing at herself, she headed inside but as soon as she stepped into her mudroom, she froze. Normally her security system chirped, the loud beeps a signal that she needed to disable it within forty-five seconds. Now there was simply the little *beep beep* of her door opening.

But nothing else.

And she was absolutely neurotic about setting her alarm every day because of what she did for a living.

For the most part the clients she dealt with were angry at someone, whether it be a spouse or whoever, but at the end of the day she was just a PI. A small weapon in whatever war they were waging against each other. Still, there were a few occasions where people had been stupid and vengeful, so she was cautious.

Easing back out the door, she hurried to her car. Instinct buzzing through her like angry mosquitos, she opened the garage door and hurriedly reversed into her driveway.

She was probably being stupid but there was always that one percent chance that— Her heart stopped for a millisecond as a masked man wearing dark gloves stepped into her garage. The door was closing on him as he took a step in her direction.

Holy sweet potatoes!

Heart racing, she pressed on the gas, flooring it into reverse.

In hindsight, she hadn't even looked back to see if anyone was in the street, her eyes glued to the man standing there.

She quickly kicked it into drive, racing down the road even as she yanked her cell phone out.

Without questioning why, she called Carson instead of 911. Sure he was the police, but she'd still called him and was surprised when he picked up on the second ring.

"Hey gorgeous," he murmured, his voice sex and sin.

She had another jolt of a different kind upon hearing him call her gorgeous, but she quickly moved past that. "Someone broke into my house. A masked man."

"Don't go inside," he ordered.

"I'm in my car, driving away," she rushed out, wild horses still galloping in her chest as she checked her rearview mirror. Everything felt so surreal right now. She knew what she'd seen and it *still* didn't feel real. Her fingers tightly gripped the steering wheel, her knuckles pale as she came up to a stop sign. She glanced all around her, fear ratcheting up inside her.

She realized she was heading straight toward Carson's place, which was also ridiculous. Or maybe not. Her instinct was telling her to get somewhere safe. No matter their personal history, in a situation like this he would keep her safe.

She glanced in the rearview mirror. No one was following her. The horses in her chest eased up a bit, but not by much.

"Get somewhere safe. I'm calling in the nearest patrol right now," he said before there was a muffled sound and she heard another voice. He was talking to someone and she wondered if he was still at whatever had called him away before. A crime scene, she'd assumed. He came back on the line again. "Where are you now?"

She quickly gave him her location as she kept driving, trying to put distance between herself and her house.

"Okay, get to the Publix about two blocks from where you are. Go sit in a brightly lit section of the parking lot. I'm three minutes out."

"Will do." She was glad that her voice didn't shake, though she had no idea how it wasn't at this point. A tremble had started in her core and she couldn't seem to stop it as she took a left-hand turn.

Someone had been *in* her house, her sanctuary. They'd broken in and done God only knew what inside. That someone had been waiting, could have attacked her if she'd ignored her instinct and gone inside.

A wave of nausea swelled up suddenly, but she managed to shove it back down. She hadn't gone inside and she was safe.

For now.

"Talk to me, Sienna. I need to hear your voice." Carson's tone was soft, soothing as he talked to her, and she realized she'd just gone silent as she got caught up in her thoughts.

She cleared her throat. "I'm here, I'm fine. I just..." She cleared her throat again as the words stuck. "Thank you for answering," she rasped out, so damn grateful that he'd picked up, that he was coming to see her.

That he'd be involved with whatever this was. Because even if she didn't want a relationship with him, she trusted Carson to help her.

"I'll always answer for you."

It didn't take her long to get to the Publix, and even though she was still terrified, panic buzzing through her like angry bees, she found a spot near the front, thankfully. So she sat in her locked Jeep and waited.

CARSON PUT his hand at the small of Sienna's back as they stepped into her house—and ignored the look his partner gave him. Because Julian Ruiz missed nothing and it was clear Sienna mattered to Carson.

Plus, he'd had too many drinks one night months ago and told Julian about her.

"As far as we can see, nothing has been overly disturbed and we've got a small team searching for hidden cameras and microphones in case this has to do with your job," he said quietly as they moved through to her kitchen.

Sienna nodded at him then glanced at Julian, but didn't say anything else. Her expression had a pinched quality and he hated that this had happened to her.

No matter what, he was going to get to the bottom of it. Because a masked man breaking into her place? There could be multiple reasons for that, none of them good.

"I just don't understand how he got in here," she murmured to herself as she opened two cabinet doors and rummaged inside.

"We found a few scratches on the lock on your back door. And your alarm was obviously off."

"No, I set it. I *always* set it." She headed out of the kitchen and straight for the living room.

"Maybe you forgot." He stayed with her, but gave her enough space to search for anything that might be missing.

She started walking around, methodically looking at everything, opening the doors to an entertainment center. The flat-screen on the wall was still in place and other electronics scattered around the room appeared to have been untouched as well. Julian had dusted for prints in a few places, but Sienna had said the guy was wearing gloves—and Carson trusted her recollection and observation skills.

"No," she finally said, referring to his statement minutes earlier. "I'm so neurotic about programing my security system. I mean, I guess there's a one percent chance I forgot to set it on the same day someone broke in—" She let out a low curse, then pulled her phone out of her back pocket.

"What is it?"

"I can't believe I didn't think of this before," she muttered to herself. "I can just check my dashboard and check the log."

He moved up next to her, ignoring her fresh vanilla scent as he looked down at her screen.

"Someone turned my alarm off in the house an hour before I got home. Manually, according to this." Her cheeks had gone white as she handed him her phone so he could see the activity log.

It was similar to the one he had, breaking down when the security panels were disarmed, armed, even when her doors opened and closed.

So this was definitely not a random break-in. Because breaking a security system took a decent amount of skill. Unless... "Does anyone know your code? Have you ever texted it to someone, given it to your mom or...anyone?"

Sienna paused, her dark green eyes thoughtful as she looked at him. "I don't think so, but I can't swear to it. I change my code every two months or so and I recently changed it. Since then I haven't given it to anyone. Though I have given my mom the code in the past when I've been out of town. She's the only one though."

"What about your brothers? Maybe you texted them?"

"No way. I love them, but..." She shook her head as she trailed off.

"Hmm." Her security panel was in her laundry room on the wall right by the door so the panel wasn't visible from any windows, which eliminated the possibility of someone spying on her that way. "Do you think this has anything to do with one of your cases? A recent one or a current one?" Maybe something to do with the yacht she'd broken into today.

"It's definitely possible. But...I don't know the purpose of breaking in here. Most of my stuff is at my office and I back everything up to the cloud anyway. So hurting me won't change the outcome of anything else. So...I need to think," she said, more to herself than him as she strode out of the living room.

He followed her, his gaze trailing down her back, over her perfect ass, and her long jean-clad legs. She moved with an innate confidence that was the sexiest thing about her.

Her dark brown hair was still pulled back into that braid against her head and she moved with purpose, every sleek line of her making him itch to touch, to stroke and kiss.

Even though he was keeping himself locked down now, it was impossible not to want her, not when he'd kissed every inch of her. It was more than physical though. He'd made it clear he wanted to date her. Hell, he'd had to hold back because he hadn't wanted to scare her, but after three dates she'd told him they would just be friends and had stopped texting or calling him. He was ninety percent sure it wasn't anything he'd done either. The chemistry between them had been combustible—still was.

"My old laptop is missing," she said as she shut the closet door of a bedroom she'd turned into a home office. Then she went over to a cabinet and opened it. "So is one of my old cameras. Damn it, my long-range camera is gone too."

There was no computer on her desk and she'd left her laptop bag in his truck—which was currently locked. "You just have the laptop?"

"A laptop, a tablet, a newer camera, my phone. And my phone and laptop are synced."

"What about paper files?" He didn't see any filing cabinets, but wanted to cover all his bases. Even if he wasn't officially going to be running this case.

"I don't keep anything like that here. But I use my office when I'm working on a case, getting things organized for my clients. I like having this personal space in case I don't want to go into the office."

He nodded, glanced around the small room. It had her stamp all over it. Eclectic art, colorful, gauzy, billowing curtains over the window, a little ceramic hedgehog with a top hat as her pen holder.

"You can't stay here tonight," he said as she continued to look around the room, opening more drawers and shutting them.

"I know," she said absently. "I'm going to call Daniel, see if I can stay with him and Kathryn."

"Just stay with me." The words were out before he could think about them, but Carson stood by them.

She straightened at that, her whole body going rigid as she turned to face him. Her eyes narrowed ever so slightly as she watched him carefully. "Seriously?"

"Look, we don't know who broke into your house. And I don't like the fact that he was masked, or the fact that he disarmed your security system. This isn't some amateur hack job. He took very specific things and it stands to reason that he hasn't got what he wants yet—so he's not done. He'll want your current laptop once he realizes what he has is useless." At least that was what Carson was guessing based on past cases and common sense. "If he decides to come after you, do you want to lead him back to your family?"

Now she full-on glared at him—and he still wanted to kiss her, wanted to smooth away the frown lines. "Well, if you're going to get all logical on me," she muttered. "I can stay in the guest room." She paused, her expression softening as she seemed to lose all her steam. "And thank you. I appreciate it." She ran a hand down her braid as she looked around her office again, sighing. "I hate that someone was in my space. It makes me feel violated."

"We'll catch whoever did this. And you're going to need to make an official statement to my partner."

She looked back at him, her braid swishing slightly with the movement. "Not to you?"

"It's unlikely I'll be directly on this case. Not with our relationship." He held up a hand when she started to say something. "You're my sister's sister-in-law, and that constitutes a relationship. But Julian will keep me in the loop. Plus...I'll also be working on it, just not officially."

She looked as if she wanted to say more, but nodded. "Can I grab some clothes and toiletries?"

"Get whatever you want. Julian will put someone on your house for now, not that I think anyone is coming back after this. At least not anytime soon."

Expression tight, she simply nodded and headed out of the office for her bedroom.

Instead of following after her, he went to find his partner and update him on what she'd found.

Whoever had decided to mess with Sienna had taken on Carson without knowing it. Because no one was going to mess with her and get away with it.

CHAPTER FOUR

Carson's gaze fell on Sienna the moment she entered the kitchen. Like that proverbial moth to a flame, if she was anywhere in the vicinity, his eyes were on her. She was like a magnet for him. A tall, sexy, smart-mouthed magnet he couldn't get enough of. "How are you feeling?"

"My brain is a little fried." She sighed and sat at his kitchen table, crossing one lean leg over the other. She was wearing little shorts and a tank top and her hair was damp against her head. It was the second time that day she'd showered at his place, though this time he thought was more to calm her down than anything else. "Are you sure you don't mind me staying here?" Her foot tapped nervously as she watched him.

"Why would I mind?"

She lifted a shoulder, the action jerky. "I don't want to put you in danger."

He snorted in response and went to the stovetop where he pulled the teapot off the burner and poured a mug of hot water for her.

She inhaled slightly as he set it in front of her. "I didn't know you drank tea," she murmured.

"I don't. I remembered you said you liked chamomile tea at night." So he'd bought some in case she ever decided to stay over. But then when he'd pushed for just a little bit more from her, relationship-wise, she'd iced him out completely. It still stung.

"Oh..." She cleared her throat. "Ah, thank you." Then she avoided his gaze and took a sip of her tea, sighing as she set it back on the tabletop. "So when do you think I'll be able to go back to my house?"

"Do you really want to go back right now?" he asked dryly.

"No." She let out a little shudder and wrapped her arms around herself. In that moment, he wished he had the right to comfort her. "I just meant like, when do you think it will be safe?"

Sighing, he sat at the table across from her. He wished he had an answer, hated that she was displaced and scared and everything was up in the air. "There are too many unknowns right now. And I don't like the thought of you going back to a place where someone hacked your security so easily."

She tapped her finger against her mug, her expression thoughtful. "I started making a list of recent cases, the ones I wrapped up."

"What about the one you're working on now?"

"I'm including that one too. But I can't imagine why my client's husband would come after me. He probably doesn't even know that I discovered his yacht and other assets yet. Or he could have—because she might have already called her lawyer."

"Hiding a yacht," Carson muttered.

She snorted in agreement. "Right? It's so obnoxious. So..." She cleared her throat, her smile dimming. "I'll get my file together and send it to you or your partner?"

"Just make it both of us." Because he'd be working this case too even if he wasn't officially on it. Nothing could stop him from finding out who'd tried to hurt Sienna.

SITTING on the guest bed in Carson's condo, Sienna impatiently tapped her finger against her mug of tea as the phone rang once, twice...

"Hey, I was just talking about you." Eileen's voice was bright and cheerful even with the later hour.

"I hope you were saying only good things."

Her client laughed. "Oh, definitely. My soon-to-be ex is almost sure to settle now. I contacted Valentina with all the information you gave me and she's reached out to his attorney."

"Already?"

"Yep. I wasn't going to sit on this. I want this wrapped up and done with. And I'm sure he does too, even if he doesn't want to settle with me."

Well, that answered Sienna's question about whether Eileen had already contacted Valentina, the attorney who often recommended Sienna's services. She'd reached out to her because she wanted to talk to all her current clients in case the break-in at her place had anything to do with anyone she'd worked for.

"I just wish I could have seen his face when he saw those pictures you took!" She let out a laugh that was just a little too loud and Sienna wondered if she'd been drinking. "It feels a bit petty but I love that he's getting this information on a Friday night. I hope it ruins his whole weekend. Bastard."

"I'm glad things are moving forward for you."

"Thanks. Hey, is everything okay?"

"Oh yeah, fine. I'd only called to see if you'd contacted Valentina about everything. I called her but she didn't answer."

"Probably because she's talking to the slime's attorney right now." Another laugh-snort of glee.

"Listen..." Sienna tried to find the right words, wanted to say this carefully. "Someone broke into my house earlier."

"Oh my God, are you okay?"

"I'm fine. The police are handling it but...I don't know if it had anything to do with any of my cases. I just wanted to let you know so you could stay safe and just take extra precautions." Sienna wouldn't be able to live with herself if she didn't say something and then Eileen got hurt.

"Thanks for the heads-up. I'm actually in Miami already. A friend of mine flew us down on her private plane and I'm staying here for a bit."

"I'm glad to hear that." She'd certainly sleep better knowing that Eileen was out of the city.

Once they wrapped things up Sienna tried Valentina again, but got no answer. After texting her, she pulled up her files and started compiling a list even as sleep pushed in on her. This bed was so comfy and inviting and her brain was more than done for the day.

She was so tempted to shut her laptop and search Carson out— maybe see if he wanted her to join him in his bed. But nope. She had more self-control than that.

Hopefully.

CHAPTER FIVE

The next morning Sienna stumbled into Carson's kitchen, the scent of rich coffee filling the air. Normally she was a morning person, but she was dragging today. After tossing and turning for ages, she'd finally snagged a few hours of rest, but it hadn't been solid sleep and she was feeling it now.

For some reason she wasn't surprised that sexy-as-sin Carson was already at his kitchen table, working away on his laptop. The man looked wide-awake with damp hair, a T-shirt that molded to annoyingly muscular biceps, and a cup of coffee steaming in front of him.

"Did you get any sleep last night?" she murmured as she headed straight for the coffeepot.

"A little bit." He glanced over at her, his gaze lingering on her bare legs for a long moment.

A shiver of delight rolled through her, waking her up as much as she imagined her first shot of caffeine would. He should *not* be able to affect her with just one look, but there it was. The man was her weakness.

"Your guest bed is soft." She poured herself a mug, inhaled the pure goodness.

"*My* bed is more comfortable." His tone was dry, pulling a startled laugh from her.

"It's too early for that kind of talk," she murmured as she turned to face him. No way were they going to talk about "them" or…whatever. No relationship talk. Because they didn't have one other than friendship. That was all. Still…his bed was soft, dang it.

"Or maybe it's exactly the right time. Maybe I can get you to finally tell me why you threw up all those walls between us after we had sex." Carson shifted in his chair, stretched out his long, muscular legs that even jeans couldn't hide. His dark hair was slightly mussed and he still hadn't shaved so his scruff was a bit longer and oh God, it looked good on him. His tattoos peeked out from his T-shirt and she had to resist the urge to look at them—to walk right up to him and take his face in her hands. To kiss him the way her entire body craved.

She could feel the full weight of his attention on her and, pre-caffeine, that was a whole lot. Clearly she wasn't thinking because she was so tempted to just throw caution to the wind and jump this man. And something told her that he'd let her. Heck, he'd welcome it. Oh no. No, no, no.

Drink your coffee, girl!

Sienna turned away from him, unable to handle that intense stare as she hurried to the fridge to grab some creamer. "Look," she said on a sigh. "You don't want *me*. You just like the *idea* of me." And it was better that they got that out of the way now.

He snorted with laughter as she turned to face him. Damn it, it was like he got sexier every single time she looked at him. "Please tell me more about this insane idea that you have."

She wrapped her fingers around the mug, frowned at him over the rim. "It's not crazy, and I'm right. You don't want me."

He laughed again, shaking his head now, as if she'd lost her mind.

"Look, I have a fairly dangerous job," she said.

"I know. So do I." He lifted a shoulder as if to say *So what?*

But she knew better. "You want someone softer, someone who works a regular nine-to-five and who doesn't get put into dangerous situations."

He simply lifted an eyebrow as he watched her. "Where the hell are you getting this from?"

"You wouldn't be the first guy who couldn't handle my job." Wouldn't be the first guy in law enforcement either. She'd tried dating someone in law enforcement before. A DEA agent, not a detective, but he definitely hadn't been able to handle her job. Not only that, but he'd tried to tell her what to do, as if she'd asked for his help.

And if things went south with her and Carson, it would be so complicated because of their families. It wasn't like they could avoid each other forever. Nope, they'd be stuck having awkward conversations every time they saw each other and just, no, no, no.

He frowned at her. "For the record, I like what you do. I think your job is interesting. I think *you* are interesting. I've never said I want you to change your job. I'm not sure where this crap is coming from, but it's not from me."

"Crap?"

"Yeah. I like that you go toe-to-toe with me. I like that you're a smart-ass. I like a *lot* about you. Even when you're driving me crazy," he said as he turned back to his laptop. Then he started muttering under his breath to something on the screen. Before she could think about responding, he said, "Tell me about Kevin Fox."

She paused before she took another sip of her coffee. It went down smooth and hot, but she focused on the man Carson had just brought up on his screen. "Fox is a loser. But he's in jail."

"What happened with that case?" he prodded.

She'd included Fox's name in her list of recent cases for Carson, but hadn't given much detail because, well, Fox was in jail.

"Not much to tell. He used to knock his wife, Hailey, around until she finally got up the courage to leave him once she was pregnant. He lost his mind when she tried to leave. He already hurt her badly, on a fairly continual basis. But he was smart about the way he abused her, leaving no marks that anyone could see, and she would never press charges."

"The guy's brother is a cop?" He looked at his screen, his expression going darker.

"Yeah. But that guy is all right from what I can tell. He had no idea what his brother was doing, but Fox made it sound like she would have no one to turn to, that no one would believe her. And she believed him. It was like he brainwashed her into thinking she was trash." Sienna wished she could punch the guy again just for good measure.

"How did you get introduced to the wife?"

"A friend of mine, an attorney, took her case pro bono. And she recommended that Hailey hire me—I also worked for her pro bono, although she made me a quilt as a thank-you."

Carson half-smiled at that.

"Anyway, I followed him for a while, got some really interesting pictures of him committing random crimes. He was just a piece of shit in general and he likely would've gotten himself tossed in jail sooner or later. He'd already been arrested and jailed a couple times, but I took what I had and turned it over to the police. Somehow he found out it was me, and when he was out on bail he stopped by my office talking trash, trying to intimidate me. He also had a weapon on him, though he didn't use it. When I refused to back down, I could see the shock on his face. He eventually took a swing at me but he missed and I broke his nose. He tried to say that I attacked him, but unfortunately for him I've got security cameras in my office for that very reason."

He lifted an eyebrow. "Damn."

"You think he might be involved?" Maybe the guy's brother had wanted revenge or something? But no, Sienna found that hard to believe. Fox's brother had seemed pretty decent, had been getting Hailey stuff for the baby, doing a lot of work around the house for her. And the break-in at Sienna's place had been too methodical, too clean. Someone had been looking for something specific and Fox was nothing more than a blunt object with no finesse. The guy was in jail anyway.

"I don't know anything at this point, but you didn't have much next to his name other than the words 'asshole' and 'deserves another broken nose,' so I wanted to ask." Amusement flared in his blue eyes and she fought the effect that had on her.

She was already on a slippery slope with Carson. Because everything he did affected her. "Sorry about that," she murmured, wincing. "I was exhausted last night. Let me look back over what I sent you." She'd tossed together a file for Carson and his partner, wanting to give them as much information as possible, but clearly she'd been half asleep while putting it together.

"Tell me about this guy, Leo Tizon. You don't have much next to his name either."

She drank more coffee, savored it. "There's not much next to him because he's a new client. He hired me because he thinks his partner is screwing him out of money. They own a bunch of food trucks and the margin of profit is already fairly slim. But he thinks his partner is siphoning money away a little at a time."

"Is he?"

She lifted a shoulder. "I'm not sure yet. But I'm pretty sure his partner is screwing his wife. So, not exactly a stand-up person."

Carson winced. "You really see people at their worst, don't you," he murmured.

She wasn't surprised by his insight. His job was different than hers, but he still saw people at their worst too. "No more than you, I imagine."

He paused and then nodded. "Yeah. I usually see people on their worst day. Or at least on a really bad one. Sometimes I have to remind myself of that when they're acting like assholes. Trauma can bring out the worst in people and they react poorly."

"Do you like what you do?" She'd never asked him before and she was curious.

He nodded and turned in his chair, once again giving her the full weight of that blue stare.

It was a little bit intimidating to be on the receiving end of all that sexiness.

"I do," he said. "I like solving puzzles. Kinda like you. And I like helping people get justice." He paused, a heavy weight hanging in the air as if he wanted to say more.

"What?"

"When I was in college, I was friends with a girl who was raped. The detective handling her case was, well, lazy. A piece of shit if I'm going to be blunt. He didn't handle the case the way he should have, treated her more like a suspect than a victim. She never got the justice she deserved and it always stuck with me. I'm not saying it's the only reason I became a detective, but it's part of it. That whole thing stuck with me. Our system is broken in a whole lot of ways and I want to be part of the solution."

She took another sip of her coffee, not surprised by his view of the world. He had a sort of code of honor she'd seen early on. It was impossible not to respect that. "How's your friend? Did she recover, emotionally?"

He smiled slightly, an affection bleeding into his gaze. "She's really good. Really happy now with her new husband. The man treats her like gold. And the guy…" He cleared his throat, a hint of anger flashing in his eyes. "The man who hurt her ended up going to jail for a similar crime. I'm not happy about what he did, but I'm glad he got caught and someone did their job for once."

"The world is screwed up," she murmured.

"No kidding." He cleared his throat. "Okay, so this new case with the two partners. Can you think of any reason the partner would come after you? Has he seen you following him?"

"No. And trust me on that. He's not very bright." She'd gotten pictures of him and his client's wife at a cheap motel. It was like something out of a bad movie. They weren't very clever about their meeting places and didn't hide their PDA even in public. They were like octopuses all over each other. Almost like they wanted to get caught.

"What about the yacht case, the one with the Bentleys?"

"I really can't think of anything new from my files. She's definitely going to get a bigger settlement, but the guy can afford it. I've looked into his financials and he is killing it. What she wants won't even put a dent in his lifestyle or income. Not really. And she already has the pictures. So does her attorney. So why come after me? What's the point?" Sienna figured the guy could have just come after her because he was a jerk, but that seemed like a waste of time.

Carson looked back at his computer and typed in some more notes. "I'm going to update Julian with everything you've told me."

"What's he working on today? Can you tell me?"

"He's following up with some of your former clients. Well, not clients, but the people your actual clients hired you to look into."

She'd figured as much. While she really didn't like talking about her clients with anyone, they all knew that if she was ever involved in a police investigation she would cooperate with the cops. That and a few other things she'd made clear up front. And all of her clients had signed off on their contracts.

"You hungry?" Carson asked suddenly. "I think I've got bacon in the fridge."

"Coffee is fine."

He eyed her. "Are you just saying that because you don't want me to cook?"

"I don't want you to go to any trouble." He was already putting her up at his place.

"Fine, then *I'm* hungry, so I'm going to make some bacon and eggs. How does that sound?"

She grinned at him. "Delicious. And if you're taking requests, I really like scrambled eggs with salsa."

He grinned at her and it softened his entire face, making all sorts of heat pool low in her belly. "I'll make whatever you want." His voice dropped an octave as he said it.

And she knew she was in trouble. This man was so dangerous to her. Wild, hot danger in the sexiest package ever.

She cleared her throat and pushed away from the countertop. "Thanks. I'm going to get changed and organize my notes a little bit better. Plus I need to check in with my current client. I know I'm sort of in lockdown right now, but I still need to work."

"Of course. Breakfast won't take too long."

She made her escape, wondering if holing up with Carson had been the best idea. Because she knew that if she asked either of her brothers, or heck, her parents, they'd let her stay with them and she'd be safe. But then she'd be caged, basically, and unable to contribute to this investigation.

She simply couldn't sit on the sidelines. And…she really liked staying under the same roof as Carson, no matter how badly she wanted to deny it.

CHAPTER SIX

Feeling more awake after getting dressed for the day and updating that file, Sienna stepped into the kitchen to find Carson eating and a plate of bacon and scrambled eggs across the table from him. "Oh my gosh, you're the best. Thank you so much for cooking. I could—" She cleared her throat as she sat, definitely not about to finish *that* thought.

"You could what?"

"I could probably eat a whole pound of bacon," she said, lying through her teeth. She'd been about to say that she could get used to this —as in, she could get used to being with him. Which was true and terrifying, so she wasn't opening up that Pandora's box. "Anything new since I saw you half an hour ago?"

He shook his head, watching her carefully. Damn that man and his detective skills. His scrutiny made her feel exposed, as if he could see right through to her innermost thoughts.

She ignored him and bit into a piece of crispy bacon, moaning slightly. It was even cooked the way she loved it. As they ate in silence, him working on his laptop as she checked through work emails, she noticed how comforting it was to be with him. Just his mere presence made her feel safe and secure.

She frowned as a text popped up from Daniel. Then one from Brodie. She winced as she read both messages from her brothers. Then one from Kathryn popped up.

Carson told us what happened. What do you need? I've got a place you can stay no problem. This one from Daniel.

I can pick you up right now. What do you need, little sis? From Brodie.

Omg! Are you okay? Carson told me what happened. Do you want to come stay with us? I've got a room and bottle of wine ready for you! From Kathryn.

"You told my brothers what happened?" She set her phone down, deciding to ignore all their messages and her phone for a moment.

"Of course." He said it as if she should have expected it. "Told Kathryn too." And he looked completely unapologetic.

She bristled slightly. "You couldn't let me tell them?"

He lifted a shoulder, a very broad, sexy one she wanted to trail her fingers over. "Daniel's married to my sister. If someone decides to target your family to get to you, I wanted to give them a heads-up. It would have been irresponsible of me not to say anything."

"You're annoying when you're right." She bit into another piece of bacon, the crunch satisfying.

"Unfortunately for you I'm right all the time."

"Keep telling yourself that." She ate another piece of bacon, tried not to moan too loudly.

He simply grinned at her before he polished off the rest of his eggs.

She'd started to ask what his agenda was for the day when his phone dinged quietly.

She knew something was wrong even though his expression barely changed as he looked at the screen. It was something about the way he went *very* still as he read whatever it was.

"What is it?" She was nosy, and if it involved the break-in at her place, she wanted to know.

"The attorney you work with sometimes, the one who recommends clients call you..." His expression was sober, his jaw going tight.

"I work with a few attorneys. Which one are you talking about?"

"Valentina Hall."

The breakfast she'd just eaten turned to stone in her stomach. Sienna cleared her throat, forced the question out even though she didn't want the answer. "What about her?"

He paused for a long moment. "She was found murdered, and her office torched."

The words were a sucker punch to her sternum. Her instinct was to ask him if he was sure, but of course he was. "When?" she rasped out.

"Yesterday, mid-evening. She called her husband, told him she'd be working late and then when she didn't come home... Well, you can figure out the rest. Julian just let me know. He doesn't like that you're linked to her and just had a break-in, and she was..." Carson shook his head slightly. "I'm sorry."

Even though she hadn't finished her breakfast, Sienna pushed the plate away. "She has kids," she murmured. It was awful regardless, but Sienna still hated the thought of those kids growing up without their mom.

Carson nodded slightly, as if he already knew.

"I'll go over every single client she's recommended and give you a comprehensive list."

It could be a coincidence that Sienna's house had been broken into by a masked intruder the same day Valentina had been killed, but she was going to go with the odds on this one. The two things were related.

She rubbed her hands over her face, trying to wrap her mind around this. "I know it's soon, but do they have any suspects? You know there's security cameras at her place and across the street, and—"

"Julian's on top of this. I promise." Carson's expression was sympathetic.

"Can I call her husband?"

"I'd wait a little bit. Julian just left the husband and he'll likely be telling their kids soon."

Fighting the nausea pushing up, Sienna stood, picking up her plate and his, taking them to the sink. Wanting to keep her hands busy, she washed the dishes as she started mentally reviewing all the clients Valentina had ever sent her. She couldn't believe that Valentina was dead, hated that her family would be grieving and dealing with the aftermath of senseless violence.

If this involved one of her cases and Sienna could help in any way, she sure as hell was going to. Because she wouldn't sit idly by and do nothing.

~

AFTER TAKING a few moments to splash water on her face and get herself together, Sienna stepped back into the kitchen to find Carson on his cell phone.

He nodded once at her, his expression hard as he spoke to someone.

She set up her laptop across from his, figuring this was going to be their workstation for the time being. She knew she should probably call her brothers but didn't feel like dealing with either of them right now. She loved them more than anything but they could be a whole lot of overprotectiveness. She texted them, and Kathryn, however, just to let them know she was safe.

"You're sure?" Carson said. "All right. Keep me informed." He ended his phone call and his expression didn't change as she looked at him. "Fox is out of jail."

Ice wrapped around her. "Are you serious?"

"Yep. Got out a few days ago. Overcrowding and some other bullshit reasons, but he's out."

Sienna stood, though she wasn't sure what the hell she planned to do. "Oh God, Hailey. His ex-wife."

"She's out of town apparently. Julian has already looked into it. She's visiting family in Canada and is out of the country for the next couple weeks."

Sienna let out a sigh, the tension in her chest unraveling slightly. "At least there's that. Has Julian brought him in for questioning yet?"

"Nope. He doesn't have a parole officer or anything to check in with, and no credit cards or cell phone that we know of, so finding him is going to be a task."

"We'll just see about that," she said as she pulled up her file on Fox. She'd made a list of all of his contacts and people he'd screwed over. She was going to find where the loser was hiding out. And if he was

behind killing Valentina, she was going to make sure he went to jail for
life.

CHAPTER SEVEN

Carson tucked his cell phone into his back pocket as he stepped into the kitchen. He'd been making phone calls all day, helping Julian as much as possible from here. Normally they worked as a team on all of their investigations and divided up interrogations and research, but his number one priority was keeping eyes on Sienna. On keeping her safe.

He had a feeling that would always be his priority.

"I found him!" Sienna did a fist pump as she looked up from her laptop, her wide grin triumphant.

He had to shake himself out of staring at her. "Found who?"

"Fox."

He shouldn't be surprised, but a thread of it wound its way through him. "Seriously? How?"

She lifted an eyebrow as she closed her laptop and stood, stretching. As she arched her back he had to force himself not to stare at the way her breasts pulled against her T-shirt. She was tall, lean, built like a runner. And he'd seen her in action before—she could outrun him any day of the week. He knew she'd participated in multiple marathons. Which didn't surprise him, knowing her personality. She was driven and couldn't seem to sit still. She'd told him that she'd been diagnosed late in high school with ADHD and the diagnosis had changed everything for her. She'd embraced that part of herself and learned how to make her ADHD work for her instead of against her.

"I probably don't want to know how you found him, right." He didn't phrase it as a question.

"I didn't do anything illegal." She tried to look offended but she ended up grinning again, looking pleased with herself. "I simply called a few people who I know had a beef with him before he went to prison. People he stole from. Turns out he's crashing at the house of someone he used to smoke weed with. The guy is in the Bahamas for the week and said Fox could lie low at his place while he got back on his feet."

"You have the address?"

She groaned. "You're going to give this to your partner, aren't you?"

"Yes."

"I was hoping we could—"

"You're not going anywhere."

She rolled her eyes but rattled off the address to him anyway, and crossed her arms over her chest. "I need to get out of here for at least ten minutes. Can we go to the gym or something?"

Shaking his head, he texted Julian before looking back up at her. "We can go to the gym here or there's a track that loops around a park close by. I know you like to run."

Her eyes lit up and he stupidly felt like a king. "You think we'll be okay doing that?"

"No one knows you're here and we won't be going anyplace with cameras…" He frowned as he looked back down at his pinging phone. "Julian is stuck in interviews right now and doesn't want to chance that Fox slips away."

"Do we need to bring him in?"

"There is no we." They could send an officer over to talk to Fox, but they had no reason to truly bring him in. And Fox understood the system, would know that. Carson needed to talk to him in person, wanted to see his expression when he told him that Valentina Hall had been murdered.

"So you're going to leave me here by myself?" Her tone and body language were challenging.

"Fine. If you come with me, you will stay in the truck the whole time. I'm just going to talk to him and ask him to come in to answer some questions. Got it?"

Her smile was way too big and way too sexy as she nodded enthusiastically. "I'll wear a hat and sunglasses on the drive over."

CARSON GLANCED around the quiet neighborhood. This was an older Florida neighborhood, the kind that had mostly retirees. Almost all ranch-style houses, jalousie windows and ADT stickers on street-facing windows even though most of them likely didn't have security systems installed.

"What did we talk about?" he asked as he put his truck in park.

"Oh my God, you're ridiculous." Sienna was practically bouncing in her seat, this never-ending fountain of energy. She'd pulled her hair up into a ponytail and it swished every time she moved. Which was a lot. "I'm not getting out. Promise."

He'd already run the license plate of the sedan under the carport and it had come back as registered to the owner of the house. The guy Sienna said was in the Bahamas. "Okay. I just wanted to make sure there was no miscommunication between us. You shouldn't even be with me, but since you've consulted with the PD before, it should be all right." She shouldn't be with him at all, especially not on an active investigation, but as of now Fox wasn't technically linked to this case. He might be once Carson questioned him, but that was up in the air.

"Just go knock on the door. Get him to come into the station. Use that charm of yours," she added.

He couldn't tell if she was being sarcastic or not and resisted the urge to lean over and brush his lips over hers. He certainly didn't have that right but the urge to kiss her was there nonetheless. Always there, lingering.

He couldn't get her out of his mind, not when she'd so thoroughly burrowed herself under his skin. This woman was in his blood at this point. And he was questioning his own sanity for continuing to want her so damn badly.

Sunglasses on, he slid out of the truck and scanned the neighborhood. He waved once at the older woman watering the yard across the street.

The woman was wearing a housedress, her gray hair curled perfectly. Didn't wave back, just watched him cautiously.

According to the computer run he had done, the owner of this house had inherited it when his mom died. And if the guy was into drugs as Fox was, it stood to reason that the neighbors didn't care for the owner or any associates.

After another quick scan of the street, he hurried up to the front door, knocked once. As he did, he realized the door was already ajar.

Nudging it open with his boot, he called out. "Kevin Fox? My name's Carson Irish. I'm with the police."

The door creaked as it swung open, and that was when he spotted what was most definitely blood pooling in the hallway from an open doorway. *Shit.*

Moving quickly, he withdrew his weapon and swept inside. As he moved, he called in backup before sweeping the rest of the house. He went room by room, methodically checking each room, but when he was done there was only one dead body sprawled on the tile of the small bathroom.

Kevin Fox with a bullet hole right through his head.

CHAPTER EIGHT

C arson looked out the window from his boss's office to the bullpen where Sienna was sitting at his desk. She was talking on her phone, likely to one of her brothers, as they'd been calling her all day.

He quickly reverted his attention back to his boss, Captain Tobias Johnson.

"I think we need to get Sienna out of town," Carson said bluntly, looking between his boss and partner. Someone had broken into her house, stolen electronics, an attorney she'd worked for was dead, and someone she'd investigated was dead. She did not need to be anywhere near here right now.

Julian simply nodded because ultimately it was the captain's decision, not theirs.

Tobias was quiet for a long moment. At six feet with broad shoulders that highlighted his high school linebacker days, his boss had a commanding presence. "I don't like any of this, especially the optics if this gets out."

Carson knew what he meant even though his boss didn't say it out loud. Sienna was a MacArthur, and one of her brothers owned a large company and had been voted sexiest bachelor a bunch of years in a row.

The other owned his own security firm and worked for one of the biggest tech companies on the East Coast. Not to mention her wealthy parents were well-known in the region for all their charitable work.

"She won't stay with her family," Carson said. "But she's agreed to go out of town with me. One of her brothers has access to a place in Miami where we can lie low." It wasn't true that she'd agreed, but he would convince her. Because after this recent murder, he simply wanted Sienna away from here. Yes, he wanted to investigate, but he trusted Julian, and sometimes it was wise to know when to step back. Right now his job was to keep her safe. Period. Because if she stayed here, she was going to be a bigger target.

And she might not like it, but in the end she would see that he was right. He just had to convince her to leave with him.

"I trust your judgment," his boss finally said. "We need to make sure we keep her potential involvement with the two murders quiet as long as possible. We need her safe. Do what you've got to do. I want all the details later, but get her out of town."

Carson was surprised at how quickly his boss was moving on this but maybe he shouldn't be. Tobias had always been a big-picture type of boss and had never micromanaged.

His boss continued, his expression darkening. "And I want answers," he snapped out. "Two people are dead. I don't want any more deaths."

"We're working around the clock." Julian's tone was neutral.

Carson simply stood and nodded because it didn't matter what they said at this point.

"She really agreed to go with you?" Julian asked once they were out in the bullpen, the door shut behind them.

He snorted softly.

His partner cracked a smile, the first one Carson had seen in a while. "Why do I get the feeling that you're going to have a hard time convincing her?"

"Shut it," he muttered as he reached his desk.

Sienna popped up immediately. "Is everything okay? What did your boss say?"

"Everything's good." Good being a relative word. But she was alive, and he was going to make sure she stayed that way.

"You're not in trouble?" she asked.

He blinked. "No. That's not why we were in there."

She eyed him carefully as if she wasn't sure she believed him. "All right. So what's our next move?"

"To get you somewhere safe. I've already talked to Daniel, and—"

"I'm not staying with my family. My parents are out of town and my brothers will smother me. Not to mention, I—"

"Can I finish?" he asked.

She bit her bottom lip, looking ridiculously sexy. "Sorry."

"As I was saying." He lowered his voice. "I want to get out of town with you. Just the two of us so you can lie low. If someone is gunning for you, they won't find you here."

"Where are you thinking of going?"

"Miami. Daniel said a friend of his owns a condo there you can stay at. It's not being rented right now so there will be no connection to your family."

"Miami? Okay."

He paused, suspicious. "You gave in really quickly."

"You were expecting an argument?"

"Yes."

"Look, I want to be smart. And I've already talked to a friend of mine. He's going to take over the case with Leo Tizon. Leo is fine with it."

Even if he hadn't been, Carson was getting her out of here. Still, she had a kind of gleam in her eyes that made him wary. "What are you planning?"

Her eyes widened as she gave him an innocent look, but he did not buy it for one second.

"Fine." She let out a little huff. "Eileen Bentley is in Miami. I can talk to her in person."

He scrubbed a hand over his face. "You're trying to put me in an early grave."

"Look, she's the last person I saw before that guy broke into my house."

"Julian already talked to her," he said. "He interviewed her thoroughly."

"Talking to her again won't hurt," Julian said from his desk, which was pushed up right against Carson's. "She was nice enough but not overly talkative. I feel like she might've been holding back. Not about her attorney's murder or anything, but maybe something to do with her husband?" He shrugged as he fixed his attention on Sienna. "If you get anything useful, let me know."

Sienna looked positively smug as she smiled at Carson. "See? You can keep me safe *and* we can get some work done too. It's a win-win."

He shot a look at Julian, who just lifted a shoulder.

"Let's get you packed and get out of here," he finally said. He wasn't letting her go see anyone when they were in Miami, but that was an argument he'd face once they got there. Sienna was just going to have to let his people do their jobs.

To his surprise, Sienna linked her arm through his as they headed out of the station.

Ah, hell. How was he going to keep his hands off her in Miami?

"So why don't you work for your brother?" Carson asked as they headed down the highway. After packing and tying up a few loose ends, they'd gotten on the road. The drive would be over five hours, but with Miami traffic, probably longer. But the farther they could get away from here, the better.

"I don't think I'd make a very good security professional."

He snorted softly. "Don't be a smart-ass. Not for Brodie. Why not work for Daniel doing what you do now? Just in a corporate angle."

"He's offered me a job a few times."

"No kidding. That's why I'm asking. Kathryn told me he's offered you a job at least once a month and you always turn him down."

"He told Kathryn that?"

"Of course. He wants you working for him. Why wouldn't he? You're smart and driven." He'd never worked with her personally, but he knew she'd assisted the PD on a few cases and everyone had great things to say about her. "Imagine how much good you could do with all of his resources. Right now you're basically a one-woman show... You know what, never mind. You'd probably take over the world if you started working for him."

She let out a low laugh, the throaty sound going straight to his dick. He rolled his shoulders once. Being in close quarters with her was wreaking havoc on him.

"What about you, you plan on being a detective forever?"

"I don't know, honestly. Right now I like it. I've got a good captain, but work life is long and I don't like the thought of locking myself in to one job forever." Something he'd never told anyone before.

"So how is it having Daniel as a brother-in-law?" she asked slyly.

He laughed lightly. "I never had a problem with Daniel. Okay, for the most part I didn't. Not until I thought he screwed up with my sister. But he treats Kathryn well and I see the way he looks at her." Daniel would never hurt her, not intentionally anyway. The man worshiped the ground Kathryn walked on.

"I know, right? They're kind of disgusting and I say that in the nicest way possible."

He laughed, liking this easy camaraderie with her. Sienna challenged him, but at the same time, things were so easy between them. He wished... Hell, he wished a lot of things. Like he could figure this woman out. Figure out how to get her back in his life in a way that didn't involve an investigation.

"Shit!" she yelped just as a big semi swerved in front of them.

Grasping the wheel, he jerked to the left to avoid a collision. His gaze snapped to the right, then left side mirror. Lines of cars were in both lanes behind them. *Hell.* He couldn't avoid it.

When the semi jerked wildly, its back end fishtailing, he winced and veered into the next lane of traffic. It was either that or a head-on collision.

Horns honked as the semi hit a truck's back end.

Gripping the wheel tight, he cut off a car, went flying into the median even as he pressed on the brakes. *Damn it!* He twisted at the last second, his side taking the brunt of the impact as they rammed into the guardrail.

The impact rattled through the vehicle, the airbags popping out with a whoosh.

They shuddered to a stop as the semi plowed ahead, crashing straight over the guardrail and smashing into the ditch between the opposite sides of the highway. Smoke billowed out from under the hood, a wild plume of it.

Cars behind them had all slammed on their brakes but it was a miracle no one had hit them from behind.

"Are you okay?" Trying to shove the airbag out of the way, he looked Sienna over.

"I'm good. How about you?" She looked him up and down too, scanning for any injuries.

"I'm fine." But his truck wasn't. Smoke was billowing out from under the hood too and when he tried to start it, the engine didn't turn over.

"I don't think we're making it to Miami tonight," she murmured.

Yeah, he didn't either.

CHAPTER NINE

"Just get in your bed," Sienna said in a grumpy tone.

Carson glanced over from the hotel window, let the curtain fall back into place. After the accident, they'd had to wait for the scene to be cleared, to deal with insurance, to make a report and then get a ride to the rental place. His truck was being towed back home to his normal mechanic, and right about now he was glad for insurance because they'd made things as easy as possible. Instead of driving into Miami tonight, they'd opted to grab dinner and stay in the nearest decent hotel.

But he couldn't stop pacing, couldn't stop looking out the window. "I don't like that our plans have been derailed." It had truly been an accident, but all the same, things had changed and an uneasy sensation had settled in his bones.

"I know. And we can just leave now if you want." She was sitting up in one of the two queen beds, her laptop on her lap.

"No. We're both exhausted." He stretched out on the bed parallel to hers, knowing he wasn't going to sleep well, but he didn't want to make her endure the rest of the drive this late at night. They both needed rest.

She closed her laptop and tucked it into her duffel bag. In yoga pants and a T-shirt, she had her hair down, literally and figuratively. He liked that she was just herself with him. That was one of the sexiest things about her.

"You want to watch TV, or just crash?" she asked as she got under the white sheets and flopped down on the pillow.

He'd rather be naked with her right now. "I'm fine either way."

"Okay. I'd rather not watch TV." She turned off the little lamp and lay back down.

He stared at the ceiling, painfully aware of his breathing and hers. Even with the outside traffic and muted noise, every shift against the sheet seemed overpronounced in the room. He'd imagined being in his bedroom with her—her bedroom. Any bedroom. But in those fantasies, they hadn't been clothed and in separate beds.

"Would you really be okay with me going into dangerous situations for my job?" Sienna suddenly asked into the dimness.

Her question startled him. The lights from the parking lot streamed in through the tiny gap between the curtains so he could see her well. "What?"

"I'm just curious. I want to know if you'd really be okay with me going into dangerous situations."

He paused as he tried to formulate his answer even as it registered that since she was asking, she'd been thinking about the possibility of being with him.

Apparently he didn't answer fast enough because she said, "See? This is why it would never work between us."

Oh, hell no. "Can you give me a second to give you an honest answer?" Without waiting for her to respond, he slid out of his bed and moved into hers.

She made a little yelp of surprise but didn't tell him to get back to his bed.

Lying on his side, he studied her as she turned to face him. She propped her head up on her hand, her eyes bright in the darkness and her dark hair spilling around her shoulders.

It was impossible not to be physically affected by her. And in this moment, he knew things could change between them. This was the opening he'd been waiting for. "I'm not going to *like* you going into dangerous situations. But I'm never going to tell you what to do with your life. For the most part I understand your job can be kind of boring, but that sometimes you get into sticky situations. Again, I'm not going to love that aspect. But I'm also not going to ask you to quit your job, because that would be like you asking me to quit mine."

She bit her bottom lip, watching him carefully. Her subtle vanilla scent teased the air, making him crazy.

"What about you? How do you feel about my job?" For the most part he got sent to calls where people were already dead or crimes had already been committed. So he was there for the aftermath. But he still faced dangerous situations on occasion. There was no way around that.

"I would never ask you to quit your job either, but...I'm not going to love that you're in danger." Then she bit her bottom lip again and he could see the wheels turning inside her head, and wished he knew exactly what she was thinking.

Taking a chance, he reached out and wrapped his fingers around her hip, flexed once. He liked holding her, however and whenever she would let him.

She let out a sort of sigh and leaned closer to him, erasing most of the distance. Not quite all of it, but this was very, very good.

He shifted a little closer, all the muscles in his body pulled tight as he erased the distance between them. She was finally opening up to him, actually talking about *them*. He wanted her so damn bad he ached.

To his relief, she slid her hands up his chest and clutched onto his shoulders as she pulled her body flush with his, erasing the final inches between them. And this was what he'd been waiting for, aching for.

They watched each other for a long moment, and when her gaze fell to his mouth he slanted his lips over hers, desperate for a taste of her. He'd been fantasizing about her for months. Hell, longer than that. Since pretty much the moment he'd seen her. Then he'd gotten to know her and it had been over for him.

As he delved his tongue into her mouth, she immediately threw a leg over his hip.

The two of them together had always been like fireworks going off.

It was pure combustion. He forgot to think, sometimes forgot to breathe—like right now as she molded her long, lean body to his.

She tried to take over and push him onto his back, but he was balancing on a razor-thin wire, all his muscles bowstring tight, so he pinned her beneath him. He savored the feel of her under him, holding on to him, moaning into his mouth.

God, he'd missed her, missed this.

She arched against him, her breasts rubbing against his chest. Only two layers of material separated them, her T-shirt and his.

As they kissed, he slid his hands under her top, his fingers skating along her soft, smooth skin.

His cock was heavy between them, a desperate throb against his jogging pants. This was not how he'd imagined their day ending. Not even close. But Sienna underneath him, and—

A car alarm started blaring, obnoxiously loud as it sliced through the quiet.

He jolted, coming back to reality as he pulled back slightly. Breathing heavily, he looked down at her.

Sienna's lips were swollen, her eyes dilated as she looked up at him. "Ignore it," she rasped out, her fingers digging into his shoulders.

He wanted to. Oh, how he wanted to. But some kind of instinct had him moving, forcing himself off her even though leaving her warm, welcoming embrace was the last thing he wanted to do. "Give me a second," he murmured.

Returning to the window, he ignored his uncomfortable erection as he eased the curtain back.

The alarm was still blaring as he scanned the parking lot. A car near the front of the hotel was the culprit, its lights flashing in tune to the alarm. Stupid cockblock car alarm.

He started to step back, but paused as something in his hindbrain registered. Something...was off. He wasn't sure what it was though.

There. One of the security lights had gone out. No, *three* were out on the big light poles across the parking lot. And they hadn't been out when they'd arrived. He'd specifically picked a well-lit spot but the three out created a sort of triangle around their rental.

The back of his neck tingled with awareness, and when he turned around Sienna was sitting up, watching him carefully. "What is it?"

"Grab your stuff."

She didn't even question him, simply grabbed her sneakers and slipped them on before tugging a hoodie on over her top.

Neither of them had unpacked their clothes or toiletries since they'd only planned to stay the night. They each picked up their bag and instead of going out the door into the hallway, he opened the door to the neighboring room.

Normally each door would be locked, but as a precaution he'd rented two rooms next to each other, the second room under a different name —courtesy of one of Sienna's brothers.

As he shut the door to the neighboring room behind them, he flipped the lock into place.

"Should we leave?" she whispered.

He shook his head and held his finger to his mouth. Then he headed to the front door, glancing out the peephole.

Nothing.

He was probably being paranoid but he didn't care. Not when it came to Sienna's safety. He checked the window again. The car alarm had gone quiet now and even though there was faint street noise and a couple cars pulling into the hotel parking lot, it was quiet enough.

As he stepped back from the window, he heard the door of the room they'd just left slide open.

Sienna stiffened.

Carson grabbed his service weapon and pointed that they should hide in the little alcove where the bathroom was.

On silent feet they both moved in near silence, not turning any lights on.

There was a slight shuffling next door, maybe the sound of the bathroom door opening, and five long minutes later the main door into the hallway opened once more.

Motioning for her to stay where she was, Carson peered out the peephole again and saw a nondescript-looking white guy pull a hoodie over his head as he hurried down the hallway.

He counted to sixty then eased the door open. He kept his weapon down, out of sight, and after a glance in the hallway, he motioned for her to grab their bags.

He kept his hand on his weapon as they raced down the hallway in the opposite direction, hurrying toward the set of stairs instead of the elevators.

Once they were in the stairwell, he said, "We need to take the batteries out of our phones."

She'd already switched phones and no one was supposed to know she was with him, but someone had tracked them somehow. And he was betting on their phones being the easiest way.

After they'd done that, they quietly hurried down the rest of the stairs. Leaving in the rental car was out of the question. As soon as they exited downstairs, he glanced around the hallway, knowing they were momentarily exposed. He had his weapon tucked beneath his shirt but he didn't like any of this.

Somehow someone had found them despite all their precautions.

Instead of heading toward the lobby and going out the front doors, they went to a side exit.

"We need to get the video surveillance. And I have a backup burner phone we can use," Sienna murmured as they reached the exit doors. "I want to call my brother. Daniel will be able to get us out of here. Or get us a car. It's better than depending on a lift service company which will be linked to one of our credit cards." Technically they could use cash, but he wasn't even sure a driver would take them all the way to Miami on the promise of cash. No, they needed their own wheels.

And they'd have to turn their damn phones back on to contact a company. Even though Carson didn't like depending on her brother for anything, he nodded and quickly scanned the side of the hotel as they stepped out into the late-night air.

Cars zooming by on the nearby main road were louder here, the scent of exhaust filling the air. A row of hedges stood between them and the neighboring gas station.

"Give me your phone," he murmured.

Without question she handed it and the battery to him.

They moved to the row of hedges, and after ordering her to sit tight he made his way to the gas station parking lot. He pieced the phone together, took out the SIM and tossed it into the back of a pickup truck before casually heading into the gas station itself.

Right off the main highway, the place was busy, so he once again scanned the parking lot, looking for the man he'd seen. Nothing. Whoever had broken into their hotel room was likely long gone or trying to track their phones.

Hurrying back out, he met up with Sienna, who was still hidden in between hedges, tucked away out of sight. Her burner phone was in hand.

"What did your brother say?"

"He's got a rental for us. We can just make the drive to Miami tonight and hole up." She chewed on her bottom lip as she glanced around and he wanted to brush his fingers over her forehead, to smooth out the worry lines.

"How far is the rental place?"

"Not even a mile." They could easily walk that.

"Let's go, then." He'd worry about his rental car in the hotel parking lot later. For now, they needed to get the hell out of here.

CHAPTER TEN

"So what did Julian say?" Sienna asked as Carson strode into the living room overlooking the Atlantic.

They'd arrived an hour ago and had settled into the Miami condo—courtesy of her brother Daniel. No one except him—and Daniel's friend who owned this place—knew where they were, which was the point.

She was all out of sorts, had barely gotten any sleep, couldn't stop thinking about that kiss she and Carson had shared, and now she couldn't get in touch with her client, Eileen Bentley. Sienna had wanted to talk to her, especially after what had happened at the hotel hours ago. It was mid-morning so Eileen should definitely be awake.

"They got the security feed but weren't able to get anything off it. The guy must have used some kind of program because it wasn't just him avoiding cameras, there were blank spaces. They also found a tracking device on my rental car."

So...whoever had done this was a pro. That ball in her stomach hardened even more. And her worry over Eileen was now simmering. Sienna stood and walked to the sliding glass door, and stared out at the glittering blue water and white sand beaches. Everything in front of her was peaceful and soothing, but nothing could soothe her edges now. "I can't get a hold of Eileen." She ran her hand over her braid once as she turned back to him.

Her whole body was humming with energy and she didn't know if she should down more coffee or try to get in a couple hours of sleep. They needed to lie low but she desperately wanted to talk to Eileen in person. There were some things that you could see and judge in person as opposed to talking to someone over the phone. Though that was a moot point now, since Sienna couldn't even get in touch with her.

"You said she was coming down here to get away. There's no reason to think that she's in danger."

She lifted an eyebrow.

"Okay, there is. I just don't like you worrying." Carson glanced at her open laptop, frowned. "What's all this?"

"All the pictures I've taken in the last six months. I know it's like searching for a needle in a stack of needles, but I decided to rescan all of them. Maybe...I don't know, maybe there's something in one of the pictures that matters?" She was just working blind at this point. "I feel like I need to be doing more, I guess." She'd left her laptop in airplane mode so it wasn't connected to the internet. Not that she thought anyone had tracked her using her laptop. That took a special type of skill.

But Carson frowned, sat in front of her laptop and pulled up the photos she'd taken from the yacht. "Who are these men?"

"You already know that this is Wesley Bentley, Eileen's husband." She'd sent a solo picture of him to Julian and Carson for their files. "I figured I'd move backward through the pictures, starting with the most recent." She touched the screen above Bentley's face. "And that's his lawyer. But I don't know who this other guy is with them. I thought you saw them at the marina?"

Carson shook his head. "I never saw their faces, just their backs as they got on the boat."

"What's wrong, then?" Because his jaw had tightened slightly and he'd gone sort of still in the way he did when he was mulling something over. It was so damn sexy.

"Nothing. Did you send all of these to Julian?"

She shook her head. "There are a lot of pictures in there that...I'm not handing over to the police."

"Why not?"

"You *know* why not. A lot of those photos are people in compromising situations, and while they're using them during their divorces, if any of those photos become part of evidence, then they become public record. I don't like the idea of that, and you guys don't have a warrant." Because most of the cases she worked on, couples ended up coming to an agreement and settling before going in front of a judge. That way none of those pictures became public record.

His frown deepened, but he said, "Can you send me this picture? This guy looks familiar. I want to run him through our databases."

"That's fine. And if there are any other pictures that don't involve people in states of undress, I can provide those too. At least on a limited basis. Why don't you just send them to yourself?"

"Thanks." He got to work on her laptop while she went to the kitchen and ended up making herbal tea instead of coffee. Because the thought of more caffeine had her heart racing, and not in a good way.

"I think I might try and get a couple hours of sleep," she said as she returned to the living room. "My system is all messed up. Unless I need to be doing anything else right now?" She could keep looking at pictures but she'd been starting to lose focus each second that passed.

"No problem. I might grab some sleep too." He started to get up and then paused before clicking on something. Then he looked at her, his expression...strange.

"What?" She stepped forward to see what he'd pulled up. Immediately her cheeks flushed hot. *Oops.*

"You have pictures of us?"

"Kathryn sent me some wedding pictures." Dang it, why did she have to sound so defensive?

"These seem to be only pictures of me and you from the wedding." His voice had dropped an octave, his expression heated.

She could feel her cheeks flushing even warmer as she fought embarrassment. She had a few images with her and her brothers and her parents, but yep, she had a whooooole lot of her and Carson. Could the world open up and devour her now, please? "Why wouldn't I have them? I look amazing in that dress."

He stood then, his eyes heated as he moved in on her like a predator stalking its prey.

She very much wanted to be caught, however.

"You did look amazing in that dress. And I desperately wanted to get you out of it that entire night."

She'd had a little bit too much to drink that night, though she'd had a lot of fun with him. And she'd asked him up to her hotel room but he'd said no because of that very fact—that she'd had too much to drink. He'd been adamant that he would never take advantage of her. Which had just made her like him even more. She set her steaming tea on the nearest flat surface as she took another step back.

She wasn't sure where she was going or why she was even moving away from him. She wanted this man with every fiber of herself.

He kept coming, a strong, lethal panther ready to pounce.

"Carson," she whispered, not sure where she was going with that. He had her all twisted up inside, and had since the moment they'd first kissed. He made her feel things she'd never experienced, made her think about settling down. Something she'd never considered before.

He seemed so perfect and that alone terrified her. Her brothers had their lives together, seemed to be so adept at handling life in general. Whereas she was a mess on the best of days and Carson seemed to have this whole adulting thing down to an art. When they'd been at the hotel a few hours ago and she'd been internally panicking, he hadn't even broken a sweat. He'd just taken charge, and that was insanely hot.

"I think it's a good idea if we *both* grab a couple hours of sleep," he murmured as he reached her, those big, sexy hands settling on her hips in the most possessive way.

She bit back a groan. Damn, but she loved his possessive streak. The sun streamed in from the sliding glass doors and wall of windows behind him. He looked like a sexy warrior from another time, with broad shoulders, scruff on his face, and the light highlighting him from behind. But it was his eyes that drew her in, snared her.

"Just sleep?" Damn it, why was her voice all raspy and unsteady?

"Later." His gaze fell to her mouth, his blue eyes flaring wild and scorching hot. "I'm still clean…haven't been with anyone since you."

"Me neither. And I'm still on the pill." They'd talked about protection months ago and nothing had changed for either of them thankfully. If he'd been with someone else…well, it would have sucked. So knowing that he hadn't eased something inside her. Freed her.

Just like always, she swore she felt the sparks arcing between them.

She wasn't sure who moved first, him or her. But suddenly she had her legs wrapped around his waist and he had her pinned up against the nearest wall, his thick cock pressing into her.

His mouth ate at hers even as he rocked his hips into her.

Heat flooded her system as she arched into him. She wished they were already naked, that they'd already gotten to that part where no clothing separated them. She didn't want to think, she just wanted to feel, to experience all of Carson. To be consumed by him.

"Too many clothes." She might have said that out loud, she wasn't sure, but he pulled back and tugged her shirt off.

Next went her bra before his mouth descended on one of her already hard nipples. Her entire body was on fire for him, a live wire, pulsing and needy.

She groaned, digging her fingers into his shirt even as she tugged at it, desperate to get it off him.

For one moment, as he leaned back so she could strip him, she mourned the loss of his mouth on her body. But as soon as she tossed his shirt to the ground, he sucked her other nipple into his mouth.

She arched her back again, wanting more of this. More of him.

He playfully bit down, sending ribbons of pleasure straight to her clit. She was lightheaded and it had nothing to do with lack of sleep and everything to do with Carson.

Broad-shouldered, tall and sexy, he had this code of honor that she respected. And he was here with her, keeping her safe when she knew the department could have easily assigned someone else to this job.

He was here because he wanted her, had been pursuing her for months.

She was tired of fighting her attraction, tired of blaming him for the actions of former lovers. Tired of pretending that she was just fine being alone. She was, but she wanted more. She wanted Carson in her life. And not just for a night or two. Because Carson was like no one she'd ever known. He treated her like an equal, wasn't intimidated by her.

"Wall or bed?" he suddenly asked as he lifted his head to look at her.

She blinked, taking a moment to digest his question. The wall or bed? Wait... *Oh.* Then she understood. The wall sounded reeeeeally hot, but... "Bed." She wanted more room to taste all of him.

He clutched her ass and hauled her to the nearest bedroom. The curtains were open, with light spilling in over the airy comforter.

Moving quickly, he pinned her to the bed, the air of the comforter going out with a whoosh under the impact of their bodies.

"Pants off," she demanded before he could kiss her again and she lost all her senses. Because he had far too much clothing on and she'd been patient enough.

He grinned at her then, the action almost boyish and softening his features. "Mine or yours?"

"Both."

He groaned and tugged his pants off first. That was when she realized he went commando and her mouth watered. Like freaking Pavlov's dog. Holy hell, he was thick and perfect and her inner walls tightened as she stared for a long second.

She sat up and reached for him, wanting to stroke him with her fingers, wanting to feel that thickness, but he moved her hand out of the way as he grabbed her pants and panties off in one swoop. Maybe she'd start going commando too.

"Hell yes," he growled before he crawled onto the bed and covered her mouth with his even as he cupped her mound.

She wasn't even sure what the "hell yes" was for, but she didn't care. He was cupping her, rubbing his fingers against her slick folds, making her absolutely crazy. She rolled her hips against his hand, needy for more.

"Gotta taste you." It came out as a desperate groan before he started kissing his way down her body, setting her on fire with his mouth until he was between her legs, growling against her clit, his tongue wicked and wild and everything she remembered.

He slid two fingers inside her, curved them up in just the right angle as he started teasing her mercilessly with his tongue. She rolled her hips against his flicks and caresses, barely able to breathe for the pleasure shooting through her.

She was so damn close, so close to orgasm and she desperately wanted him inside her first. They'd been building up to this for months, even if she didn't want to admit it. Which, she didn't care anymore. She wanted all of him. Needed all of him like she needed her next breath.

"I want to..." Before she could finish, an orgasm punched through her fast and hard. Pleasure spiraled out to all of her nerve endings until she was a trembling mess against the comforter, her arms and legs jelly.

He looked up the length of her body, but didn't look smug. No, he still looked hungry.

Carson crushed his mouth to hers even as she reached between their bodies. She started stroking him as she guided him to her body. Not that he needed the help. He was primed and ready to go.

Far too slowly he pressed himself against her slick folds and just... teased her. He sort of pulsed there, just pushing the tip in and out and driving her crazy.

Not known for her patience, she rolled her hips upward, sucking in a breath as he completely filled her.

He growled against her mouth and started thrusting inside her.

She loved the sensation of being filled by him and was cursing herself for keeping her distance from him. For putting up walls and shutting him out.

She wasn't sure how long he thrust inside her, how long they met each other stroke for stroke. But she knew the moment he was going to come because his entire body went rigid above her. All his muscles went taut, his tattoos flexing with it.

But he seemed determined to make her come again as he reached between their bodies and started stroking her clit.

She hadn't thought she was capable of another orgasm but being filled completely by him, after fantasizing about him—them together—

for months, she fell over the edge again, pleasure punching through her, taking over every last thought.

As soon as she did, he let go, coming inside her as he growled against her mouth. Time seemed to go still as they both climaxed, until they collapsed on the bed in a heap of pleasure.

Smiling up at him, she cupped his cheek, wanting to savor every second of this. The way he watched her, stared down at her, sort of awed her, leaving her speechless.

"Be right back," he murmured, suddenly disappearing.

Before she could mourn the loss of his warmth and presence he was back with a washcloth, his steady hand between her legs.

She...had to bite back a sudden bolt of emotion. Tears threatened at how gentle he was being, combined with everything they'd been through. And she knew she shouldn't be surprised but damn. This man was going to completely undo her.

"Shit," Carson suddenly cursed, setting the cloth down.

That was when she heard the ringing sound. What the hell was that? Her brain was all hazy, and as she tried to figure it out Carson eased off the bed.

"I've gotta grab that. It could be a development in the case."

Oh, his *phone*. She hurried after him, ignoring the stickiness between her thighs as she raced from the room, not bothering with clothing.

"Yeah," he said into his phone. He swore softly. Then there was a whole lot of silence and though his expression barely changed, there was a flicker of surprise in his eyes. "What does this mean for us?"

Sienna stood close to him, wishing she could hear whoever was on the other end.

He reached for her, pulling her close against him and she pressed her body flush against his. He was this big, soothing wall of steadiness. Everything about him was real and dependable. And in the past she would've thought those qualities weren't sexy, but she liked that she could depend on him. That he meant what he said.

That he always had her back. Even though it meant she was falling way too hard for this man. A man who could very easily break her heart.

"Okay, just send me the information," he said quietly. "We're not going anywhere. The place has enough food for a few days, so we'll just hang tight."

"What is it?" she demanded as soon as he ended the call.

In response he brushed his mouth over hers, then tried to deepen his kiss, but she pinched his side as they stood there naked in the middle of the living room.

The way he watched her had her toes curling against the tile. "That was incredible. You're incredible," he added. Then his expression sobered. "That was Julian," he said as he guided them back to the bedroom.

He grabbed his jeans and tugged them on as she sat on the end of the bed. "That guy in the picture with your client's soon-to-be ex-husband and attorney? The unknown man is Graham Jordan. He's bad news. Apparently the Feds had him under investigation for money laundering and a whole list of other crap. It sounds like they wanted to turn him against his boss, who is also bad news, but doesn't concern us in this situation. They'd been building a case against him, and had been planning to bring Jordan in when he 'died.'"

"But...Jordan's not dead, right?" Obviously not, if she'd just taken a picture of him.

"Nope. So we have strict instructions to sit tight."

"That's it?" She grabbed the blanket on the end of the bed and wrapped it around her.

"This is in the Feds' hands now. They're looking for Jordan and believe he targeted you because you took those photographs of him. He was friends with Wesley, or business associates I should say. The Feds believe he was tying up loose ends with you and Eileen's lawyer since you both saw those pictures."

Sienna nodded slowly. "What about Kevin Fox, then? He had nothing to do with the Bentleys."

Carson shrugged, seemingly unconcerned.

"That's all I get? A shrug?"

"Look, I'm *not* unconcerned. I'm very concerned about your safety, in fact. And that is my only priority. Julian's very good at what he does. And part of me wishes I was with him, working on this case right now, but I would much rather be with you, making sure you are safe. They'll figure things out, and with the FBI's resources they'll find Graham Jordan."

Well when he put it that way, he warmed her from the inside out.

"They also think Wesley Bentley is dead as well," he added.

She blinked. "Wait, what?"

"Yep." He sat on the bed, pulled her onto his lap. "They found a lot of blood at his house. And it's definitely his—they've already tested it."

"My head kind of hurts with what this might mean." She continued talking as she worked through everything. "So, if he's dead, it means there's definitely no divorce. And no way those pictures become public record. But why not go after Eileen instead of Wesley to make sure there was no divorce?"

"Maybe getting to Wesley was easier, more convenient. With Wesley dead, there's definitely no divorce, and no need for anyone to get their hands on those pictures now. That said…" He cleared his throat, looking as if he didn't want to continue. "She might still be in danger. She's seen the pictures. Even if she doesn't know who Jordan is, he might not want to take the chance that she recognizes him."

And Sienna had taken the pictures. No wonder someone had broken into her house, stolen her electronics. Too bad for them, they'd grabbed the wrong stuff. "So what does this mean for me?"

"We sit tight. That's it."

Gah. Not the answer she wanted, but she knew it was all she was getting for now. As she digested this new information, she leaned into him, resting her head on his shoulder. "I'm glad I'm here with you," she murmured. "I mean, I'm not glad about the circumstances."

"So I'm not just a way to pass the time?" There was a surprising hint of vulnerability in his voice.

She lifted her head to look at him, saw that same vulnerability mirrored in his gaze. "Definitely not. If I had to be with someone else through all this, there's no one I'd rather be with than you," she said, meaning it—right before she kissed him.

CHAPTER ELEVEN

"I've never seen you like this." Carson's voice was carefully neutral as he looked over at Sienna by the window.

"I don't like being cooped up like this." When she got cooped up without a purpose, she started to pace. It helped expel her energy. They'd had lots of sex last night, then again this morning, and then they'd done an actual workout in the living room. But she was still keyed up.

"We've been here *one* night." Now his tone was dry as he looked up from his laptop. Every fifteen minutes or so he would get down on the ground and do sit ups or push-ups, keeping his body moving. So he really wasn't that much different than her.

She just got more visibly antsy, apparently. "Yeah, and I hate it. I mean, I don't hate being here with you, I just don't like feeling useless. And I can't find any more about Kevin Fox. I don't know how he ties into all this and it's bugging me." At least his wife Hailey was still in Canada.

Carson had started to respond when his phone rang. "Yeah?" he answered.

She recognized the ringtone and knew it was his partner.

Carson said a handful of "yeahs" mixed in with grunts that could have meant anything. Then his expression darkened slightly before he ended the call.

"They found the guy?"

"No. Julian is in town. He's with the lead agent on the case tasked with hunting down Jordan."

"They're here in Miami?"

"Yeah."

"So why do you look like your cat died?"

"I can think of a few reasons why they're here—and want to see us. You specifically."

"Me? They said that?"

"Yeah. The Fed brought Julian along and my partner didn't say much on the phone—probably because he knows I'm not going to like what they have to say."

"What do you think they're going to say?"

He scrubbed a hand over his face and looked away from her, out the window. "I don't want to speculate, but they'll be here in an hour. Do you want to change or something?" His gaze flicked back to her, appreciation in his blue eyes as they swept over her little shorts and sports bra.

"Change? Like what, into a frog?"

He snorted. "You know what I meant."

"What's wrong with my outfit?"

His jaw clenched slightly and she suppressed a laugh. She wasn't actually going to wear this to meet some federal agent, but she liked messing with him a bit. "I mean, I guess I can take my panties off underneath the shorts? Would you like that?"

He barked out a laugh even as he stood and basically stalked her across the room. "I'm going to take them off right now."

"That better be a promise."

~

SIENNA COULDN'T STOP the nervous energy humming through her as Carson let his partner and the woman with him into the condo. Definitely a federal agent.

Both Julian and the woman scanned the place in the way those in law enforcement did. They swept everything with a critical eye before Julian introduced them. "This is Special Agent Annie Collins." He indicated the petite redhead in the dark blue pantsuit and killer heels.

Carson shook her hand once before Sienna did the same, except Sienna actually smiled, whereas Carson looked all surly.

The woman returned her smile and it looked genuine. Sienna was good at reading people—it was why she did so well at her job. So at least they were off to a good start.

Carson gestured that they should all sit in the open living room. The living area and kitchen in this condo were connected, so it felt a whole lot bigger than it actually was.

"You're not using Sienna as bait," Carson said into the quiet of the room, even though his body language screamed *don't screw with me* as he sat right next to Sienna.

And wrapped a possessive arm around her shoulders.

She was surprised by the possessive display as much as by what he'd just said. They hadn't talked about how they were going to act with each other before his partner got here, but Carson was making his stance clear. Also, bait? What the heck was he talking about?

The federal agent looked mildly surprised as she glanced between the two of them then shot a look at Julian, who had an incredible poker face.

The other detective was about the same height as Sienna and had a similar runner's build. But he had bronze skin, giving him a sun-kissed glow, and probably used more hair products than she did. The times she'd seen him, he always looked so put together and now was no different.

"We're not going to use her as bait," Agent Collins said.

"Then why are you here?" Carson asked bluntly.

Normally Sienna would have a hundred questions but Carson was handling things perfectly so she was going to sit back and see what happened. For now anyway.

The woman cleared her throat once. "We currently have Eileen Bentley with us."

Sienna shoved out a breath. So that was why she couldn't get a hold of her client. Which was better than what she'd been imagining. "Is Eileen okay?"

"She is. She's stressed that her soon-to-be ex-husband was killed, and that it's very likely tied to their divorce proceedings. She's worried about you, but she's hanging in there."

"Good."

"What we want from you is simple. We just want you to make a phone call to her. We have a feeling we know who Graham Jordan hired to come after you—the man we think killed Bentley as well as Valentina Hall."

"You don't think he's behind the murders himself?" Sienna asked because she simply couldn't help herself. She really did like puzzles and mysteries. But more than anything, she wanted justice for Valentina.

"No." Then the agent paused and seemed to weigh her next words. "At least not all of the murders. Jordan has gotten his hands dirty before so it's *possible* he's involved directly. Either way, definitely indirectly. We're going to catch him, it's just a matter of time."

Sienna nodded, watching her carefully. Since she didn't know anything about the agent, she was going to have to go on instinct with whether she trusted the other woman or not. Thankfully Carson's presence was soothing, and when he gently squeezed her shoulder, she leaned farther into him, savoring his warmth.

"Like I was saying," Agent Collins continued. "We just want you to make a phone call using a clone of your phone. We want our target to trace it to where Eileen is staying. We've got her set up in a safe house where we have eyes on her. We want to catch Jordan's hired guy in the act. He works for money so we think he'll flip on Jordan."

"What if Jordan comes himself?" Sienna asked.

"Then we take him down and get him to flip on the guy he hired."

"That's it? You just want me to make a phone call?" That seemed too easy.

"Yes. You guys were tracked to that hotel using electronics, that much we know. So it stands to reason that the man he hired has the skills to track Eileen as well. She's had her phone off, but he'll be monitoring, waiting to find her."

Sienna looked up at Carson. His jaw was clenched tight, but not as bad as before. "What do you think?" she asked.

He looked surprised, maybe that she'd asked him. "As long as you don't screw anything up," he said to Agent Collins, "then this is fine."

"We just want this to be authentic. We have a script for what we want Ms. MacArthur to say to Eileen. She's going to say she wants to meet up with Eileen—it won't really be her," she hurried out when Carson started to argue. "We've got a body double. We just need to get one of these men out in the open. From there we're confident we'll be able to bring both of them down with no more loss of life."

"They're really prepared," Julian added, looking pointedly at Carson. "They know what they're doing."

Sienna knew sometimes different law enforcement agencies didn't get along with each other, but it was pretty clear that Julian trusted the Feds. Or at least Agent Collins. If he did, then she was going to as well. "I'm in. I have no problem making a phone call. I want to bring down Valentina's killer. She was such a good person." A good mom. Sienna swallowed hard, pushing back the bubble of emotion that threatened to spill over. Now was definitely not the time.

"Okay, then. We're ready to do this now," Collins said. "I brought the clone with me. And I guarantee it won't be traced here to you. It'll ping off a nearby beach, making it look as if you called from a random stretch of white sand."

"Let's do this." The sooner the Feds caught these monsters, the sooner everyone could go back to their lives.

CHAPTER TWELVE

Sienna realized she was humming to herself as she scanned the takeout menu for the fancy barbecue restaurant at the bottom of this high-rise. Though fancy barbecue seemed like an oxymoron.

She didn't care that she was humming and acting like, well, like she'd never been this dang happy before. Because being with Carson made her ridiculously happy. She wondered if maybe it was just that the situation they were in was intense, but no, she'd wanted him long before this. And she knew he'd wanted her too.

After calling Eileen and playing her part in all this, they hadn't heard anything all day from Julian or the Feds and she was really, *really* trying not to stress out.

Sienna and Carson had of course had sex, then gone to the gym downstairs for an intense workout, and now Carson was in the shower. She'd insisted on him going first because she'd known he wouldn't let her actually shower if she joined him. Plus she'd needed to cool down.

Picking up her cell phone, she'd started to call the restaurant when a very faint click reached her ears.

She froze, her fight-or-flight instinct kicking in. That was the front door opening.

There was no way to get out of the kitchen without revealing herself

—unless she jumped over the countertop. Because the exit from the small kitchen was right into the hallway—which would give whoever had just broken in a full view of her. And a chance to shoot her if they were carrying.

Dropping the menu from cold fingers, she scrambled over the countertop, trying to be as quiet as possible.

At this point, stealth be damned, she just needed to get to her weapon. Which she had stupidly left in the bedroom.

Her bare feet were quiet against the tile as she raced down the short adjoining hallway to their bedroom. She would only have seconds and she was too afraid to call out to Carson. No, she needed to get the pistol first.

She pulled the weapon from the top drawer of the only dresser and started to hurry into the bathroom to warn him, but froze when she heard soft footsteps on the tile behind her.

Moving quickly, she backed up against the wall and, using the mirror from the dresser, watched as a man wearing a long-sleeved black T-shirt and a balaclava over his face—weapon up—strode down the hallway.

Blood rushed in her ears but she kept her eyes pinned on the target. He couldn't have seen her yet.

She would only get one shot at this. And she had to make it count. She'd practiced shooting in a controlled environment but she'd never actually shot anyone before and could admit she was terrified.

As he drew nearer to the room, the shower stopped.

The gunman swept into the room, his body angled toward the open bathroom door.

Gripping the pistol tight, she felt as if she was having an out-of-body experience as she whipped around from behind the dresser, pistol up. "Drop your gun!" she screamed, way louder than she'd intended.

The man, with his weapon pointed directly into the bathroom, froze. His entire body was poised as he gave her the side-eye.

She could see it from his body language, no way was he dropping his weapon.

"Do it!" she shouted even as he started to turn toward her.

She fired on instinct. It was either him or her. Or Carson. Hell no!

Pop. Pop. Pop

Glass shattered as he shot at her, his body jerking back as her bullets made contact.

"Duck!" Carson shouted.

She listened, crouching and lowering her weapon as Carson slammed into the guy, tackling him to the ground.

She was barely aware of moving as she jumped over the bed, kicking the man's gun out of the way as Carson slammed his fist against the guy's jaw with a sickening thud.

The guy slumped, his whole body going limp under the assault.

In moments, Carson had the man facedown, his body pinned against the tile. He was holding the shooter's arms behind him at an angle that looked incredibly painful had the guy been conscious.

"Get my cuffs! Top drawer," he ordered.

With trembling fingers she managed to grab his silver cuffs and toss them to Carson. After that, everything happened so quickly. Carson called Julian, asking for backup.

She was trembling, blood rushing in her ears as she tried to keep it together, but in reality she could barely move from where she was rooted by the dresser.

"He has a vest on." Carson's voice ripped her out of her thoughts as she stared at the man on the ground who still hadn't moved since Carson punched him.

She blinked. "What?"

Carson placed his big hands on her shoulders, his eyes searching hers. "He has a vest. You didn't kill him. He might have some broken ribs—and maybe a broken jaw—but he'll live. Julian is on the way with an ambulance."

She wasn't sure why that mattered but for some reason it did. This guy had come here to kill both of them but still...she didn't want to be responsible for taking another's life.

Throat tight, she nodded. "You really need some pants," she whispered.

Carson looked stunned for a moment before he barked out a short laugh. "You're probably right."

CHAPTER THIRTEEN

Sienna wrapped her fingers around the mug of hot coffee even though it was late at night as she and Carson sat in the office of Special Agent Collins.

The local Fed station was a lot different than the police department back home. It was quiet here, the walls gray, and everyone was in suits even with the later hour. There was a decent amount of activity, but everyone seemed to work quieter.

"Thank you for everything you've done to help us," Agent Collins said, looking between the two of them.

They'd been brought in to make an official report—the Feds had originally separated them so they could make their statements—and Sienna just wanted to leave. But she nodded politely because she also wanted more details. "Can you tell us anything about that man or...I guess anything that happened with Eileen? Is she okay?"

The woman paused, then seemed to come to a decision. "The man who broke into your place is Miles Hunt. He was hired by Graham Jordan to help him eliminate anyone who'd seen the images of him. They've worked together in the past, so it isn't a surprise that's who he hired. But they've both already tried to flip on each other. They're both trying to make deals. Hunt swears he didn't kill your attorney friend. He says Graham did that himself and I tend to believe him. That kill was too messy, especially with the added arson. The others were much more professional and lined up with what we know about his alleged past. We've been after him for a while too."

"Did you know Hunt was going to come after Sienna?" There was an underlying edge to Carson's tone even though his body language was casual as he sat with her on the other side of the agent's desk.

"No. He..." She cleared her throat. "The phone we had her use was secure. He tracked your partner. Something we didn't consider since he was with me most of the time. But it's how Hunt found your location. That's on me and I apologize. The only consolation I can give you is that he won't be getting out of jail for a long time."

"Will we need to testify?" Sienna asked.

"Doubtful. He's working on a deal right now. He's got a lot of information not just on Jordan, but others. He's hopefully going to give it in exchange for no trial and a prison of his choice."

"Are either of us in danger?" Carson asked.

"No. There's no reason to come after either of you now. Sienna was just a contract to him. And he's going to be turning on a lot of former clients. If anything, he's in danger of..." She cleared her throat instead of continuing. "We have no reason to believe you're in danger anymore. You're free to go."

"Thanks." Carson stood before she'd finished speaking.

Sienna set her coffee on the desk and stood with him. "Oh...I know I've asked about this, but what about Kevin Fox? Was his death involved with—"

"It had nothing to do with this. From what we can tell, he was killed by someone he pissed off before he went to jail. At least that's what it's looking like according to the local police department. It was just a coincidence that he was one of your clients and got killed around the same time as the others."

Well there was that, then. Sienna's head hurt as they strode out the office door.

"You want to get a place for the night? Or head straight home?" Carson asked her.

It would be a decent drive up the coast of Florida but she wanted to be home, wanted to sleep in her own bed—with him. She wanted this whole mess behind them. "Home."

～

CARSON GRABBED Sienna's duffel bag from the back seat of the rental before they strode up the front walk to her house. The sun was just peeking above the horizon, illuminating everything in oranges and pinks. It was early enough yet that the humidity of the day hadn't set in and there was a decent breeze blowing through the trees.

They'd stopped at a diner to grab some food then driven straight here, and while Sienna had tried to sleep, she hadn't been able to get any. He left his bag in the rental car, unsure if she wanted him to stay or not. The drive home hadn't been awkward, but now that they were back to reality, he wondered if she was going to place him back in that box she'd kept him in before.

"I just remembered I need to call my brother and tell him about his friend's condo." She sighed softly.

"Daniel isn't going to care. He'll just be happy that you're alive." So was Carson. When he'd heard her scream from the bedroom, telling that bastard to drop his weapon, it had shaved a decade off Carson's life. Punching the guy hadn't been enough. He was only sorry he hadn't actually broken the guy's jaw.

"True enough." She cleared her throat as they stood there on the porch. "Do you have to work today?"

"I...have no idea." He hadn't even talked to his boss. Julian had taken over everything, had told him to just call him when he got back to town.

It was Tuesday morning but he doubted his boss wanted him to come in, considering everything that had happened. Still, he would need to check in officially.

"This feels kind of weird to say, but even with everything that happened I still had fun with you. You know, when that guy wasn't shooting at us."

He snorted at her words and leaned down to brush his lips over hers.

"Do you want to come in, or…?" She left the question hanging in the air but the exhaustion on her face told him everything he needed to know—she just wanted to sleep.

Frustration slid through him even as disappointment joined in. He wasn't going to force himself into her home when she was just being polite. He'd made mistakes with her before and he didn't want to do that again. She'd just been through a lot, had shot someone. It didn't matter that the guy had been wearing a vest; she'd shot with the intention to kill. He shoved back all his possessiveness, shoved back the need to demand she let him stay. "No, but I'll call you. You need to get sleep and I've got to check in with my boss."

"Okay. Talk to you later, then." She wrapped her arms around him, giving him a hug then a quick kiss before hurrying inside her house, shutting and locking the door behind her.

The sound of the lock clicking into place made a weird sort of sensation settle in his bones.

As he walked back to the car, he couldn't stop the hollowness filling him. He didn't want to leave. He had the sudden thought that he wished they lived together, which was insane. But he wanted to wake up to her face every morning. Wished that right about now they were both crashing in a bed they owned together.

But it was way too soon to be thinking about that. Right?

CHAPTER FOURTEEN

Carson waited as long as he could. And maybe he should have given Sienna more than a few hours, but screw that.

He'd decided not to give her the chance to put walls up between them again. Hell, he never should have left earlier, but he'd been sleep-deprived and unsure of what to do about her.

Not anymore. Well, he was still sleep-deprived, but he didn't care. He knew exactly what he wanted.

When he pulled into her driveway, he saw both her brothers' vehicles there and gritted his teeth. He hadn't wanted to deal with her family right now, but it was what it was.

Moments after he knocked on the door, Daniel answered it, frowned at him. Brodie was right behind him, not exactly frowning, but... watching him intently.

"You don't need to answer the door!" Sienna called out from somewhere in the house, annoyance tingeing her voice. "I'm more than capable."

Her brothers ignored her.

"What are you doing here?" Daniel asked.

"Is everything okay?" Brodie continued.

"I'm here to see Sienna." He'd barely gotten the words out before Sienna appeared.

She was quickly followed by his own sister, Kathryn, who looked surprised to see him. But then she grinned almost knowingly.

"Can I talk to you? Alone?" he asked Sienna after giving Daniel a pointed look. Brodie was just hanging back by this point. Then Carson handed Daniel the coffee and bag of pastries he'd brought for Sienna. "And put these in her kitchen. Don't touch them. They're not for either of you."

"Someone is testy this morning," Kathryn murmured as Sienna stepped onto the front porch with him.

"Did something happen with the case?" she asked as she shut the door behind her.

In response, he cupped her face and slanted his mouth over hers. He'd definitely made a mistake leaving before. He should have taken her straight to bed and held her in his arms while they both crashed.

She moaned against him, leaning into his body as she kissed him back with a fierceness that matched his own hunger. Blinking, she finally looked up at him, her expression dazed. "Not that I'm complaining. At all. But what was that for?"

"I wanted to stay earlier. But I wasn't sure if you wanted me to, and for the first time that I can remember, I felt like a teenager, unsure of myself. And I don't want to leave things up in the air between us. I know I could've called but I wanted to see you in person. I'm in love with you, Sienna," he said bluntly, because it was the truth. "I let you put walls between us before and I'm not doing that ever again. Right now I'm laying it out there and letting you know that I want more than just dating you. I want to be exclusive. I want to be able to stay over. I want you to stay over at my place. I want you to take up half my closet or more if you want. I want to worry about you when you go off to work—"

She grabbed him by the front of his shirt and yanked him to her, kissing him hard and long. He wrapped her up in his arms, savoring every sweet kiss as he pressed her up against the front door.

"I love you too," she rasped out finally. "And I wanted you to stay earlier too, but I was sleep-deprived and you're *really* hard to read. I didn't want to be all needy and have you stay out of a sense of duty or whatever. But I'm so glad you're here now."

"I knew I should've stayed," he murmured, kissing her again.

The door flew open and Daniel glared at him. "Why don't you just come in here? It's better than making out on her front porch for the whole neighborhood to see."

Sienna simply rolled her eyes but wrapped her arm around Carson's waist as he tugged her close to him. "You better not have touched my pastries," she said, jabbing Daniel in the ribs with a light punch.

"I might've." He grinned, completely unrepentant.

Carson locked the door behind them, kissing her on the head as they strode toward the kitchen. He loved this woman and she loved him back.

It was almost too much to believe. Soon he was going to figure out a polite way to ask her brothers and his sister to leave. Or maybe he'd just forget being polite and tell them to get the hell out so he could have Sienna to himself.

EPILOGUE

Four months later

Carson held his wife in his arms—his wife, something he would never get tired of saying—as they danced at their wedding.

Her family had wanted longer to plan a wedding but that had been unnecessary, and Sienna hadn't cared one way or the other. So they'd settled on a December wedding, which meant he got to end this year as a man married to the woman of his dreams.

"What are you thinking about?" Sienna murmured, burrowing closer against him.

"Our honeymoon."

She threw her head back and laughed, the sound music to his ears. As always.

She was stunning today, no surprise. In her strapless white dress, her hair down in gorgeous waves, it had taken all his restraint not to thread his fingers through her thick tresses. But only because his sister had warned him that even though her hairstyle looked simple, he would mess everything up. Then Brodie's fiancée had threatened him with a curling iron—so he'd listened to the women.

But soon he was going to mess up Sienna's hair, strip her dress off and bury his face between her legs. Very, very soon.

"I have a feeling you're thinking something dirty for sure," she murmured before going up on her toes and kissing him.

"Maybe a little." He grinned against her mouth as the music played around them.

Both their families were there as well as a decent-sized crowd, but all of his focus was on her. The woman who had definitely made him a better man.

They'd been living with each other practically since the moment they got back from Miami, and while he sometimes worried about her at work, he knew she could take care of herself. He was honored to be married to such a strong, wonderful woman.

A smart-ass he would never let go.

Dear Readers,

Thank you for reading The MacArthur Family Collection. I hope you enjoyed it! If you'd like to stay in touch with me and be the first to learn about new releases you can:

- Sign up for my monthly newsletter at: www.katiereus.com

- Find me on Facebook: facebook.com/katiereusauthor

- Follow me on TikTok: tiktok.com/@katiereusauthor

Happy reading,

Katie

ABOUT THE AUTHOR

Katie Reus is the *New York Times* and *USA Today* bestselling author of the Endgame trilogy, the Red Stone Security series, the Redemption Harbor series. She fell in love with romance at a young age thanks to books she pilfered from her mom's stash. Years later she loves reading romance almost as much as she loves writing it.

However, she didn't always know she wanted to be a writer. After changing majors many times, she finally graduated summa cum laude with a degree in psychology. Not long after that she discovered a new love. Writing. She now spends her days writing paranormal romance and romantic suspense.

COMPLETE BOOKLIST

Ancients Rising

Ancient Protector

Ancient Enemy

Ancient Enforcer

Ancient Vendetta

Ancient Retribution

Ancient Vengeance

Ancient Sentinel

Ancient Warrior

Ancient Guardian

Darkness Series

Darkness Awakened

Taste of Darkness

Beyond the Darkness

Hunted by Darkness

Into the Darkness

Saved by Darkness

Guardian of Darkness

Sentinel of Darkness

A Very Dragon Christmas

Darkness Rising

Redemption Harbor Series®

Resurrection

Savage Rising

Dangerous Witness

Innocent Target

Hunting Danger

Covert Games

Chasing Vengeance

Sin City Series (the Serafina)

First Surrender

Sensual Surrender

Sweetest Surrender

Dangerous Surrender

Deadly Surrender

Verona Bay Series

Dark Memento

Deadly Past

Silent Protector

Linked books

Retribution

Tempting Danger

www.ingramcontent.com/pod-product-compliance
Lightning Source LLC
Chambersburg PA
CBHW050139120726
47903CB00002B/412